SPECIAL MESSAGE TO READERS

This book is published under the auspices of

THE ULVERSCROFT FOUNDATION

(registered charity No. 264873 UK)

Established in 1972 to provide funds for research, diagnosis and treatment of eye diseases. Examples of contributions made are: —

A Children's Assessment Unit at Moorfield's Hospital, London.

•

Twin operating theatres at the Western Ophthalmic Hospital, London.

•

A Chair of Ophthalmology at the Royal Australian College of Ophthalmologists.

•

The Ulverscroft Children's Eye Unit at the Great Ormond Street Hospital For Sick Children, London.

You can help further the work of the Foundation by making a donation or leaving a legacy. Every contribution, no matter how small, is received with gratitude. Please write for details to:

**THE ULVERSCROFT FOUNDATION,
The Green, Bradgate Road, Anstey,
Leicester LE7 7FU, England.
Telephone: (0116) 236 4325**

**In Australia write to:
THE ULVERSCROFT FOUNDATION,
c/o The Royal Australian and New Zealand
College of Ophthalmologists,
94-98 Chalmers Street, Surry Hills,
N.S.W. 2010, Australia**

Jean Saunders began her career as a magazine writer. She has written about six hundred short stories and over eighty novels. She is past chairperson of the Romantic Novelists' Association and she frequently speaks at writers' groups and conferences. She is married with three grown-up children and writes full time. She lives in Weston-Super-Mare, Somerset.

DEADLY SUSPICIONS

The discovery of a mutilated hand had closed the investigation into the disappearance of sixteen-year-old Steven Leng. Now, ten years later, the victim's mother is still determined to find out what really happened to her son. She contacts private investigator Alexandra Best, who discovers more about the incident in the woods that originally sparked off the mystery. Alex becomes convinced that Steven was murdered and her investigations lead her to the Followers, a religious group that appeared to fascinate Steven. Alex treads a dangerous trail that finally leads to a dramatic denouement.

Books by Jean Saunders
Published by The House of Ulverscroft:

LADY OF THE MANOR
GOLDEN DESTINY
WITH THIS RING

JEAN SAUNDERS

DEADLY SUSPICIONS

Complete and Unabridged

ULVERSCROFT
Leicester

First published in Great Britain in 2001 by
Robert Hale Limited
London

First Large Print Edition
published 2003
by arrangement with
Robert Hale Limited
London

British Library CIP Data

Saunders, Jean, *1932* –
Deadly suspicions.—Large print ed.—
Ulverscroft large print series: suspense
1. Women private detectives—Fiction
2. Cults—Fiction
3. Detective and mystery stories
4. Large type books
I. Title
823.9′14 [F]

ISBN 0–7089–4938–X

Published by
F. A. Thorpe (Publishing)
Anstey, Leicestershire

Set by Words & Graphics Ltd.
Anstey, Leicestershire
Printed and bound in Great Britain by
T. J. International Ltd., Padstow, Cornwall

This book is printed on acid-free paper

1

In Alex's opinion, it was the office party from hell. In any case, she had never been part of the scene where workmates gathered together for their annual jollities in an entirely false environment from the norm.

The unreal situation was compounded by the inclusion of spouses and girlfriends, who were definitely not part of the in-crowd. And that included Alex. She worked alone and liked it that way. And she wasn't sure, even now, why she had accepted Nick's invitation to the pre-Christmas party.

And now he had wandered off, Lord knows where, leaving her with a drink in her hand and fair game for all the creeps who thought they were God's gift, in or out of uniform.

'How's my favourite Private Dick?' she heard a well-oiled voice slur.

She turned slowly, giving him the full benefit of her green eyes at their grittiest, and moved neatly away from his groping hands. That was another thing: these parties always seemed to bring out the lech in even the mildest nerd, and this guy was a nerd, *yes*, but mild, *no*.

'I was never your private anything, Sergeant Thomas,' she said, as cool as ever.

He gave a boozy chuckle. 'Oh, come on darling, loosen up and be friendly for once. I hear you're leaving us soon.'

She looked at him coldly.

'That's right, but I doubt that you'll miss me.'

'Can't take the pace, eh?' he sniggered. 'I always said you'd take fright sooner or later.'

'I am *not* taking fright.'

Bastard, she thought, making her rise to his bait.

His arm slid around her more tightly.

'How about a dance for old times' sake, then?'

'We don't have any old times, creep. And by the way, your wife's looking for you, so piss off.'

She had the satisfaction of seeing his head swivel around as if it were on a spring, and she moved quickly away from him, searching for Nick, and wondering how soon she could decently suggest that they get out of here.

She groaned, seeing him deep in conversation with the Chief Constable's wife. He had to do his social bit, of course. DCI Nick Frobisher was always on duty and aware of his responsibilities. This was very much *his* scene. The three Services had combined for this year's annual shindig instead of having the usual exclusive Policemens' Ball (other guests invited). But glancing around, the groups were still very much in their separate factions: Police, Fire, Ambulance . . .

Somebody bumped against her, knocking her glass and spilling a little of her drink on her black cocktail dress. In such a crush these things happened, and thank God she was drinking her usual vodka and lime, so it was unlikely to stain, Alex thought, with more hope than certainty.

The woman who had bumped into her apologized profusely.

'It's all right,' Alex said. 'It will soon sponge off — '

'I'm so sorry, and that dress looks wildly expensive.'

There was a note of almost desperate envy in her voice. It wasn't a local accent. More West Country, Alex noted.

'I'll be mortified if you won't let me see to it in the Ladies' Room,' the woman rushed on.

'Really, it's not necessary — ' and if she didn't catch Nick's glance soon, she had the feeling she was going to be trapped with this one for ages.

Next minute she felt the hand squeezing her arm.

'It would make me feel so much better. You *are* Alexandra Best, aren't you? The Private Investigator?'

The way she said it made Alex look at her more sharply. There was a hint of pleading in the faded eyes now, and Alex knew at once that the collision hadn't been accidental.

She hid a small sigh. This wasn't fair. It was out of office hours, and she was nobody's unpaid Agony Aunt. A doctor friend had once told her of his feelings when people discovered his identity on holiday, and he'd be presented with all manner of minor ailments for an instant consultation . . . all for free, of course.

'I had a dress made out of similar material to yours once,' the woman went on wistfully, with an apparent change of tactic. 'So I know it will spot if it's not attended to right away. And I really must buy you another drink as well.'

There was no way she was going to let her go, Alex realized, and with one last raging look in Nick's direction, she followed the woman to the grandly named Ladies' Powder Room, praying it would be too busy for private conversations.

But it was temporarily empty with no sign of an attendant. Just her luck. Like policemen, attendants were never around when you wanted one, she thought, wincing at her own feeble attempt at a joke.

'I'm Jane Leng, by the way,' the woman said. 'My husband Bob's about to retire from the Fire Service. Now let's get to that mark on your lovely dress.'

She became fussily attentive, but Alex's intuition told her it was only a matter of time before the real reason for contacting her came out, and she didn't have long to wait.

'I always hated my husband's job,' Jane Leng said, with a definite catch in her breath.

'Well, that's understandable.' Alex was brisk, hoping this wasn't going to be a weep on the shoulder half-hour, and that someone would appear soon to break up the unwelcome twosome. She wasn't uncharitable, but there were limits.

'It's not all *London's Burning* and cute nicknames, you know,' she went on accusingly, as if Alex thought it was. 'More like *The Towering Inferno* at times, and some of the things Bob's had to deal with in his day would turn your stomach.'

'I can imagine. Well, thank you for your help, Mrs Leng, but I really should be getting back to my escort.'

She elevated Nick above the status of friend and sometime lover, in the hope that her own cut-glass accent would deter this rather annoying woman.

'He has nightmares.' The voice was jerkier now. 'After ten years he still has nightmares. *Dreadful* nightmares. They won't go away. They keep tormenting him.'

'Ten years?'

The question left Alex's lips before she could stop it. She groaned inwardly, knowing she shouldn't ask. She didn't really want to know, but was unable to resist her curiosity about something she knew instinctively this woman was bursting to share. And there had to be a reason why she had chosen a Private Investigator to confide in. That she *had* been chosen, Alex was perfectly sure now.

A group of giggling young women came into the Powder Room, glancing at them oddly, and as Alex looked back at their reflections in the large mirror, she realized what an unlikely couple she and Jane Leng made.

She was tall and willowy — except for the hips that Nick generously said only emphasized her slim waist. Her colouring was dramatic — pike-straight red hair and green eyes enhanced by the long emerald earrings and slinky black cocktail dress. And there was Jane Leng, small, middle-aged, worried, wearing a blue crimplene dress of uncertain vintage. A highly unlikely confidante for a

27-year-old career woman with a classy up-market voice, and a growing reputation for doing the business as far as her PI clientele went.

Even as she assessed them both, Alex was angry at herself for being so mean-minded. The woman and her husband clearly had a problem, and should be seeking the help of a social worker or counsellor, not herself.

As they left the Powder Room and joined the throng of revellers in the hotel ballroom, she spoke firmly.

'If your husband's having these problems, I'd say he should get professional help. Has he seen his GP?'

'Oh yes. GPs, specialists, counsellors, head doctors. None of them do any good. No, it's you I need to see.'

'Well, this obviously isn't the time or place, Mrs Leng,' Alex said more gently. 'I don't see how I can help, but if you think I could, why not make an appointment at my office for an hour's consultation at the usual rates?'

That would surely put her off. Most casuals backed off at once if they thought there was payment involved.

'Would one day next week be all right? I want to get Bob sorted out before he has too much time on his hands to brood.'

Alex groaned. It was nearly Christmas, she

had wound up everything at work, and had intended spending the next couple of weeks clearing out her flat and office in preparation for moving down to Bristol and the new Shop-front Premises with Self-contained Flat above.

She still thought of it all in capital letters in estate agent's jargon — and her heart would still give a little blip every time she thought of the move she was making. And it was nothing to do with getting cold feet, or the sleazy characters you met in this kind of work. They were everywhere, anyway, and you expected to take the rough with the smooth . . .

'How about Tuesday afternoon?' she heard Jane Leng say determinedly. 'I'll be doing some last-minute Christmas shopping so Bob won't expect me home for hours. He knows what I'm like when I'm dithering about what to buy.'

Alex gave in. 'Tuesday will be fine. I'll give you my card and I'll expect you at two-thirty. Does that suit?'

'Thank you, Miss Best. I'm ever so grateful — ' but Alex had twisted away quickly to avoid having her hand wrung.

* * *

'Where the hell have you been?' Nick said, grabbing her. 'I've been looking everywhere for you. I began to think you'd run out on me. I know you don't care for this kind of thing too much, but it's our last chance for a big night out, Alex, and I wanted you to enjoy yourself.'

'I am enjoying myself,' she said mechanically, 'now I've got rid of your Sergeant-bloody-Thomas's clutching hands.'

'Take no notice of him. He's had too much to drink, and it's a sure bet he'll get tongue pie from his wife when he gets home tonight. Who was that woman you were with earlier?'

She smiled up at him sweetly as the conversation took a swiftly different turn. He really did look terrific in evening dress, dark and slightly foreign-looking, almost James Bondish in a Pierce Brosnan eat-your-heart-out kind of way.

And she might have known he wouldn't have missed a thing. He might have said he'd lost sight of her, but he had an uncanny way of registering exactly who she had been talking with and for how long. His super-keen detective brain had a way of mentally picturing a scene and storing it away for future use.

'I thought you knew everything that went on around here. She was a fireman's wife, a bit out of her depth, like me.'

Nick laughed. 'You were never out of your

depth, darling, not since you left AB behind in Yorkshire, anyway.'

As the band struck up an old-fashioned waltz, he swung her on to the dance floor and pulled her close. She was tall, but he was taller. As she felt his warm breath on her cheek her heart beat faster, and not only because she was aware of every horny part of him.

'What made you think of her?' she asked.

'Just the hope that when you go down to the sticks you're not going to revert to being sweet little Audrey Barnes again. I much prefer the feisty Alex Best I've come to know and love.'

'You can't say that,' she said with crushing logic. 'You never knew me when I was Audrey Barnes.'

'I know damn well that the softer part of Alex that listens to sob stories has more to do with being born Audrey Barnes than a sophisticated PI,' he said. 'But I'd hate it if she ever lost that gentler quality too. And whatever you're looking for, you won't find it by running away.'

'Don't do this, Nick,' she said, in TV-script lingo.

'Do what?' he asked innocently.

'Don't start making me want to stay, when you know very well I've made up my mind to go. I need to make a fresh start, and there's no going back on it now. New year, new beginning.'

'Until the next bad case comes along, and you can't handle it. Give it up, Alex, and marry me.'

She ignored his comment on her ability, hearing his voice become rougher with passion, and she knew that lower ranks weren't the only ones who'd had too much to drink. She also knew that Nick wanted her — had always wanted her — but marriage wasn't on the cards, and in their sober moments, they both knew it. He'd know it in the morning too, and be thankful she hadn't said yes.

'We've gone through this before, Nick. You know I love you, but not enough to marry you, no more than you'd want to marry me if you were thinking straight.'

'OK,' he said, infuriatingly cheerful. 'I'll just have to sleep with you then.'

'And from the state of you, that's probably all you could manage,' she said with a grin.

'Don't underestimate the power of the law, sweetheart,' he said meaningly. 'So if you've had enough, let's go.'

* * *

It was pouring with rain by the time a taxi got them back to her flat, and she didn't have the heart or the strength to turn him away. It was the last big social occasion she would share with him, and maudlin thoughts of how much she was going to miss him were starting to infiltrate, despite herself.

They spent the night in her bed, wrapped in one another's arms, as close as two peas in a pod, and as chaste as nuns, until the incessant rumble of the early morning traffic awoke her. And alerted her to the fact that he was leaning up on one elbow, looking down at her.

'Time to get up,' she croaked, her throat dry from breathing in too much second-hand cigarette smoke last night.

'No, it's not. It's Sunday morning,' Nick reminded her. 'And that woman you were with last night was Bob Leng's wife.'

Alex blinked into the daylight, realizing they were both naked, and that one of his fingers was idly circling her nipple. She pushed his hand away at once, annoyed that he was disgustingly awake so early in the morning, when she still felt in need of a hundred years' sleep.

'What are you talking about?' she asked huskily.

'Bob Leng. Fireman. Screwed up to hell

after an incident ten years ago.'

It was the phrase 'ten years ago' that did it. And why did they always mention *incidents* in that brush-off way, when Jane Leng obviously thought that whatever had happened to her husband was of volcanic proportions?

'His wife said something — '

'I'll bet she did. She's been around every copper on the force trying to make somebody listen to her ramblings. You don't want to let her get at you, Alex.'

'She won't. I'm leaving town, remember?'

She threw off the duvet and marched to the bathroom, ignoring her kimono in her annoyance. She took an ultra-quick shower, and came back swathed in a large towel, to find Nick still lounging in her bed.

'So what did she want?' he said, never one to let go easily. Like a cat with a mouse, Alex thought. Only in Nick's case, more like a tiger stalking its prey . . .

'I've no idea,' she said airily. 'She was worried about her husband having nightmares and wanted somebody to talk to, that's all.'

'I hope you told her you're too busy.'

The words were too casual. He was clever, but so was she, and this was more than idle curiosity. In her desire to avoid a direct answer, she let herself slip.

'Alex might be, but Audrey wasn't ever too busy to resist letting someone confide in her. I'll be glad to get away from here to where life is more *normal* and people don't question every motive.'

She fumed, even as she heard the cutesy words leave her lips. She had left her old persona behind in the Yorkshire Dales years ago, and it had been Nick who had dredged it up again last night. He leapt out of bed, rampant with anger if not morning-glory libido, and shook her.

'I knew it. You really did let that last big case get to you, didn't you? The bastard's not around any more, Alex. He can't harm you, and he's never getting out of that prison.'

'Well, thanks for reminding me. I never even think of it any more, and he's *not* the reason I want to get out of London. Do you think I'm going to be constantly on the move every time a lunatic tries to kill me?'

'You tell me.'

'I'm not that stupid. I know it's part of the price we pay in this kind of job, so don't soft-soap me, Nick. If it had anything to do with all the unwelcome publicity that case attracted I'd have given up long ago.'

He bent down and kissed her lips, and she

made no more than a token resistance. He was a bloody gorgeous man, she admitted. So why the hell was she letting him go?

'God, you're beautiful when you're angry,' he said, stifling a laugh. 'I suppose sex is out of the question?'

His humour got her back on track.

'Right out. Go and take a shower and let me get dressed,' she said, giving him a shove.

'All right. And then you can tell me exactly what Bob Leng's wife said to you.'

'Only if you'll tell me exactly what this so-called incident was all about,' she replied smartly. 'Fair's fair.'

While she was dressing, she tried to imagine what it could be. Firemen had many gruesome jobs, just like policemen. Often worse, in fact, because they had to go into burning buildings and drag people out who were more dead than alive. They had to drag out corpses, and bits of bodies. Once, she had heard of a fireman who had got stuck in a drain trying to rescue a child, and the trauma of finding the child choked to death on dirt and his own vomit had stayed with him for the rest of his life.

Nick came back, casually draped in a towel, his broad shoulders gleaming with traces of water, his dark hair still dripping on her carpet. She ignored it. What the hell? It was going to be left for the next occupant, anyway.

He dropped the towel with his usual confidence, and shrugged into his clothes. Every time she saw him naked she was never less than impressed . . . but now wasn't the time, and she turned away as her treacherous hormones stirred.

'So tell me,' she demanded over a breakfast of instant coffee and toast.

She refused to register that even this meagre feast gave out a sense of cosy domesticity. It was like one of those perfect TV adverts, where vicarious aromas of steaming coffee and warm toast practically shrieked love and harmony at you. She could get to like it . . . and she squashed the thought.

'You can't stay long, Nick,' she went on, glancing at her watch. 'I've got a hell of a lot to do.'

'It's Sunday, remember? Day of rest and all that?'

'Not for me. I've still got boxes to pack.'

'I could help you — '

Like how? Persuading me back to bed . . . ?

'You could hinder me, you mean. And stop putting off the answer to my question. What happened to Bob Leng?'

'OK. He was involved in a shout ten years ago. A gang of kids had set fire to an old makeshift hut in the woods where druggies and winos used to sleep rough. The kids threw fireworks into the hut, doused it with petrol and set light to it, then stood back and watched the fun.'

'Good God. What happened?' Alex said, horrified.

'Well, the fireworks went up like rockets, of course — pardon the pun — which luckily alerted people in the village nearby to contact the fire brigade. But the hut quickly burned to the ground. There had been a long hot spell of weather and the woods were tinder-dry, so you can imagine how quickly the fire spread.'

'Was anybody inside the hut?'

'They didn't think so at the time.'

The way he paused for effect invited the obvious question.

'*But*?'

'But later on, there was a bit of a hassle about a group of kids from the local Comp school. It was the summer holidays, and they'd gone camping on Exmoor, but after six weeks some of them failed to return home as expected. A storm in a teacup really, as most of them eventually turned up, though a bit hetup, clearly expecting an ear-bashing from their parents, and rightly so.'

'But was there any reason to connect them with the druggies and the fire at the hut?'

Nick shrugged. 'Oh, it was the same lot all right. No doubt about that. They'd been seen hanging around the hut before. You know what kids are like. They see the glamour of living rough, doing your own thing, whatever the hell else they call it. In the sixties, they used to call it 'finding themselves'. Bloody nonsense. Anyway, these kids had frequently been warned off getting involved with them, and especially about experimenting with drugs. They get regular talks in schools from us nowadays, for whatever good it does. Unfortunately, what Bob Leng found was far less glamorous than a packet of speed or a few Ecstasy pills.'

'Why didn't the police move these druggies on?' Alex said, ignoring what Bob Leng had found for the moment. 'It sounds to me as if they were condoning their presence.'

'Not at all. They were never found to be in possession, and they'd long gone by the time of the incident in question.'

'All right. So what did Bob Leng find?'

Nick glanced at her. 'Sure you want to hear this?'

She nodded. 'You can't stop now.'

'It was his dog who actually found it, ferreting in the undergrowth one morning when he was taking him for a walk in the woods near the burned-out hut. There was this hand.'

He stopped, waiting for her reaction.

'*And*?'

'And nothing. Just a hand. Bob didn't recognize it for what it was at first because it was half-eaten away and covered in filth and slime. He thought the dog was worrying something alive until he realized the thing was heaving in the dirt because it was crawling with maggots.'

'Oh, Christ!' Alex whispered.

'You can imagine his horror when he saw what it was. He was never the most stable of men, in quite the wrong job for someone of his temperament. It turned his guts, and he went ranting to the police like a madman to come and check it out. It had to be sent to forensics, and it wasn't an easy check, as you can imagine. It had been there for some weeks by then, probably through all the hot school holidays.'

'So what's your point?' Alex said, trying her best not to picture that putrifying, disembodied hand.

'The point is, Bob Leng kept going back over the events in his mind, and he was convinced that he might have helped towards destroying evidence that would have led to a murder conviction. It began as a routine fire call, but now it began to look as if there might have been a more serious crime committed than just kids larking about.'

He glanced towards her, seeing her questioning face.

'In case you don't know, a fierce attack with water hoses blows the ash of burned bodies to smithereens. Destroying the evidence. Leaving no trace.'

Alex began to feel sick. 'So did this hand belong to one of the missing kids then? If it wasn't one of the druggies, was it one of the Comp school campers?'

For a second her words sounded appallingly like something out of St Trinian's, but she knew it was anything but . . .

'That's what they concluded,' Nick said grimly, and she knew how much the police hated crimes involving kids. Even those with the strongest stomachs could be deeply affected, needing counselling. Not that she thought any of it did any good, but this wasn't the time to voice her opinions on that score.

'But there was no reason to think the druggies were murderers, was there? And what about the other kids? You said *most* of them returned home.'

'All but one. Steven. They were all questioned, of course, but they all swore that after a big bust-up he hadn't gone on the camping trip. Apparently that was nothing unusual. He was sixteen. Only child. Good grades at school. Very self-sufficient,' he added, in clipped police procedural note-form. 'Always threatening to go off to India or some such nonsense. The other kids reckoned he was in a bit of a sixties time-warp. Big fan of John Lennon and all that guru rubbish. When the truth finally came out, it left his parents in shreds.'

'It was the boy, then? The hand, I mean. Did they ever find the rest of him?'

And what if they hadn't? What did anyone do in such circumstances? Hold a burial service for a hand? In a shoe-box? The thought was so ludicrously terrible that Alex didn't know whether to laugh or cry.

'Never,' Nick said. 'His mother cracked up, and his father took to drink. Classic, isn't it? Hell on earth for them, of course. The guy was lucky to keep his job at all, though in a much lesser capacity than before.'

'Yes, but what about Bob Leng?' She had to get her mind away from the vision of that hand and those poor bloody parents . . . 'Where does he come into all this? Why does he still have nightmares after ten years?'

'I thought you'd have guessed by now, babe. Steven Leng was his son.'

2

Ten years ago Alex had been living in the Yorkshire Dales with her parents. Ten years ago she had still been Audrey Barnes, farmer's daughter, and had been a long way from reinventing herself after his death and the legacy he'd left her.

It hadn't been on the scale of lottery money, but it was enough for her to realize a dream — that of moving to London and turning herself into Alexandra Best, Private Investigator.

She discovered she had a talent for adopting whatever accent she needed, and it was almost natural to her now to sound more estuary-English than broad Yorkshire. It went with the job. Regional accents might be 'in', and TV presenters might make a million out of using them, but people in trouble had more faith in a woman PI who spoke crisply and with style . . .

As the words came into her head she gave a small smile, remembering one of her father's favourite old TV sitcoms, *'Allo 'Allo*. Although the pet phrase of the French undertaker played by Kenneth Connor was '*swiftly* and with style', she remembered. And with the thought, her smile faded.

She shouldn't be having frivolous thoughts now, after what Nick had told her. She was still shocked to think that ten years ago Bob Leng had been the one to find the gruesome remains, or rather *remain*, of his son. How could anyone get over something so terrible? No wonder he still had nightmares. And no wonder his wife wanted to speak to someone about it.

All the same, Alex really didn't want to get involved with Jane Leng, and it did no good to try to revive old crimes, whether real or imaginary. The police would have wrapped up the case long ago and wouldn't exactly welcome a female PI poking into their files.

She couldn't even remember hearing or reading anything about it at the time, although it must have been headline news. But why would she, ten years ago, when she had still been Audrey Barnes, helping her father on a remote Yorkshire farm, and not overly interested in unsavoury crimes? Nor yet avidly watching TV crime series or devouring the *Self-Help Manual of Detection* she had later discovered at a car boot sale. Ten years ago, she hadn't had the remotest notion that maybe she too could solve crimes . . .

'Damn you, Jane Leng,' she muttered when Nick finally left her that Sunday, and had told her as much as he chose to about the 'incident'. 'But by Tuesday I'm going to find out everything I can before I get your version.'

Since Nick was so scathing of Jane Leng's continuing approach to anyone who would listen, she decided not to ask him for any more information. She needed to keep an open mind. He'd be able to search out any police records still on file, but as soon as she showed too much interest he'd be on her like a ton of bricks, and tell her to stop wasting her time.

The hell of it was, she'd been born too damn curious for her own good. She needed to know if the Leng boy's killer had ever been found — or if there had been a killer at all. Nick's view — and the general consensus at the time — was that it was probably no more than a tragic accident which occured during the firework incident at the burned-out hut. And that was the eventual conclusion. No foul play suspected. No trace of the rest of the body, possibly due to the efforts of the firemen, which would certainly have traumatized Bob Leng. But no body, no inquest. QED.

At any rate, it could still be a missing

person case and not murder at all. But if it wasn't, and the kids had closed ranks to cover up what had happened, one or other of them might eventually crack. They would all have been questioned closely by the police, but there could still have been a bad apple among them that the others had vowed to protect. Kids could be devious as well as being adept liars, no matter how many doting mummies and daddies might think otherwise.

So why did all Alex's instincts tell her there was more to this than a closed case? She answered her own question: because she had become addicted to watching too many bloody crime movies and TV programmes and preening herself when she solved them before the final credits came up, that's why. And because there was no satisfaction in leaving a crime unsolved. She applied logic to what she already knew. If the Leng boy had actually gone to India he must have had a passport. He must have got a plane ticket. People must have seen him, registered his details. Nobody simply disappeared without trace these days.

But logic also told her that the police would have checked on those things. So that was a non-starter. Therefore her first stop on Monday morning was the reference library to get out every microfiche newspaper record of a long-ago incident where a boy's mutilated hand had been found.

* * *

When she found what she was looking for, she saw that it had made national news at first, but then became more localized. Murder was clearly not suspected. It seemed to have been assumed that there had been an accidental death — despite losing most of the body. But the local papers had made far more of a splash with the human interest stories, interviewing Bob and Jane Leng at length, until she could imagine them at screaming point from the intimate, painful questions.

Alex's mother had always hated such intrusive stories, while her father had tried to dissuade her from taking what he called an unhealthy interest in criminal affairs, so they had probably played it down at the time.

She made copies of the relevant articles and took them home to study. It wasn't her case . . . there *wasn't* any case, she reminded herself, but by now she was completely caught up in the horror of that day when Bob Leng had made his discovery.

She also had far too much to do to get

involved with some neurotic woman's problems. But on Tuesday afternoon she was in her office before two-thirty, and awaiting her client.

* * *

Jane Leng arrived flustered and nervous, armed with various plastic bags with the names of Oxford and Regent Street shops emblazoned on them — including Hamleys, Alex noted.

'Please sit down Mrs Leng,' she said, trying not to wince as the faint whiff of perspiration wafted towards her. Jane had obviously had a busy day.

'I see you've finally done your Christmas shopping,' she went on, smiling to put her at her ease. 'Do you have young relatives to buy gifts for?'

It was none of her damn business, but it was an ice-breaker, since the woman looked as if she would rather be anywhere else than here. Now that she was confronted with the business-end of a PI's world, Alex guessed she had begun to realize what she was taking on.

'It's for Steven,' his mother said. 'I always buy him something nice at Christmas. He's not a child any more, but it will be his birthday on the same day, you see. And a son's always a boy to his mother, isn't he?'

It wasn't so much that she always bought a gift for her dead son, as the fact that she spoke of him in the present tense. The woman was clearly as cracked as her husband . . . and then Alex saw the anguish in Jane Leng's face, and handed her a box of tissues.

'It's all right,' she said gently. 'I know what happened to Steven, Mrs Leng, and I can understand your need to keep his memory alive.'

'He is alive, Miss Best.'

'Well, of course he is to you — '

'You don't understand.' She dabbed her eyes with a handful of tissues. 'But if you know what happened ten years ago, then you'll know that Bob's dog found something.'

'Yes,' Alex said, determined to be as businesslike as possible now. 'And also that it was positively identified as belonging to Steven. Forensics can't lie, Mrs Leng.'

'Well, in this case, they did. I know they did. I know Steven's still alive, because I've seen him.'

Oh no, not again, Alex thought. Her last case involved oddballs, and she'd vowed to keep well clear of them.

The memory of the psychic Eleanora

Wolstenholme and her equally weird daughter Moira, whose respectable florist trade hid her sleazy other life of high class call-girl, was something she'd rather forget. Particularly as the outcome of it had resulted in the traumatic court case where she had been called as a witness, facing the cold-blooded eyes of the High Court Judge killer who'd tried to kill *her* too. That was headline news, if you like, and pushed her into an unwelcome limelight for a while.

She gave Jane Leng a more sympathetic smile now.

'I'm sure you know it's a common phenomenon to imagine you see the face of a loved one who's passed over, Mrs Leng,' she said, cringing inwardly at the twee terms she thought the woman would appreciate.

'Oh, I know all about that,' Jane said, more briskly than before. 'It's what everybody says, but they don't know what they're talking about. Bob says I'm driving him back to drink again, because he insists I'm going mad and I'll probably be committed before I'm done. But I know what I saw.'

Christ, it was getting worse, Alex thought, wondering how long this interview was going to last. She'd offered an hour's consultation, and so far they'd hardly got through five bloody minutes, and she was already wondering if she was dealing with a madwoman.

'Would you like some coffee?' she asked in desperation, but Jane Leng shook her head. 'Tea, then?'

At the same negative reponse, Alex knew there was to be no respite.

'All right. So you think you've seen Steven — '

'I don't think. I know. Why does nobody listen to me?'

'I'm listening, Mrs Leng.'

God, she was Frasier Crane at his best now. 'So why don't you tell me where you've seen him?'

'On the television. In the middle of a football crowd.'

'Is that the kind of place Steven liked to be?'

'No, not at all. That's what makes it so odd. He preferred different sports, and his school was progressive like that. They were a Grammar once, you know, and they kept up the old standards. They promoted things like fencing and squash, and even fishing instruction. He was good at that. He liked being by the river. But I know it was him I saw. I know my own son, don't I?'

'When was this sighting, Mrs Leng? Was it recently?' Alex said, noting the unconscious snobbery in her mention of a Grammar school.

'Last year. And before you ask, I went to the police, and they said they followed it up, but I'm sure they didn't. Bob won't believe me. He'd like to forget all about Steven, but I can't. And now he's started getting the nightmares again, even worse than before, and he says it's all my fault.'

She grabbed another handful of tissues, and Alex made a silent note to replenish her supplies.

'Do you have any photos of Steven?' she asked next, not sure exactly what this woman wanted of her, and hoping she didn't want anything more than to talk. Sometimes all people wanted was another pair of ears to listen to problems when their nearest and dearest wouldn't, or couldn't.

'Oh yes, dozens,' Jane said predictably. 'The house is full of them, and that's another thing. I refuse to put them away, and Bob can't bear to look at them. Life hasn't been easy for us, Miss Best. We have — problems.'

That was probably the understatement of the year, thought Alex. But Jane was rummaging in her handbag now, and produced a large envelope.

'I brought some with me. I knew you'd

want to see them.'

'I haven't said I can help,' Alex said quickly. 'In fact, I'm not sure what it is you think I can do.'

'Find him, of course. And find out whoever was responsible for planting that horrid hand in the woods and putting about the wicked story that he'd died.'

She was completely gaga, Alex decided. Deranged. You couldn't fabricate forensic evidence, and DNA was so accurate these days it was virtually impossible to make a mistake. Even the flimsiest evidence could prove conclusive: a fragment of clothing, a pubic hair, the length of time maggots had been devouring a body, fingernail shape, dental impressions, old scars . . . the list was endless, and impregnable. She had only witnessed an autopsy a very few times, and didn't particularly want to do so again, thank you very much, but she couldn't help but be awesomely impressed by what she had learned.

She studied the face of the boy in the photographs. He was a handsome lad, dark-haired and studious, with strong, open features. And apparently never in any bother at home, Nick had told her. Not the kind to go incognito for the rest of his life after missing out on an end-of-term camping trip, she would have thought.

And yet there was this other side to him — the side that was addicted to John Lennon songs and the Indian guru nonsense. A schizophrenic, perhaps. One of those people with multiple personalities.

If so, it was getting too deep for her. It was something only a professional could deal with.

'Did Steven have any medical problems?' she said carefully.

'What sort of medical problems?'

'I don't mean anything serious. For instance, I know that schools still have regular visits from what was called the nit nurse, scrutinizing everybody's heads,' Alex said, trying to lighten the atmosphere. 'Sounds horrible, I always think. But nowadays they also have attendant psychologists to sort out any small social problems among their pupils — '

'Steven wasn't mad. He may have been a deep thinker, but he wasn't mad.'

'And was he popular? Did he have plenty of friends?'

'Good Lord, yes. He was always one of a group, in and out of school. There was nothing peculiar about our Steven.'

Alex noted that she was now referring to him in the past tense. It was probably a slip of the tongue, since she seemed utterly convinced he was still alive. While Alex was just as convinced that he was not.

But she could understand his mother a little more now. She couldn't warm to her, but it must be the worst thing in the world to have the mystery of her son's disappearance hanging over the family for ten years; to be incomplete; unable to say goodbye properly, though presumably her husband had done so long ago, which must make the tension between them even more unbearable at times. All those heartbreaking photos around the house that she couldn't bear to put away, when he couldn't bear to look at them . . .

There was something else she should query, but before she could do so, Jane Leng had spoken again.

'I understand you're moving to Bristol,' she said, throwing her off balance with the change of direction.

'Well yes, I am, in a couple of weeks' time, as a matter of fact.' And hopefully, that would be the end of this . . .

'You'll be able to look into it all for us then.'

'Mrs Leng, it was all a long time ago, and I can't believe you really did see your son,' she said quietly. 'Are you sure you want to pursue this? Isn't it just prolonging the agony for you and your husband? And it will be difficult for me to communicate with you — '

'That's what I wanted to tell you. We're moving back home to Chilworthy when Bob retires in February. South of Bristol, near Chew Valley in case you don't know it. That's what makes it perfect. As soon as I heard that nice Mr Frobisher telling somebody about you moving, I knew it was fate. I believe in fate, don't you?'

'I do indeed,' Alex said mechanically. The hell of it was, fate didn't always do what you wanted it to. And damn Nick for being so indiscreet. But how was he to know?

'So will you take on our case, Miss Best?' Mrs Leng said more grandly, clearly liking the sound of the words. She was a homely woman with homespun ways, and Alex suspected this was probably the most daring thing she had ever undertaken on her own.

'And if you're worried about payment, it's no problem. Bob's getting a very nice golden handshake when he retires, and we're splitting it down the middle. The old fool will squander all his on drink,' she added spitefully, 'but I'm spending my half on finding Steven. I don't care how much it takes, or how long. I just want him home.'

God, it was tragic how two people, who had presumably once been close, could tear one another apart. It was pretty obvious there was no love left between them, and in Alex's mind there were worse things than physical abuse. There was the slow, painful disintegration of a marriage.

She hardly knew what else to say, but she reminded herself that she was a professional with a job to do, and if this woman wanted her to do some investigating, she would do it. It would take her a while to get established in Bristol, so this would tide her over nicely. And if that was a hell of a cynical way of looking at it, sometimes it was the only way to get through.

'Then we have a deal, Mrs Leng,' she said, to let her know the interview was over. 'I'll give you my new business address, and you can contact me there.'

'Thank you,' she gushed, still using up more tissues than was necessary, in Alex's opinion.

'In the meantime, let's all try to enjoy Christmas,' Alex said, not sure if this was going to cheer her up or not, but making sure the woman knew she had a life outside business hours. 'I'll start things moving as soon as I get to Bristol, and hopefully I'll have something to report the next time I see you. I must stress, though, that you mustn't expect miracles.'

'Oh, I already think of you as my miracle, Miss Best!'

She gave Alex a brilliant smile, and just for a moment Alex saw the echo of the once-pretty woman she had been, before Bob Leng and his drinking and the loss of her son Steven had worn her away as surely as the encroaching sea wears away rocks.

* * *

After she had left, Alex forced herself to remember again that she was a professional in a bloody hard world, and there was now a hefty cheque in her possession. Once she had banked it, the first thing she was going to do was call Nick and treat him to a flash night out on the town. There wouldn't be many more occasions for doing so, and the encounter with Jane Leng had left her uneasy, and longing to do something normal.

Nights like these, the song said, and if he got the wrong idea about her invitation, then so be it, she thought. A healthy dose of R and R, which was the army's term for Rest and Relaxation — and Nick's way of referring to a night of rampant sex — was just what was needed to forget all about the neurotic Lengs and their problems.

* * *

'Hell, Alex, I can't make it tonight,' he said, in answer to her call. 'Why didn't you call me before, babe?'

'It doesn't matter,' she said, more sick with disappointment and resentment than she had a right to be, considering she had no intention of making their relationship a permanent one. 'I was tired of packing, that's all, and needed some good conversation.'

'If that's all you needed, I'm not sorry I'm busy,' he teased. 'And no, I don't mean that. You're always good to talk to — as well. How about Friday night instead?'

'Friday's the night before Christmas Eve. Everything will be booked up, and I really wanted to treat you to a meal, Nick, to thank you for everything . . . ' Her voice trailed away, knowing she sounded pathetic. At a loose end so close to Christmas? But then so, apparently, was he.

'Tell me where you want to go, and I'll get us a table,' he said arrogantly. 'The power of the law, remember?'

For once, she didn't bite. So what if he had influence? She named the best West End restaurant she could think of, and ignored his small whistle.

'Have you come into money or something?'

'Something like that. I'll see you Friday then. Book a table for eight o'clock and pick me up around seven, OK?'

'Yes, Ma'am,' he said smartly, before ending the call.

She was still smiling when she hung up.

Christmas Day wasn't going to be a lonely affair, either. She had friends. She had plans. Before leaving London for the south-west, she was finally going north, back to her roots to spend Christmas with an aunt who'd been asking her for years if she was too proud now to visit her old relatives. And Alex's new second-hand Suzuki (one careful lady owner, non-smoker, vgc) was going to be put through its paces.

She hadn't been back to Skeldale for years. It would be odd to see them all again. Her cousins would be grown-up now, strangers in many ways, and her aunt still refused to address her occasional letters to anyone but Miss Audrey Barnes, c/o Miss A. Best. It was quaint and old-fashioned, but it reminded Alex of who she was. Sometimes it was important to remember that.

But Friday night was for Nick, and she dressed up to the nines in her trademark black, and got the required reaction.

'Why the hell am I letting you out of my life?' he moaned dramatically the minute he saw her.

'You're not. You just keep in touch, you hear?' she said, swallowing hard, because she was feeling far too emotional, damn it. And with Christmas parties going on everywhere, and people wallowing in nostalgia, it was hard not to wonder if she was doing the right thing after all. She had everything she needed right here. But she was going, and that was that.

The restaurant meal was hugely over-priced, but she didn't care. She was treating a good friend — her best friend — and by the time the taxi took them back to her flat they were both mellow with champagne.

'You can't stay, Nick, much as I'd like you to,' she giggled, fumbling for her key. 'I have to be off early in the morning to visit the folks back home.'

'Lucky old hayseeds,' he commented.

'No, they're not. They're just family, even though they think of me as the black sheep because I never write, I never phone, I never visit — '

'Good God, bring out the violins,' he grinned, as they finally fell inside the door of her flat. 'Well, if you won't let me stay, you'd better fill me up with black coffee or I'll never find my way home.'

'You're not driving!'

'I drove here, so I suppose I'll have to drive home.'

Alex gave a sigh. He couldn't risk it and they both knew it. He'd be staying over. They both knew that too.

'I want to ask you something, if you can be sensible for a minute,' she said, when she got out of the clinch that was seriously holding up the coffee-making.

'Ask away, Ma'am,' he said.

'It's about the Leng boy.'

The atmosphere between them dropped a couple of degrees, and his hands slid away from the interesting places they had been moving towards.

'Christ, Alex, leave it alone. Don't get involved.'

'I *am* involved. I've agreed to look into it. Did you know Jane Leng is convinced she's seen her son?'

'So what's new?' he said with a resigned air. 'The bloody woman's obsessed. She needs psychiatric help, and so does Bob, if you ask me.'

'Because he's having nightmares?'

'Because he's going to kill himself, and her too, if she doesn't let it go. He's violent when he's drinking, and they'd have chucked him out of the fire brigade long ago but for a few sympathy votes.'

'About Steven,' Alex said quickly, before she lost the thread. The violent angle was something new, though, and she must remember it. 'He had plenty of friends, according to his mother. Do you think the group of schoolfriends he was meant to be camping with were involved in a cover-up?'

'Doubt it. They were questioned minutely. But if you must look for scapegoats, why not the druggies? Why not the other group he was messing with? They were all clean — '

'*Whoa* a minute! Hold on, Nick. What other group?'

She remembered instantly now what she had intended to ask Jane before the woman went off at a tangent. *Steven was always one of a group, in and out of school* . . .

'Those bloody Followers.'

'Followers? What — stalkers, you mean?'

Nick snorted. 'No. Jesus groups and all that rubbish. You know the sort. Like the Moonies. The Sunnies. Religious cults. *Crackpots*. These just called themselves Followers. Couldn't think of anything more inventive, I reckon.'

'And Steven was involved with them?'

'I didn't say that. He was attracted to them. Spent time with them, apparently, which caused plenty of aggro at home with his father. If you've met him, you'll know what I mean. Once seen, never forgotten.'

'I didn't meet him at the party.'

'Big geezer. Disagreeable face. Typical mugshot features. Could double for a TV gladiator or a wrestler, whichever turns you on,' he added for good measure.

'Neither, as a matter of fact.' But the more she heard about Bob Leng, the more she was losing sympathy with his nightmares. It seemed more likely they were a case of the DTs.

'Look, can we forget these morons and make the most of tonight?' Nick said, putting his arms around her. 'I can think of far better things to do. And you're not really going to turn me out on a cold winter's night, are you, babe?'

She wasn't, and she didn't. But first thing next day she turfed him out early, knowing she had to forget all about problem clients for the next few days, because she had to drive to Yorkshire and revert to being Audrey Barnes again.

3

Skeldale never changed. It was as comfortable as an old coat, and as predictable as breathing. When she reached the top of the hill leading down to the valley, Alex got out of her car to stretch her legs and felt a prickle of unexpected tears blur her eyes. It didn't take much to make her feel like Audrey Barnes again after all. Just this.

The whole valley was like a Christmas card scene, coated with a sprinkling of snow now, and glittering like sugar frosting in the wintry thread of sunlight, Alex thought theatrically.

'*'Tis two overcoats colder up here*,' her father used to say prosaically, with the satisfying implication that the south was soft, and southern folk weren't hardy enough to stand it anyway.

The isolated farmhouses in the valley below looked snug and cosy with smoke rising from their chimneys. But icicles hung from the more shaded bushes, and the cold had already penetrated Alex's fashion boots.

'*Daft, I call it, wearing stuff like that*,' she could almost hear her Aunt Harriet say, with a disapproving look at her footwear. She made a bet with herself as to how soon she would say it. And who would be the first to ask when she was coming back home: Aunt Harriet or Uncle Bill.

She got back in the car quickly, reminding herself that she had chosen to leave, and she didn't belong here any more. Only in her heart. But you had to move on, and there wouldn't be much call for a PI among these farming folk — especially those who had known you since you were knee-high to a sparrow.

She blotted out the stupid memories, and drove on to her uncle's farm, stamping away the snow before she went inside, to be enveloped at once in her aunt's embrace. Then it was the turn of Uncle Bill, who held her away from him for a few scrutinizing minutes before he nodded sagely.

'You need a bit o' fattening up, our Audrey. You're nowt but skin and bones. Don't they feed you in London?'

'Leave the lass alone, Bill,' her aunt said. 'And let her get rid of them fancy boots. Daft, I call it, wearing stuff like that in these parts!'

Alex burst out laughing. God, they were straight out of *Wuthering Heights*, and she loved them.

* * *

But it wasn't all beer and skittles and *déjà vu* . . . Christmas Day was scratchy with the cousins. Amy was still as pasty as a suet dumpling and had got progressively fatter as she reached forty. Her farmer husband was her double, and Alex thought that if ever they wanted to cast an adult production of Tweedledum and Tweedledee, here they were.

They argued like hell all the way through Christmas dinner (never called lunch in these here parts), and her cousin Jed, whom she always thought was the spit of cousin Jethro in *The Beverley Hillbillies*, eyed her with suspicion now and then, occasionally spouting a remark which he'd clearly practised a dozen times in his head.

Shamefully, Alex knew she was stereotyping them. But how could you help it, when they were already caricatures of all the worst country thickos ever portrayed on screen?

'You're real citified now, our Audrey. What's to do with that job of yours then?' Jed said finally.

'She's a glorified tally-man,' Amy's husband Vic put in spitefully. 'That's about it, ain't it, lass? You go round collecting debts from them that can't pay up.'

'That comes into it sometimes,' Alex

agreed, prepared to keep calm and hoping her eyes weren't spitting fire at this lout. 'I also try to solve crimes.'

He snorted. 'Hell's teeth, that's what the police are for, ain't it? Who'd want a flashy young lass like you poking into their affairs?'

'Thank you for that,' Alex said sweetly.

He stared at her suspiciously. 'For what?'

'Calling me a flashy young lass. I've been called worse.'

Jed sniggered, clearly crowing over his brother-in-law, and his father clipped him around the head for his trouble.

Jesus, she had to get out of here, Alex thought wildly. How the hell did she ever come to be part of such a family?

She caught a brief sympathetic look in her aunt's eyes, and she knew. Aunt Harriet was her mother's sister, and you couldn't be responsible for your in-laws. They were all the product of their environment, and if Alex ever doubted herself for getting out of it, she didn't any more.

Her mobile rang while they were watching the Queen's Speech on the television. She instinctively knew Aunt Harriet would think of the occasion in capital letters. It was a wonder they didn't put on hats and stand up smartly to attention when they played *God Save the Queen*.

She snatched up her mobile and went out of the sitting-room before she had to face too many disapproving eyes at the intrusion.

'Hey, kiddo, I hope this isn't a bad time. I just wanted to wish you a happy Christmas, and hope it's all going well with the old folks at home — '

'*Christ*, Nick, am I glad to hear you. Can you invent some dire emergency to get me back to London pronto?'

'That good, eh?' he said.

She could hear the smile in his voice, and the sound of glasses chinking somewhere in the background. There was the sound of laughter too, male and female, and she knew he wasn't having such a soulless time as she was.

She gritted her teeth. 'I'm joking, of course. Take no notice,' she lied. 'It's probably a touch of last night's hangover talking.'

Actually, Uncle Bill's home-made elder-flower champagne had one hell of a kick to it, and a few bottles more should get her through the next few days.

'Do you really want me to send out an emergency call?'

It was so bloody tempting . . . but then she remembered the trouble Aunt Harriet had gone to over her room, and how Uncle Bill had fussed over her not getting enough to eat down south, and she knew she couldn't do it.

'Of course not. I've still got people to see and places to go. But thanks for the call, Nick. And have a great time.'

'I'm doing that already,' he said with a laugh, before the line went dead.

She'd just bet he was. She could imagine it. All the singles got together and had a whale of a party on Christmas Day. She wondered whose bed he'd end up in tonight, and blotted out the surge of jealousy.

She'd made her bed and had to lie in it, same as he would. And that was something she preferred not to think about.

'Sorry about that,' she said brightly, rejoining her family in time to see Uncle Bill switch off the TV.

What now? Pass the parcel? Charades? But wasn't this whole bloody day one big charade?

'Heard about that bit of trouble you had last year,' Vic said suddenly. 'Nearly got strangled, didn't you?'

'Thanks for reminding me,' Alex said, feeling the familiar jolt in her heart. 'Bit different from being just a tally-man, wouldn't you say, lad?'

She was fast falling into the lingo, but she knew better than to use the classy accent that was more natural to her now. They would hate it and be embarrassed by it. To them, she was still 'our Audrey' and while it both amused and irritated her, that's what families did, she thought.

'We don't want to talk about that,' Uncle Bill said briskly. 'But why don't you tell us what you're up to now, Audrey-love?'

Audrey-love? For a minute she thought she'd been thrown into the middle of *Coronation Street*, where Tracey-love, the frequently absent daughter of Ken Barlow, always used to emerge from the bedroom a different actress. Which was just what *she* was, Alex reminded herself. Acting out the part of Audrey Barnes, instead of Alex Best. Or was it the other way around?

She took another slurp of Uncle Bill's plentiful supply of elderflower champagne, which was his contribution to Christmas cheer, and wondered what they would say if they really knew what she was up to.

Oh, I'm currently investigating a crazy woman's idea that her son is still alive after being assumed dead for ten years. At least, his hand was dead. God knows what happened to the rest of him. He was involved with druggies and winos, and possibly a religious group, and his schoolfriends might hold the secret . . . and there was something about a burned-out hut in the woods that some kids had ignited with fireworks . . . just a run-of-the-mill job . . .

As they all looked at her expectantly, she wondered if she had really said the words out loud.

'I'm looking into a young boy's disappearance,' she said lamely.

'That's a job for bobbies,' Vic snapped. 'Not for a — '

'A flashy young lass like me?' Alex said. 'Well, the police have had their chance, and now it's down to me.'

'Well, it sounds like a nasty kind of work,' Aunt Harriet said. 'And best left to the men, I say.'

'Oh, Aunt Harriet, that's so outdated — '

'Mebbe 'tis, but so am I. Now then, who wants mince pies and cream?' she said, dismissing it completely.

That summed it all up, Alex thought later. Time-warp, comfy-cosy. Nice to come back to but not to stay. She lay in bed with everything loose, feeling as if she was floating on a sea of cream and elderflower champagne and would never fit into her jeans again. All those weeks of trying to slim down and firm up her wayward thighs were coming to nowt.

She giggled into the darkness. Oh yes, two weeks here, and she'd be back to where she started — which was why it was going to be no more than two more days. Then back to London, back to packing, and off to Bristol to begin another new life. It no longer sounded as bleak as it sometimes did. A new challenge was just what she needed. Coming back here had done her favours after all.

* * *

Since half the country seemed to take the entire week off after Christmas, Alex had persuaded the 'Man With Van' she found in Yellow Pages to move her stuff two days before New Year's Eve, by blatantly using a husky voice over the phone. What the hell? You used what methods you could to get results. And when he and his mate called to the flat, she gave them her sexiest smile, and didn't miss the way they assessed her tight black jeans. *Too* bloody tight now, Alex thought, swearing to lay off everything remotely smelling of chocolate for the foreseeable future.

Nick had helped to bring all her office equipment to the flat, so everything was boxed up and ready to go.

'I'll be following behind you in my car,' she told Man With Van briskly. 'You've got the address, haven't you?'

'Sure have, lady.' He consulted a grubby sheet of paper. '17, Whiteleigh Road, Old Market, office premises downstairs, flat above. Right, love?'

'Right,' she said.

Suddenly she didn't want to prolong this any longer. She had insisted that Nick should stay away. This flat held many memories for her, good and bad. The raunchy times she had spent with one Gary Hollis, virile biker; Nick's chameleon-like personality — the hard-nosed copper, the tender lover; Charmaine, the model-cum-wannabe-actress in the flat below, to whom she had donated some of her CDs; other friends who had come and gone . . . and the horrific, evil man who had tried to strangle her for revealing his crimes.

She shuddered, finally glad to lock up the flat and leave it as anonymously as she had arrived.

* * *

Four hours later, she had finally seen off Man With Van and his assistant after persuading them to put up her bed and get most of the furniture in place, and paying them way over the top for the privilege. She'd also bought them a meal in a motorway service station (how the hell did they pack so much food away?) and since given them cake and soft drinks, as she hadn't yet tracked down her coffee and kettle. Besides which, she didn't want them settling in. But paying for their time had been worth it. Once the heating had come on, the place seemed less like an icebox than it had when she arrived, and by the time she had unpacked most of her other things, the new flat was looking and feeling reasonably like home.

She took a breather, made some coffee at last and glanced at the small collection of letters that had been lying on the mat inside the office door.

Junk mail followed you everywhere, though most of it was addressed to the previous owner. The gas and electricity people requested her to read the current meters and send back the information on the enclosed cards.

There was a jokey 'New Home' card from Nick, with the message inside that if she got fed up living in the sticks, she could always come back to his place, and there was a letter in handwriting that looked vaguely familiar, addressed to Miss Alexandra Best.

The letter inside was handwritten as well, and one look at the signature told her what she should have guessed. She'd seen it once before on a cheque, and Jane Leng wasn't going to let go of her now that she had found her.

She hadn't even moved in properly yet. Her computer and printer and fax machine weren't even plugged in, and if she had any sense she shouldn't bother reading this letter until she'd had something to eat and got her breath back. But she wasn't like that. Some people could ignore the phone ringing, or delay opening mail, but not her. She had a child's curiosity to know what was inside.

'Dear Miss Best,' Jane had written, 'I know you'll be busy what with Christmas and all, and me and Bob won't be moving back to Chilworthy until Feb, like I told you, so I won't be calling on you until then. But I thought you'd want the names of Steven's friends at the time in question. Yours faithfully, Jane Leng (Mrs Bob Leng).'

Alex thought it a sad little letter. Humble and hopeful at the same time, and sure that Alex Best, PI, would perform the miracle that the police couldn't, and find her son alive and well. *Sans* one hand, of course.

And pigs might fly. The unconscious irony didn't escape her as she glanced down at the list of names Jane had included. Steven's friends. There was a TV play or film with a similar title. *Peter's Friends*. She remembered it now. Stephen Fry et al. Marvellous, funny, racy and poignant . . .

But back to the present, even if she was so damn tired she could sleep standing up. In the last few days she had driven to Yorkshire, back to London, and now here, with all the traumas of Christmas and moving thrown in.

The Suzuki was a gem, but she had a right to be tired. And Jane Leng had a right to get full value for the generous fee she was paying her. Alex gave the list of names her full concentration.

Cliff Wilkins
David Wilkins
John Barnett
Keith Martin
Lennie Fry

Nothing there to stir the senses, she thought. And no other details, just a list of names. The first two could be related. Brothers, perhaps. Alex sighed, her brain beginning to fuzz. She really should get to bed, and in best Scarlett O'Hara style, think about it tomorrow.

Unfortunately, she was intrigued now. Names made the whole thing more real. It brought five people into focus, even if she knew nothing more about them, and the stack of local phone directories that the previous occupants had kindly left behind in the flat were staring at her like a reproach.

She plonked them down on her sofa beside her. It wouldn't hurt to just take a look and see if any of the names were listed. One thing she was sure about: the boys had attended the same comprehensive (once Grammar) school, and hopefully, would still be local.

'And this is the one and only thing I'm doing for you today, Jane Leng,' she muttered firmly, resisting the urge to go one better on Scarlett and say that not only tomorrow, but next year was another year . . .

* * *

She rewrote the names alphabetically in a notebook and went through the phone book. There were four Barnett, Johns, with Bristol addresses. Others lived in Bath, Portishead, several in Weston-super-Mare, and in Somerset villages with names Alex had never heard of. This one looked like involving a long weeding-out process.

There was no Fry, L, although there was a large number of Fry subscribers, and she supposed Lennie could have been a nickname anyway.

Martin, Keith William, had his name in full

and sounded important. She checked the business addresses and found that he had a hardware shop in Bath.

Wilkins, Cliff and David, had the same address and phone number, confirming her thought that they could be related. Yellow Pages supplied the information that they operated a haulage firm. Not bad for twenty-six-year-olds.

She found herself yawning, and decided that was enough for one night. She'd made a start, though on what, she didn't really know. It was all going to be a non-event, anyway. Steven Leng was long dead, and eventually his mother was going to have to face up to it.

Uneasily, Alex wondered how the news was going to affect her once there was no other option. It was probably the only thing in her empty life that kept her going. With a drunken husband who gave her no support whatsoever, and precious little affection, she guessed, her entire world was going to collapse if and when Alex discovered anything. The temptation was suddenly huge to fabricate her findings, going through the motions but holding back from anything that might be conclusive, thus leaving the woman with some hope. But that would be just as cruel, and anyway she couldn't and wouldn't do it. She had ethics.

* * *

Winter sat lightly in the south-west, with none of the bitter winds and early snowfalls of the Dales. Apart from the early morning chill in the air, and the thin sunlight, it could almost have been an early spring. Not bad for December going into January.

It didn't bother Alex that she didn't know anyone yet with whom to celebrate New Year's Eve. It was the one time of the year she hated. Her father had died at that time, and it always seemed a depressing occasion.

Instead, she decided to take a couple of days off, the same as everybody else, and explore her new home on foot. It would be good for the figure too, she thought nobly. To begin with, there was a huge area of green above the city, known as the Downs, and Brunel's graceful suspension bridge that spanned the river Avon. It was a businesslike city with a lot of history behind it, and Alex liked that.

She was gazing down at the ribbon of river far below the bridge when she heard the roar of a powerful motorbike along one of the many linking roadways over the Downs. For a minute she felt a sense of *déjà vu*, wondering if she would turn around and see Gary

Hollis, bike courier, one-time lover, coming towards her.

Crazy, of course. The guy pulling up near her now was nothing like Gary. He was older, for a start, in his thirties, she guessed, with streaked blond hair falling over his forehead beneath his helmet and ruggedly good-looking. The outdoor type, and a dedicated biker, she guessed.

'Some view, isn't it?' he said, nodding below.

'Pretty impressive,' she agreed.

'You don't sound like a local. Live around here, do you?' he said.

'I do now. Still finding my way around, as a matter of fact.'

'I could help you in that,' he said with a grin. 'The name's Phil, by the way.'

'Alex,' she said, realizing she'd hardly spoken to anyone but shopkeepers for the last few days. He was friendly enough, even if it did sound like a pick-up. But, she was over twenty-one, and not averse to male company.

'So what do you do, Alex? Are you a model or something?'

'Nice of you to think so! No, it's something far more boring. I'm a private investigator.'

She didn't usually come right out with it. It often put people off. They imagined she was about to start probing into their affairs, and uncovering secrets they'd rather keep hidden. But hey, she was proud of what she did, so why shouldn't she show it!

Phil was staring at her admiringly now. 'On a case, are you?'

She laughed. 'No. Just having a breather.'

'Do you want to come to a party tonight? All kosher, of course. You don't want to be alone on New Year's Eve, do you?'

'I do, actually.' He had some nerve!

'No worries. Some other time then.'

Before she could say anything else he had revved up the bike and turned it around to go roaring off. She didn't know whether to be glad or bloody annoyed at his offhand manner. He could have tried persuading her.

She turned her attention back to the river below, and seconds later she heard the roar of his bike again. It skidded to a halt beside her, causing an older couple of walkers to tut-tut. He was laughing at her now.

'Only kidding, Alex. Really, it would be fun. A group of uni students and tutors are getting together at the Greenbelt — it's a nightclub just outside town.'

'Uni students? Kids, you mean?'

'Hardly. And did I forget to mention that I'm Head of Sports? Philip Cordell if you want to check me out. Here, you can have my card for starters. And if you fancy learning a bit of karate, I'm your man.'

The card he handed her certainly looked impressive enough. Her mouth twitched. 'Actually, I did a course on karate myself once — and isn't a nightclub called the Greenbelt a bit lowering for an expert like you? I'd have thought you were a *black* belt.' And muscly with it . . .

'I am,' he grinned. 'So what do you say? Do I pick you up around nine o'clock? Sort of initiation into city life, you might say. Where do you come from, anyway?'

'London,' she said dryly.

And then she relaxed. Why not? Why the hell not? It was a sure bet Nick wouldn't be staying in tonight wallowing, and she needed to meet people. It also occurred to her that if Phil was a tutor at the university, he might well know something about the people she was going to trace — and about the Followers. She felt her heart beat faster. Fate was a funny thing. It sometimes found you even when you weren't looking for it. Even when you damn well wanted nothing to do with it.

'Nine o'clock then? Give me the address and I'll be there.'

'On the bike?' she asked. And wouldn't it be wiser to suggest meeting at the Greenbelt?

But since she didn't have the faintest idea where it was . . .

'In my car. Don't worry, I wouldn't want you to ruin your best bib and tucker on the babe machine,' he said, his grin revealing a good set of cared-for white teeth. She was doing the horse-check again, she thought.

But she acknowledged that he was pretty fanciable, even if he was as arrogant in his own way as Gary Hollis ever was. She liked his style too, and she gave him one of her newly-printed cards, feeling her heart give a jolt of pleasure at the thought that she needn't spend the night in her own company after all.

'You might be able to help me sometime,' she said casually. 'I've got a list of people I want to trace. Nothing vital. Just contacts for a friend.'

'Why not? I've got a couple of weeks spare for the vac, so I'll be happy to join forces with you.'

He roared off on the bike again, leaving Alex wondering if she had done a stupid thing involving him, even in so small a way. She didn't want anyone joining forces with her, although she had seriously begun to wonder about taking on an assistant — a dogsbody — and Phil certainly didn't fit that description.

No, she thought, walking on across the Downs, and ignoring the thought that the well-toned body of a Head of Sports tutor would be anything but a dogsbody . . . What she wanted, if she wanted anyone at all, was a bright girl who was a whizz with computers and the Internet and could be trusted with the private nature of the business. Maybe she should advertise. The more the idea came into her head, she knew it wasn't such a bad idea. And Phil might well have connections. New Year's Eve certainly wasn't the best of times to assess anyone — but uni students should also be intelligent and keen and looking for something more interesting than the usual boring jobs.

She began to feel uplifted. An assistant could be useful in many ways, if only to take calls and field off unwanted enquiries when she was out on the job. It would be quite good to have someone to share the puzzles that her work entailed too. She would still do the legwork herself, of course. It was her show. Miss X would just be someone to do the office chores. She found herself smiling, and realized that people were smiling back at her. It must be something to do with the extended holidays, and the fact that a stronger sun was lightening the sky.

Without thinking, Alex began humming

beneath her breath, glad she was here; glad she had had the courage to make the move, and scornful of any suggestion that it had been her last traumatic case that had prompted it. And even more, she had already met a dishy man who was taking her clubbing that night.

It was time to forget about work and the Jane Lengs of this world for the time being, and start thinking about what she was going to wear to wow him.

4

Friends and acquaintances knew of Alex's preference for wearing black. It was her trademark colour. The contrast it created with her sleek red hair and stunning green eyes made her look even more dramatic. She wasn't too proud to admit that she liked the attention it attracted — though she could be as chameleon-like as DCI Nick Frobisher when it came to altering her appearance and her accent for professional purposes. It was part of the job.

But tonight, she was going to wear a glittery, slinky black sheath of a dress, with heels that made her even taller. Phil Cordell must be well over six feet, she had noted, so together they would make quite an entrance.

'God, you're vain, aren't you, kiddo?' she asked, grinning at her reflection on her way to the bathroom for a shower, imagining Nick saying the words, and knowing what he would say next, too.

'Are you sure you want to go out tonight, babe? I can think of much better things to do staying in . . . '

Alex turned away with a sigh. She did miss

him, and she was already wondering why on earth she had agreed to go out with a stranger to a place she didn't know. It would probably be filled with under-twenties and she'd feel out of it. But then, so would Phil — except that he would know people and she wouldn't.

What a wimp she was being, Alex thought furiously. It wasn't her style, and she had better buck up her ideas pretty quickly if she didn't want the evening to end up like a damp squib. She took a few deep breaths and stepped under the shower, letting the hot water refresh her, and paying as much attention to her appearance as if she was meeting Nick.

* * *

'Wow!' was all Phil Cordell said when she opened the door to him, right on time.

That was the word all right.

'Is that wow *good*, or wow I'm-dressed-all-wrong-for-the-place-we're-going-to?' she asked him.

'Wow *great*, and you know it,' he said with a laugh.

He didn't look so bad himself, smartly casual in a black jacket and trousers and a beige silky rollneck sweater. And she still liked those impossibly white teeth — providing they weren't like the stars and came out at night.

'I'm ready then,' Alex said brightly, resisting a giggle before her thoughts ran away with her and she turned this meeting into a farce. Not that she had any intention of letting it become anything more than friendly, she had decided. He was good-looking, and hopefully great company, but she didn't want to start a new relationship. Not yet. If ever. Well . . . not ever was a long time, and she wasn't dead yet. But she could play it cool when necessary, and a sixth sense told her it would be wiser to do just that. She had been wrong before.

'You'll like these kids, Alex,' Phil said casually, as they walked out to his car. A People Mover, she noted. Nice. Good for carrying lots of students about. Darkened windows for anything else that might be going on inside. She wished away the thought.

'I hope so,' she said, in answer to his comment. 'Where I used to live, there was an actress-cum-model in the flat below, and her parties weren't exactly my style.'

'Really? Druggies, were they?'

His words startled her. 'No, they weren't, actually.'

Why did people naturally assume such

things? You could think the same about students. Many people did. Drugs weren't her scene and never had been, and she hoped she wasn't going to be disappointed in Phil and his crowd.

'Good. We have a real downer on that kind of thing at college,' he said.

'I thought you were Head of Sports at the university,' she said.

'Did I say that? No. St Joseph's College. It's a teacher training college. But I know a lot of the uni students. Some of them have come on to us.'

He glanced at her as the car took them smoothly out of town.

'Does that make a difference? I didn't take you for a snob, Alex.'

'Good Lord, no. I just got the wrong end of the stick. That's all.'

She pushed down her small feeling of unease that had risen up due to the fact that she was sure she hadn't got the wrong end of the stick, that he was a virtual stranger, and that she didn't have a clue where they were going. For all she knew . . .

'Sorry about that,' Phil went on. 'I'm afraid St Joseph's is rather smaller fry than the uni, but a lot of my friends are tutors there, and we usually get together at this time of year. We have a lot more mature students too, of course,' he added.

She almost said thank God for that, but stopped herself in time. She didn't want to sound like somebody's maiden aunt.

'So what's this case you're on now?' he went on casually.

'I don't remember saying I was on a case.'

He laughed. 'I think you rather neatly ignored it, but my guess is that you are. You don't strike me as the kind of woman who sits around twiddling her thumbs waiting for business to come in. So what kind of things do you investigate? Straying husbands, that kind of thing?'

'Sometimes. And straying wives. Men don't have the monopoly on it.'

'Uh-oh — touched a nerve, have I? Bit of a feminist streak in there somewhere, is there? Still, I like that in a woman. Shrinking violets went out with the suffragettes.'

Alex laughed back. She couldn't quite make him out, but it was New Year's Eve, for God's sake, and she was hardly being abducted by aliens.

'How long have you lived in Bristol?' she asked him.

'Oh — half my life. Man and boy — or should that be boy and man?' he said easily. 'From student to tutor, single, married and divorced.'

'Thanks, but I didn't mean to be that personal.'

'Well, you didn't ask, but now you have it in a nutshell. In case that was what was bothering you.'

He was more astute than she realized. 'It wasn't. I just thought if you've lived here a long time you may have heard something about the Leng case that happened ten years ago.'

He whistled, and for a moment Alex could have been in the company of one Gary Hollis, who'd had a habit of driving her mad with his tuneless whistling. But something told her that this guy had little in common with Gary except for being a keen biker. All Gary's brains were in his jeans, she thought with a small surge of memory that wasn't altogether unwelcome.

'So that's it, is it? The mad Mrs Leng has got you on the case, has she?'

'You know her then? And why do you call her mad?' Alex demanded, feeling her heartbeats quicken at Phil's response to her question.

'I don't know her, but most people know *of* her. Every now and then she writes a letter to the local rag, knowing she'll get more sympathy than from the nationals, demanding that the case is reopened since she's sure she's seen her son yet again. Sometimes it's on TV, and sometimes it's in the middle of a crowd. My guess is they use her letters when there's nothing much else to put in the paper.'

'Don't you find that a bit sad?' Alex said, defending her.

'No. She's led that husband of hers a devil of a life, by all accounts, making him think their son was still alive, when everyone knew he was dead.'

'Did they?' This conversation was starting to get interesting.

'Well, so they say,' Phil amended. 'But listen, we don't want to talk about that all night, do we? We're nearly at the Greenbelt, so let's enjoy ourselves, OK?'

He seemed mighty glad to end the discussion on Jane Leng and her dead son. Or was this her feminine intuition going haywire, just because she wanted to think she'd struck lucky in finding someone who just might know something so soon, and without even trying?

Come on, Alex! She didn't believe in coincidences, and in any case, she knew she'd get nothing more out of him right now, because they were turning into the grounds of the nightclub. Neon lights blazed out, and even from here the music screamed loudly enough to burst the eardrums and rattle the chest. Talk was obviously going to be limited. But there would be time enough later to find out just what Phil Cordell knew — or surmised.

⋆ ⋆ ⋆

The Greenbelt wasn't exactly tacky, but it wasn't the West End either, and Alex knew she had better not start comparing, or she certainly would be marked out as a snob. The most refreshing thing was to find that Phil's party friends weren't all mad-brained teenagers, and there was a fair sprinkling of tutors among the students. As he said, some of the ex-uni ones had turned to teacher training and gone on to St Joseph's. They all seemed to accept her as Phil's new girl, and for the time being, she let it go at that.

She approved of the fact that he drank very little, knowing that he would be driving home after midnight. What she hadn't expected was that a few of them assumed he'd be driving them home as well, which gave them plenty of leeway to get well and truly plastered by the time midnight had struck.

There were hugs and boozy kisses all around, and then she felt herself clasped in

Phil Cordell's arms and held tight to his chest.

'You know I fancy you rotten, don't you, Alex?' he whispered in her ear.

'No, you don't,' she said, superior as ever. 'We hardly know each other.'

Oh God, here was her maiden aunt stuff again, and she knew that her ice-cool voice frequently raised the libido instead of squashing it.

Phil whispered against her mouth now. 'I mean to do something about that. Unless there's someone else? If so, where is he, tonight of all nights?'

He was a confident, easy talker, his blond-streaked hair, height and physique oozing sex-appeal. He was every student's dream tutor, especially on the sports field. All those muscles, and those pecs . . .

But just as quickly as she had fancied him, Alex knew that she didn't — and couldn't. He just wasn't her type. She gave him a cool smile as they were jostled and pressed together by people still kissing and screeching out 'Happy New Year' to one another as if their lives depended on it, by streamers and balloons cascading down on them, by the explosion of party poppers all around them, and by the heavy pressure of his sinewy body against hers.

'There is someone, as a matter of fact,' she told him. 'He's still in London, but he's coming down as soon as he can get a few days off,' she invented.

'What the hell does he do if he can't get away for New Year's Eve?' Phil said, almost surly, and again Alex was reminded of Gary Hollis — except that Phil was more powerfully built, and a black belt in karate.

'He's a policeman. A Detective Chief Inspector, if you want his full title,' Alex said, awarding Nick his impressive status.

'Jesus Christ. That's almost incestuous — you a private investigator and him a copper.'

'No more so than you and other ranks spending time together.'

'See what I mean? You even use the same jargon. *Other ranks*!'

'Are we having an argument?' Alex said pleasantly. 'If so, one of your students has been asking me for a dance, and I think now might be a good time.'

He squeezed her to him very tightly for a moment, and she could feel the pressure on her ribs. And then he was all sweetness and light again.

'I'm sorry, Alex. This isn't the best of days for me. You couldn't have known it, but today's the anniversary of my divorce. I shouldn't be taking it out on you, but the fact is, my ex-wife ran off with a copper, so it's no wonder I've got no love for the breed, is it?'

So she was here on a bloody therapy trip for him, was she? Poncing her around like an accessory, to prove to the world that he could still pull, even if his wife had left him for somebody else.

'I think I should go and have that dance with Brendan now, don't you?'

'All right. And I'll get the drinks in for when you've put him through his paces,' he said, grinning as if he'd said something terribly witty. 'And I hope you won't hold all this against me?'

'Not a chance,' she said sweetly.

There was no way he could mistake her meaning, and she wasn't going to make any move towards seeing him again either.

* * *

Two days later, the hangover had subsided and she was thinking coherently again. She had told Nick over the phone that yes, she'd had a good time on New Year's Eve, Bristol was fine, and she wasn't missing the Smoke at all.

Now she was at her desk, looking gloomily

at the ad she was trying to compose for the local paper.

The last thing she wanted to do was to advertise her presence too obviously. On the other hand, there were two ways of looking at that. One, she wanted the business. But two, she didn't want every weirdo calling at all hours of the night and day, thinking it must be a hell of a kick to work for a private eye. All that sleaze going on, with their lascivious little fingers poking into every pie and reporting it to their best mates for the price of a pint.

She pushed her hands back through her hair in annoyance at her own paranoid thoughts, making her fringe stand up on end, until she heard the ring on her doorbell, and hastily smoothed it down again.

For her own peace of mind, and a modicum of security, she'd had one of those smoky glass doors installed which enabled her to see who was outside, while they couldn't see in. It was a gawky young man, tidily dressed, who didn't look as if he was all set for rape and pillage. Not that you could tell these days.

She spoke into her intercom, released the door catch, and told him to push it open. The cautious, rusty-haired young man stepped inside, fidgeting with the envelope in his hand.

'Are you a postman or something?' Alex said, when he seemed too tongue-tied to speak.

'Heck no,' he said, thrown off balance for a few seconds. 'Oh, you mean the letter. Sorry, Miss. I didn't know what to expect. When Mr Cordell said you were a private investigator, I imagined — well, I don't know what I imagined really — certainly not — not — well — '

By now he was bright red up to his ears, and the colour seemed to merge into his hair. Alex immediately felt sorry for him, identifying with the problem at once. Red hair could be a curse at times. She knew it only too well. It could take years to control that quick rush of blood to the face, if ever.

'Why don't you sit down?' she said, more gently. 'And I take it you're referring to Philip Cordell? Of St Joseph's College?'

'That's right,' the boy said, breathing more easily. 'If you'd read the letter Miss, it will explain everything.'

She ripped it open. It was short and to the point. It was just to introduce Ray Smart, who had always lived up to his name in college, and was keen for some responsible work experience in his gap year before going on to university. He was hot on computers, Phil added, which might be an advantage in her business, and he would personally vouch for his discretion and trustworthiness.

Alex looked up, conscious that Ray Smart's gaze hadn't moved away from her. She knew that look. He was dazzled, if not instantly smitten, and she wondered if it would be such a good idea to take him on. She hadn't envisaged a male assistant, though a female would probably be far more likely to keep her phone line tied up with chatty calls to boyfriends and God knows who else, she thought cynically. This boy didn't look as if he'd ever had a girlfriend, or knew what it was all about. He was weedy and earnest, and if he was as hot on computers and as trustworthy as Phil said, then he was probably highly suitable for the job.

'Mr Cordell gives a very good report of you, Ray,' she said at last.

'I hope so. He's always been a bit of a hero of mine.'

Good God, he was the epitome of a kid with a crush on a teacher now — and that was probably all he was thinking about with regard to her too. In which case, she could certainly expect loyalty — and somebody wearing a skin-tight black sweater and ski-pants must be a bit of a shock if he'd been half-expecting to meet a female Sherlock Holmes.

'You know what the nature of this work is, don't you, Ray? I presume Mr Cordell will have told you that much. It's essential that everything that goes on in this office is totally confidential.'

'Oh yes. I'd die before I revealed anything outside it, Miss Best.'

'Well, I don't think you need go that far,' she said, hiding a small smile.

He was so bloody intense she hardly knew how to handle him. But at least he was taking the whole thing seriously. Some gap year students she had met took the whole year as an excuse for one big rowdy party. This guy seemed sincere, enough. Her dad would probably have called him a swot.

'Where do you live, Ray?' she asked next.

'Eastville. With my parents. My dad's an insurance agent, and my mum's a home help.'

'Right.'

No sweat there then, and he was looking so anxious now she was starting to feel a bloody heel at the thought of turning him down. But since he came well recommended, she could always hire him on a temporary basis. She was mentally giving herself the options, already knowing what the answers would be.

'We could start on a month's trial, Ray, but I can't say any more than that at this stage. I hadn't definitely decided I needed an assistant at all,' she lied, 'so how does the arrangement suit you? Unless it's too temporary, and you've got anything else in mind?'

She almost hoped he'd say yes, but from the way he shook his head so vigorously, you'd have thought his life depended on getting this job. Maybe the parents were sticklers for not letting their little boy be seen as a wastrel. Perhaps they insisted that he earned his keep during this year. Whatever.

'Right then, you're hired,' Alex said, putting out her hand to shake on it, and surprised to feel how clammy his was.

She drew back as quickly as she could, resisting the urge to wipe her fingers down the sides of her trousers.

'So when do I start? Today? Now?'

'Let's leave it until Monday, shall we?' Alex said, wondering if she was going to have to wet-nurse him all the way. But Phil *did* say he was hot on the computer, didn't he? That was what had drawn her to him, even though he looked as useless as a bent penny. First thing next week she would put him to the test by asking him to track down anything he could on the Followers.

'You can sort me out with the Internet stuff,' she added. His face lit up at once and she knew she'd said the right thing.

'Fantastic. Anything you want to find out, I'll get it for you, Miss.'

'Good. And for pity's sake call me Alex. Otherwise I'll begin to think I'm your headmistress.'

The smile vanished from his face and he just managed to stutter out her name as he reached the office door.

'All right — er — er — Alex. I'll see you on Monday then.'

'Nine sharp,' she called after him, but he was already gone.

Ye Gods, what have I done? she wondered weakly. She rummaged in her desk drawer until she found Phil Cordell's card. It would be courteous to call him and thank him for putting Ray on to her. However, that would open up communications again, and although he had initially offered to be around for his two weeks' vac, she had the feeling that idea had cooled by now. Anyway, Ray still had to prove himself. There would be time enough to contact Phil and report, when she had seen what the boy was worth. She put the card back in the drawer again and closed it firmly, and opened the file on Jane Leng.

Jane Leng was turning out to be a bit of an enigma. On the one hand she was the doting mother, desperate to believe that her son hadn't died. On the other, she was the monstrous wife, killing her husband with her obsession, as surely as he was killing her with his drunkenness. It was too cruel to think that they deserved one another, but in Alex's opinion, they damn well did. Instead of Steven's death drawing them together, it had had the effect of driving them further and further apart.

But sorting out their marital problems wasn't the purpose of Jane's hiring Alex, nor her problem. She just wanted the truth about Steven, as if it wasn't staring her in the face with all the weight of police and forensic evidence — except for the lack of a body to prove once and for all that he was dead, of course. And that was the one thing Jane couldn't accept. The final proof was missing. In her eyes it was unfinished.

Alex closed the file and shrugged into her leather jacket. It was time to make a start. She switched on her answering machine and left her office, armed with a local map, and made her way to the local newspaper offices. It wasn't far, and she decided to walk, making the most of the clement weather while it lasted. She needed to find out everything she could — not only about the reports of the events ten years ago, but she was curious to see the letters Jane Leng had been bombarding the paper with ever since.

There was nothing much moving at the offices that day, and New Year's Eve was clearly having a lengthy recovery time here. She was passed on to an older reporter in answer to her queries, who looked none too pleased at being disturbed from whatever activities he had been engrossed in. The arrival of a glamorous PI in the town wasn't enough to create a stir, even if she had advertised the fact, but it was part of the job to use her female assets whenever the need arose. And it arose now.

'I hope I'm not disturbing you,' she said, giving the guy the full benefit of her green eyes, and passing over her card. 'I've been given permission to look in the archives for some information I need.'

'Then I'm your man, and we aim to please, Miss Best,' Charley Adamson said, reviving from his reverie with a smirk that passed for a smile. 'So what is your desire?'

She smiled sweetly back at these clumsy attempts to be gallant, wondering if he always spoke in clichés, and told him she was interested in seeing some of the letters written to the newspaper by poor Jane Leng over the years.

That did it. Charlie gave a guttural laugh, which started him coughing and spluttering, and had Alex stepping back a foot or so to escape it all.

'Don't waste your sympathy on that one, dearie,' he almost honked. 'She's as daft as a brush, still thinking she can see her boy around every corner.'

'You don't believe it then?'

'Do you? I'd have thought a young lady of your credentials would have known better.'

'I didn't say I believed it. I was merely asking if you did.' She wasn't falling for that one. A reporter was always a reporter, and he'd be mentally noting her responses to his artless questions, just as she was noting his.

He laughed. 'No, I don't believe it. The boy's long dead, and it's time the silly woman let him rest in peace.'

Or in pieces, Alex supplied in her head.

'So can I take a look in the archives, then?' she persisted.

'Oh well, if that's what you want, I daresay we can manage that. Come and see my etchings,' he chuckled, in what was apparently meant to be winsome.

What was it about men? Alex wondered. They took one look at a woman, and they were either young enough to be bursting out of their jeans with testosterone, or old enough to think their age allowed them to get away with anything — even corny lines like that. But she guessed he was harmless. If she made as much as one move in the same direction, she guessed he'd go scuttling away in fright. Most ageing would-be gigolos did.

She followed him down into the bowels of the building, only half-listening to his comments that the kids upstairs (presumably anyone under twenty-five) had everything on computer now, of course, but you couldn't beat the old hands-on methods of turning crackling, yellowing newspaper pages, and breathing in the essence of past events and crimes.

'There's passion in them thar pages, my dear,' he went on, putting a pseudo-Western drawl into his voice, 'them old crimes and reports come to life through the pages far more than they do on any newfangled screen.'

Alex had a sneaking empathy with those feelings, although it was something you hardly dared say to the Internet nerds these days for fear of ridicule.

You mean you're not connected yet? Good God, what planet have you been living on, Alex?

Well, she was now, even if she wasn't exactly conversant with it all yet. She found herself revising her first opinion of Charley Adamson. He was a real newspaperman, one of the old school. And chatty with it.

'So how far back do you want to go, Miss Best? I'll tell you summat for nothing too.

Whenever they get stuck upstairs, they send me down here to ferret out the lost bits of news. Progress ain't everything, and I'm a bit of a ferret myself, ain't I? If it's here, I'll find it.'

He chuckled at his own joke, clearly priding himself on his knowledge.

'You're a treasure, Charlie, and please call me Alex. I've a feeling we're going to be down here for some time.'

As long as it took, she said mentally to Jane. *Until I put together the pieces of your personality — if not your son.*

5

Charlie proved to be a godsend. As well as finding all Jane's letters over the years, he had his own tame computer nerd upstairs. Neville put all the letters into one file and printed them out for her to take away. Progress wasn't all bad news, Alex thought humbly, ignoring the superior attitude of said Neville, and the undoubted whiff of something suspiciously like pot that wafted all around him. It was none of her business, and who cared as long as it got results?

In any case, the make-it-legal brigade would sneer at her for still living in the dark ages. Or the Yorkshire Dales.

She left the offices, promising that the next time she came in for information, she'd stand Charlie a pint and a pie at the local of his choice. It was the least she could do, and it made for good public relations — even if she had to include the revolting Neville as well.

* * *

Jane had been very thorough in her vicious attacks on the ineptitude of the police, and the lack of interest in her precious boy once the coroner had decided he could give no verdict other than accidental death. That was how she put it in her letters, no matter what the official terms would have been. She accused anyone and everyone for being in on a cover-up, without naming anyone specifically.

Occasionally the paper published an answering letter. It usually told her mildly to give it a rest, since it was doing no good, and only hurting herself and her husband to keep resurrecting it all. It was the kind of response that could have been kindly meant, or a threat. Especially as it was usually signed 'a well-wisher'. How corny could you get? Alex thought to herself.

But in the end, Jane's letters told her little more than she already knew, which was hugely disappointing. If she had hoped to unearth some great revelation that the police had missed, she was foiled, because there was nothing more than the ramblings of a sad and embittered woman.

She wondered how long it would be before Jane got in touch with her again. She and her husband were moving back to Somerset when Bob retired in February, she remembered, and she had no doubt that Jane would be pestering her for news the minute she got the chance. So before then, Alex had better have something ready to report, if only to get her off her back.

Nick called her while she was still wishing fervently she'd never got tangled up with the woman in the first place.

'How's it going down in the sticks? Found any missing haystacks yet?'

He was so brash and breezy it made her bristle; assuming naturally that she had done no such thing as finding anything interesting; that there was nothing much doing in the back of beyond, anyway, and that London was the only place to be . . . and he of all people, should know better. If she was getting all that from an inflection in a voice, she must be in dire need of physical company!

'I'm very busy, as a matter of fact,' she said coolly, 'and you just caught me before I left my office.'

'Oh yeah?' She could hear the grin in his voice now. She could imagine the smile curving his mouth. 'What is it today? Somebody lost something at the village jumble sale?'

'It's not that provincial,' Alex snapped. 'And you're being very snobbish, Nick. Anyway, there's nothing wrong with the country — not that Bristol is the kind of country I was brought up in, as you never forget to remind me.'

'Hey, calm down, babe! I was only teasing, or have you lost your sense of humour along with all your best mates?'

'What best mates?'

'Yours truly, for one. But that's a situation that's about to change next weekend, if you play your cards right.'

'Go on.' As if she couldn't guess what was coming.

'Well, it all depends if you've got room in your flat to put up a close friend for the weekend.'

'How close?' But she couldn't help smiling back into the phone now.

'Your call, darling,' Nick said, his voice dropping even lower. 'I just want to see you again — and I might just have a bit of news to interest you.'

'Oh yes?' Alex said more sharply, her attention caught far more than the prospect of sharing her flat with Nick for the weekend. That could wait.

His laugh was soft and sexy. 'Didn't your daddy ever teach you the joys of anticipation? On all counts, sweetheart. And with that thought in mind, I'll see you around eight on Friday evening.'

The next minute he was gone, leaving her fuming at the phone. Damn cheek, expecting her to be ready and waiting . . . as she would be, of course. What else did she have to do? And if he'd read *that* little piece of her mind, he'd be less than flattered, Alex thought.

But when she let her feathers unruffle, she knew she would be enormously glad to see him. It had only been a few weeks, but already it seemed like a lifetime since she left London, and if she had ever thought it an impersonal city, she was learning that any city could be just as impersonal if you didn't know people. It was a mistake to be isolated.

On impulse she called her aunt and uncle, and was even pleased to hear her Aunt Harriet's caustic tones at the other end, though she was certainly not bothering to hide the surprise in her voice at this unexpected communication.

'There's nowt wrong with you, is there, lass?' Harriet said suspiciously, 'only when we don't hear from you from one year's end to the next — '

'You only saw me a few weeks ago, Aunt Harriet,' Alex protested.

'Aye, and that was the end of one year, and this is the beginning of the next. Or don't they count the same number of days in a year down south?'

Alex gritted her teeth. Nothing changed — except herself, she thought.

'I just wanted to wish you all a Happy New Year, that's all.'

Oh well, if that were all, then the same to you, but 'tis an expensive way of doing things, when you could have said the same at Christmas before you left.'

'So I could,' Alex said in a strangled voice. 'Goodbye then, Aunt Harriet.'

She put down the phone again, staring at it resentfully. But it had been a worthwhile couple of minutes: it reminded her of just why she'd had to get away from them all in the first place.

'I'm a snobby pig, if there is such a thing,' she told herself out loud. And then she relaxed. 'But I'm a happy snobby pig because Nick's coming down for the weekend!'

* * *

Before then she had work to do. By now she had checked out all the John Barnetts in the phone book, and concluded that he had to be one of the Weston-super-Mare ones. One of those had sounded far too elderly to qualify, and there was no reply from the other. But that was the one she was going to suss out.

Before that, she went into a couple of nearby shops to buy bread, milk and the morning paper, and made friendly overtures to the girls behind the counters. She told them she was new in town and asked for directions to the library, the nearest post office, the bank, the supermarket (not too tactful, in a corner grocer's shop) and other places of interest. She got a friendly response and a few smiles, and thought that life wasn't all bad. One of the girls was especially keen to chat, and said if she ever needed a guide around town, to call on her. Name of Mavis, Alex noted by the badge on her lapel.

'Mavis, I might just do that, since I don't know many people here yet,' she told her.

'Don't forget then,' the girl urged. Her accent was broadest Bristol, but such things never bothered Alex, since she could as easily lapse into her native Yorkshire at the drop of a hat. (Why hat, she found herself wondering?)

'I won't. See you soon,' Alex promised.

People said that all the time, didn't they? And rarely meant it.

But maybe she should mean it. Maybe it would be good to find a woman friend who was uncomplicated and had nothing remotely to do with the kind of world she lived in. And how about *that* for a kind of backhanded snobbery?

But she didn't mean it that way, and once she had found her way out of the city in her car, she found herself humming as she eased onto the open road and followed the signs for Weston-super-Mare. She could have taken the motorway, but from the look of the map it seemed more of a devious a route to reach it than driving smoothly out of town through Nailsea and Backwell and Congresbury and onto the mini-metropolis that was Weston-super-Mare.

Alex headed for the seafront through the main road into town with its plethora of B & Bs, and her eyes widened with pleasure at the vast open bay, fringed with sand, with its pier splitting the curve of the bay in two. The tide was in, and there were small boats at the sheltered end of the bay, bobbing majestically on the little waves. She had already learned that the tide went out a very long way, so she was catching it at its best, despite the greyness of the January sky. The weather was still mild, but she imagined that with a gale blowing and the sand being whipped up to sting the eyes and ears, it would be a very different picture.

There was free parking along the seafront during the winter season, so once out of the car she decided to take a bracing walk along the wide promenade. She needed the exercise, but bracing was definitely the word for it, and after half an hour she took refuge in a small café near the grand edifice of the

Winter Gardens. After she had been fortified by a steaming cup of coffee and a toasted bun she enquired the way to Alfred Street.

As so often happened, the local waitress looked completely foxed by the question, as if she knew no more of the town than the street where she lived. And the Bingo Hall, Alex guessed, letting her prejudice slip for a moment.

'You can walk to Alfred Street from here,' the portly guy behind the counter called out. 'Do you know where the Odeon is — and Tesco's?'

Alex had to confess that she didn't, and the guy brought out a tattered and well-thumbed town map, clearly not averse to spending a few minutes with this vision on a dull morning, when tourists were few and far between. Alex ignored the general smell of cooking grease around his person, and shuffled to one end of the plastic bench seat as he sat down beside her.

He stabbed his fingers on the map until she got the general route, and realized it wasn't very far at all. All the same, she'd had enough walking for one morning, and decided to drive. She thanked him and was glad to get out.

Now for John Barnett, with any luck. And, remembering that like all Steven's old friends, he would have been throughly vetted in the past, she needed a tactful line of questioning if she wasn't to scare him off altogether.

* * *

Alfred Street was a narrow residential street of small stone houses. Alex found the house that she wanted, and rang the bell. After a few minutes a woman looked out from behind the net curtains, took one look at Alex and swished them back into place again. When she didn't appear at the door, Alex rang the bell again. She didn't look like a Jehovah's Witness, for God's sake, nor a canvasser doing a survey on the smoking or reading habits of the neighbourhood.

Eventually the door opened a fraction, and as she saw that the woman was elderly and moved carefully behind a walking frame she was instantly contrite at her uncharitable thoughts.

'I'm so sorry to disturb you,' she said with a bright smile when the woman didn't say anything. 'I was hoping to have a few words with John Barnett. He does live here, I believe? This is the address I was given.'

For a few seconds Alex thought the woman was going to explode. Her face was already the colour of parchment, but within seconds it went a fierce shade of red. She clutched at the walking frame as if it was a lifeline, and Alex hoped desperately that she wasn't going to have a heart attack here and now. She had done a First Aid course, and knew how to cope in an emergency, but it was a different situation when you thought you had caused the bloody emergency!

'I seem to have taken you by surprise, Ma'am, and I've obviously come at a bad moment,' she said quickly. 'Is Mr Barnett at home — and if not, is there anything I can do for you?'

And who was she in regard to him? Lodger? Grandmother? This *was* the address in the phone book — unless the house had changed hands since it had been updated and the news hadn't reached BT yet. But she doubted that this was a new tenant. From the look of her and her drab clothes, and the glimpse of old-fashioned furniture inside the hall, she had been here since the year dot — whatever that was.

When the woman continued to stare at her, saying nothing, Alex tried again.

'Look I really am sorry to disturb you, and I'll go away just as soon as possible. It's just that I do want to contact Mr Barnett — John Barnett — '

'You can't do that,' the woman said, speaking for the first time.

At least it was contact of a kind, and Alex spoke more quietly.

'Is he at work, maybe? If you could possibly give me an idea of where I might find him I'd be very grateful — '

'He's in the cemetery.'

Alex felt her heart leap. He was *dead*? But why hadn't Jane Leng told her that when she gave her the list of Steven's friends? But she remembered quickly that Jane had given her nothing more at all except the list of names. Everything else, so far, Alex had found out for herself. Maybe Jane didn't even know. Nick hadn't mentioned this little bit either, Alex thought resentfully.

As she struggled to find a suitable reply to the information, the old woman sniffed audibly. 'What is it you want?'

'I'm working on a a kind of project for the university,' she invented wildly. 'We're presently gathering information on old Grammar school boys for a statistical dossier, and are interested in the kind of work they did after leaving school, and also in any photographs we can find of them and their classmates. But I'm so sorry to hear that John Barnett is no longer with us.'

She made the project sound as grand and

as far removed from the truth as possible, and dangled the bait in the hope of being given as much information as this woman could tell her. If John was a relative, then surely she'd want his memory preserved in as good a light as possible.

'You can come in, if you like,' Alex was told grudgingly. 'I've got my albums, and you can have a look.'

Bingo! Old people always kept photo albums.

'And you are?' she asked, as she stepped inside the front door and was immediately assailed by the stale smells of an old person's home.

'His granny. His folks don't live here any more. They moved away when my son — John's dad — got a job over in Cardiff.' She sniffed again as if this was comparable to going to hell. 'This was always my house, anyway, and John stayed here wi' me, until it happened.'

'What did happen, Mrs Barnett?' Alex asked carefully, after following her to a sitting-room crammed with the collected paraphernalia of the elderly.

Huge potted plants in the window practically shut out the daylight. Tables were cluttered with newspapers and magazines and there were knick-knacks on every surface.

There was a fine film of dust over everything. Alex felt a burst of pity that overcame the distaste she felt and sat down on the edge of a sagging armchair as Mrs Barnett sank down heavily on another.

'I told you. He died.'

'Yes, but you didn't tell me how. Did he have an illness? I'm sorry if I seem to be probing, but it would be such a help for our records, you see, if we can find out what happened to our old Grammar school boys. I'm sure you mourn the passing of the old system as much as any of us.'

Well, that was a bloody daft thing to say, Alex told herself severely. If this old lady was mourning anything, it would be the passing of her grandson, not any old school system. She was on delicate ground and she knew it, but she had to keep up the pretence that this was for a project or she would get nowhere. Old people could be very protective of their privacy, and she guessed this one was no exception. She realized Mrs Barnett was staring at her now, but she was relieved to see the normal colour — or lack of it — was evident in her face now.

'He didn't have no illness,' she was told, scorn in her voice. 'He was as strong as an ox, my John. Could have been anything he wanted. Worked on the railway to keep himself afloat, but he was studying figures at night school to make summat of himself. He would have done it too.'

'So what happened?' Alex said, forcing herself to be patient. When they got that reminiscent look in their eyes, she knew there was no hurrying them.

'Well, he was coming home late on that motorbike of his, wasn't he?' Mrs Barnett said, with a flash of anger in her eyes. 'Nasty things, motorbikes. I always told him they'd be the death of him, but what happened weren't his fault. He wasn't the madhead they said he was. The road was muddy and slippery after a lot of rain, but I know my John wouldn't have taken any chances. It was the car driver who was the madhead, going too fast and forcing him over the edge. You can still see the gap in the hedge where he went over on to the rocks below, if you know where to look. Smashed him and his precious bike to pieces, it did.'

She was retelling it almost by rote now, as if it all had to come out in a series of short sentences, or it would never come out at all.

'I'm so sorry,' Alex said, almost in a whisper.

The woman blinked, as if only just remembering she had a listener.

'Bless you, but it was a long time ago now — '

'How long ago, Mrs Barnett?'

'Four years and a bit. Just before Christmas, it was. And that Toll road can always be a death trap at night, can't it?'

Alex agreed that it could, with no idea where or what the Toll road was, but meaning to find out the minute she got out of there.

'They never found the driver, of course. I daresay they were too busy with other crimes to bother too much about one poor boy being pushed over a cliff.'

And six years after Steven Leng died — allegedly — and four years ago now and just before Christmas — Alex supposed there would have been no reason for a piece about John Barnett being killed in a motorbike accident to be reported in great detail in a Bristol newspaper. Unless she had specifically asked Charlie Adamson and Neville to suss out anything about Steven's friends — which she hadn't.

'Do you want to see the albums?' she heard Mrs Barnett saying now.

'Oh — yes please, if it's not too much trouble.'

Alex saw that there was a whole stack of them on the lower shelf of a coffee table alongside her, and guessed that she spent many hours looking through them.

'My home help keeps telling me to put these away,' Mrs Barnett went on, 'but they're my bit of company, see?'

The words were said so matter-of-factly they all but stifled Alex. She had spoken to plenty of elderly people during various investigations, but this one seemed so resigned to her lot that it was sadder than most. In Alex's opinion it was a damn sight better to be in a Home than being alone, with nothing but visits from a home help and a stack of photograph albums. And the telly, she noted.

She resolved again that she should get out more. Not just in the professional sense, which was an essential part of the job, but in making friends, meeting people, having a social life.

'These are all photos of my John,' Mrs Barnett was saying now. She handed over a brown album, with the single word *John* on the front cover.

This was exactly what Alex was looking for, despite being slightly appalled to realize she was looking at an entire life between the pages of the album. There was John as a baby in his mother's arms. John with his parents and a much younger-looking grandmother. John as a toddler on his first tricycle. John in his first school blazer and satchel. John at the beach with bucket and spade, with Weston pier in the background. John at junior school. John with his arms folded in football gear. John with a group of school friends. John aged somewhere around seventeen astride a motorbike, beefy and handsome.

There were duplicates and variations of many of the photographs. Alex asked if she could borrow one or two, especially the group photos, promising faithfully to send them back later, and was reluctantly given them.

'He was obviously a popular boy,' she said to his grandmother.

Mrs Barnett gave her a gratified smile. 'He was. He and that crowd of his used to go camping and exploring, even going down them pot-holes on the Mendips,' she said with a shiver. 'There was nothing fearless about my John, until the happening, of course.'

'The happening?' Alex paused, her heart beating faster at the expectancy of what she might hear now. The happening had to be the incident when some foolhardy kids had blown up a derelict hut, which had led to the eventual discovery of Steven Leng's hand.

Mrs Barnett looked at her suspiciously.

'You did say this was for a — what was it — a project about the Grammar school boys?

Then you'll know what happened to one of the other young-uns.'

She wasn't daft then. She still had her marbles.

'Steven Leng,' Alex said, nodding. 'Of course. It must have been terrible for all the other boys, Mrs Barnett.'

'It fair turned my John's brain for a while,' she muttered, as if talking to herself. 'He was never the same after that, as if all the stuffing had gone out of him. It took a long while for him to pull himself together, what with all the questioning and all that, and the other lads bullying him.'

'Did they?' The woman was obviously getting tired now, but this was too interesting for Alex to leave it there.

'He never said so, but I knew. I reckon they were afraid of getting into trouble for dabbling in drugs. Not that I'm saying my John did, mind, but some of them others were always out for a lark, and he went along with whatever they said. And you never know these days, do you?'

'No, indeed. Well, I'll leave you in peace now, Mrs Barnett, and I do thank you for your patience. You've been a great help.'

'Have I? I suppose that's all right then. Just remember to send my photos back when you've done with 'em, and you can see yourself out, can't you?'

She could, and she did, breathing in a great gulp of fresh air as she went back to her car, and turned off the little tape recorder that had the entire conversation on it. Normally, she asked permission to record an interview, but she had the distinct suspicion that Mrs Barnett would have clammed up if she'd revealed it and she wasn't risking it.

It had been a shock to discover that John Barnett was dead, but even more interesting to find that he'd been pushed off the road and over a cliff. How significant was that? *Did he fall or was he pushed?* Well, he was obviously pushed, but was it done deliberately? That was the sixty-four thousand dollar question. And where and what was this Toll road?

She parked up on the seafront again and went back to the café she'd used before. It was nearly lunchtime and she needed sustenance now, and ham and chips sounded good. While she was waiting for it to arrive, she asked the owner for more directions, this time to the Toll road.

'You thinking of moving down here or just visiting, Miss?' he asked. 'Sand Bay ain't the best place to be at this time of year. It's cold and windy.'

When she looked mystified, he brought out

his town map again, and pointed to a long stretch of coast road leading from the town to an area called Sand Bay.

'That's the Toll road, alongside the woods on one side and the cliffs on 'tother. You want to watch the bends in the road if you're going along there. It's quite narrow and folk have been known to go over.'

'Thanks. I'll keep it in mind.'

She decided not to enquire further. She didn't need to find the exact gap in the hedge where a motorbike had plunged over the cliffs four years ago either — if it still existed. It was more likely that the foliage would have grown again by now, and it was only a grandmother's horrific memory (or imagination) of the scene that still remained.

But once she had eaten a plateful of ham and chips and immediately wished that she hadn't, she drove out towards the Toll road to Sand Bay, cruising along slowly since there were no other cars around. It would be a picturesque route in summer, but she noted how perilously easy it would be for a motorbike to be forced off the road on one of the sharp bends, especially if it were a slippery road and in the dark. Yet she didn't find it difficult to imagine that John Barnett's accident might well not have been an accident at all, but something far more sinister, if he had become as bullied, as vulnerable and anxious, and possibly as unpredictable as his grandmother had unwittingly told her.

6

On Friday evening Nick swept into her apartment with his usual panache, and she was immediately enveloped in his embrace.

'Have you any idea how much I've missed you?' he demanded, when he allowed her to draw breath.

'It's only been a couple of weeks, but I think I'm getting the idea,' Alex said with a laugh and a surge of pleasure that was completely disproportionate to the just-good-friends syndrome.

After she had been thoroughly kissed, he held her away from him for a moment, letting his hands run down the length of her arms and making her tingle.

'A couple of days is too long,' he said.

'Oh, come on, Nick,' she said, wriggling away from him. 'Don't tell me you've been pining for me. I know you better than that, remember? You were never short of female company.'

'True,' he said, his face relaxing into a grin and not bothering to deny it. 'But the one I want isn't around — '

'There's a song about that, isn't there?'

Alex said. 'Something about when the girl in your arms isn't the girl that you want, then *want* the girl that you have. Or something like that. I'm probably getting it all wrong.'

'You always did,' he said, more lazily now.

'Coffee? Or something stronger?' she asked, before she started to read things he wasn't saying.

This was a weekend visit, no more, and the last thing she wanted was for him to start making her regret this move to Bristol.

But God, it was good to see him, and hear him, and be with him. They had a history, no matter how chequered and how often they had pulled in opposite directions — which was frequent. For all their similar ideas in bringing villains to justice, there was a huge competitiveness between them too. It got the old adrenalin going though, and maybe that was what she was missing.

She brought her thoughts up short. She wasn't missing anything, and she wasn't going to appear like a wimp, either.

'Something hot and strong,' Nick said in answer to her question. 'But I'll settle for coffee right now.'

She laughed as she went to the kitchen. Her spirits lifted as she heard him roaming around, opening doors and sussing out her new place. Being proprietorial, staking his claim to be here. And oh yes, she had missed him too.

'So how goes the work?' he asked next, when she had brought in coffee and biscuits. 'Anything interesting in the wind?'

'I went to Weston the other day,' she told him.

'Bored already then? I didn't think it would take long.'

Alex looked at him coolly. 'Not at all, thank you, big copper from the Smoke! I went to check out one of Steven Leng's friends, if you must know — '

'You haven't given up yet then?'

'Did the police ever follow up on what happened to any of them?' she said, ignoring the little frisson of annoyance in his voice. But he should know that she was as tenacious as he was when it came to having a suspicious mind.

Nick shrugged. 'Why should they? The case was over long ago, apart from the wretched Leng woman's obsession. And that's all it was, babe, an obsession. Don't let it become one of yours as well, will you?'

He was half-joking, but she knew that look in his eyes.

'All right, but after she had sent me a list of their names, they became more real to me, and I wanted to know what happened to them. As you said, I didn't have much else to do down here in the sticks, so where was the harm in it?'

She spoke innocently, knowing the kind of response she'd get.

'Waste of time,' he said crisply. 'Still, I suppose you had to do something other than twiddling your thumbs before you knew you'd made a mistake and came back home.'

'I found one of Steven's school friends,' Alex said, ignoring the barb. 'At least, I found what had happened to him.'

She left it dangling in the air, knowing he wouldn't be able to resist any more than she would have done, if the boot had been on the other foot.

'All right. Let's get it over with. Who was it, and what happened? Is he a missionary in Outer Mongolia now?'

'He's dead. Killed riding his motorbike and forced off a coastal road by a car that didn't stop. Case unsolved. Case closed. Interesting, don't you think? Out of the six original boys, two down, four to go. Like Agatha Christie's *Ten Little Niggers* — except that that wouldn't be politically correct now, would it?'

Nick sat up in his chair, his shoulders tense.

'Alex, you're making a case out of all this

when there isn't one. When did this happen, anyway?'

'Four years ago.'

The way his lips twisted told her more than words that he thought she was mad. Wasting her time. Steven Leng's disappearance was well in the past, and this other boy's death could have had nothing to do with him — unless the remaining five boys in his group had kept in touch, and the others realized that John Barnett was losing it. Presumably he would have seen, or at least known about Jane Leng's newspaper letters. People involved in any kind of crime or mystery always gathered up as much information about the follow-up as they could. It was masochistic, but it was human nature. Maybe Jane's letters had begun to unnerve him, making him want to tell what he knew . . . to get it off his conscience . . . whatever it was.

'Can we leave the subject strictly alone for one night at least?' Nick was saying now. 'I can think of better ways to spend the weekend with my girl than by going over pointless stuff like this. It's not what I came here for.'

'What did you come here for then?' Alex said, before she could stop herself and realize how provocative the question was. Or maybe she did know . . .

* * *

She awoke in the early hours of the morning, still wrapped in his arms, the taste of him still on her lips, the lusty pleasure of him still filling every part of her, and with the vague notion that she certainly hadn't intended any of this, even if he had.

She lifted the heavy weight of his arm from her breast, slid out of bed and left him sleeping while she took a shower. She gasped at the shock of the cold water before the heater kicked in, but the morning freshness also alerted her senses to the fact that DCI Nick Frobisher never did anything on the spur of the moment, or without some ulterior motive. He was never off duty, either, apart from certain times when she had to admit that thinking about crime — past, present or future — had been furthest from either of their minds . . .

So he must be here for some other reason than to make love to her.

The aroma of fresh coffee filled her nostrils, and she stepped out of the shower wrapped in a towelling dressing-gown for January comfort.

In her small kitchen she lounged against the door, resisting a smile when she saw Nick wearing her red silk kimono, his bare legs sticking out beneath it, his dark hair still ruffled with sleep and the vigours of the night, and looking ridiculously and endearingly house-trained as he poured out two mugs of coffee.

'What do you want, Nick?' she asked.

His smile was seductive. 'I thought I'd already had it.'

'Apart from that.'

He gave an elaborate sigh, 'Alex, darling, do you really think I'd use sex as a means of getting information from the girl of my dreams?'

'Cut the crap, Nick,' she said. 'I know you too well, remember?'

'Yeah, I guess you do. Every nook and cranny, you might say.'

She marched across the kitchen and grabbed her mug of coffee from the worktop, taking a slurp far too quickly, and wincing at not giving it time to cool down a little. But it was time to let Mr God-damn-perfect know he wasn't the only guy in the world.

'I was actually seeing someone else this weekend,' she lied. 'It's not too late for me to call him and say the date's still on. I do have a life down here.'

'Is that what you want?' Nick said.

'It's what I've got. What I want is to know why you suddenly appeared out of nowhere. And what was this mysterious something you were going to tell me?'

She hadn't even remembered it until this minute.

'I came to find out how you were getting on — as someone who cares about you,' he added. 'And to tell you there was a hell of an upset with the Lengs recently, and your name was the cause of it. I could have told you on the phone, of course, but why not come and visit my old friend, I thought — '

'*My* name?' Her heart gave a jump. 'What do you mean?'

'Got your attention now, haven't I?' he teased. 'It seems that Bob Leng and his missus had the mother and father of all fights after he found your card and he practically threw her out of the house for hiring you. She came to us in a panic, sure he was going to do her in, and asking for police protection. The silly mare's been watching too many cop shows on telly, if you ask me.'

'You didn't take it seriously then?' Alex said.

Nick shrugged. 'The pair of them have been at each other's throats for so long, it's a way of life for them now. They don't seem to have much else holding them together.'

'Only the memory of Steven.'

He hesitated, and then said what he had come to say.

'Alex, I just want you to be aware that Bob Leng can be violent, and he's been led a hell of a life by his wife in the last ten years. If he threatens you in any way, go to the local nick and report him, OK?'

'It's hardly likely, is it?'

'It's possible. I just wanted to warn you not to do anything stupid.'

'I won't, and I'm grateful for your concern, honestly.'

'Why wouldn't I be concerned? I care about you more than you know.'

He sounded so sincere she felt her throat catch for a moment. She did know, and she cared about him too, but not enough to become the little wifey with slippers at the door every evening . . . and that was stereotyping, if you like, she thought in disgust.

Then his mood changed, the way it always did.

'So what are we doing this weekend? Are you going to show me the delights of Bristol apart from the ones I've already seen, that is? On the other hand, we could always go back to bed.'

* * *

They spent a couple of hours at the Zoo and mingled with the many lone fathers and their kids on their regular weekend escape route; they went over the SS *Great Britain*, and admired the amazing reconstruction of Brunel's great ship; they spent the evening at the theatre watching an obscure play that bored them stiff; and ended up at a local karaoke tavern before finally falling into bed, exhausted.

'I'll have to get back early today,' Nick told her on Sunday morning. 'I'll take you out for lunch and then I'll be off.'

'Right,' Alex said, with the vague feeling that this wasn't the way she wanted it, or planned it. Maybe it was the thought of losing him again so soon, but she knew there was more to it than that. They had never fallen into this pattern before. She had only slept with him a couple of times before, for God's sake, and she didn't want him thinking this was the way it was going to be from now on. They were bloody good together, but she didn't want to be a weekend fling whenever he felt like — OK she did.

'So what's wrong?' he asked, looking down at her.

'Nothing. Except that I don't think we

should make a habit of this Nick. I could get to like it,' she added, softening the blow to his ego.

'Would that be so bad?'

'You know it would. We're mates, and we always said we were going to keep it that way.'

'Funny, but I don't remember ever saying any such thing.'

'Well, I'm saying it, and now I'm going to have a shower and get dressed and then I'm going for a walk. Are you coming?'

She dared him to make anything of that, praying that he wouldn't cheapen everything, and slipped out of bed before waiting for any answer. When she returned to the bedroom, he was already dressed and raring to go. She groaned, remembering how fit he was (she had plenty of evidence of that), remembering his vigorous five-mile walks and his one-time entry into the half-marathon. But he wouldn't let her get out of a walk now.

In the end, absolutely wilted, she was almost relieved to see him go, even though she felt as if he was taking a little part of her with him. He represented everything she knew, while Bristol was still a bit of an alien country.

She mentally shook herself for being such a spineless idiot in even thinking that way. And anyway, he had certainly given her something else to think about. The violence of Bob Leng, for a start. She had never actually spoken to him, but his presence seemed to be felt by all who knew him — his wife, in particular. And she wasn't looking forward to meeting the paranoid Jane Leng again.

Alex sighed, knowing she had got herself into this, despite all Nick's warnings. Common sense told her she should have listened to him, and one of her father's sayings came into her head too:

You always did let your heart rule your head, Audrey . . . you rush into things before you stop to think of the consequences . . .

And that was no way for a PI to behave.

'Thanks, Dad,' she muttered. 'But you never came across the Jane Lengs of this world, did you? Nor anything like the world I'm involved in now.'

She paused in her flat tidying, remembering the gentle soul he had been at heart, despite the rigours of farming life in the Dales. He would have had no comprehension of the seedy characters she sometimes had to deal with, nor the dangers she put herself in. Nor would her mother . . . and Alex was in danger of getting maudlin again, when this was the life she had chosen, and the one she relished — most of the time.

She threw herself into cleaning the flat.

Housework wasn't her favourite occupation, so when it happened it wasn't so much spring cleaning as an all seasons blitz rolled into one. And how the hell could anyone have got the place in such a muddle in so short a space of time? She resolved to be tidier, knowing it was unlikely to happen. It was just taking her mind off losing Nick, that was all.

Much later the sound of the buzzer on her intercom was a welcome break in her gloom, which she was now putting down to the aftermath of being part of a couple. She answered the buzzer quickly, and didn't recognize the bright young voice for a moment.

'I saw you saying goodbye to a very dishy bloke 'safternoon. Is that really you? The private investigator who's moved in recently, I mean?'

'Yes, it is — but who — ' Alex said, half amused, half annoyed. She was tempted to say she didn't work on Sundays. Police did. Conscientious PIs did. She couldn't afford to be really off duty, any more than Nick was. She hoped she had sounded more professional than she felt at that moment.

'Oh, sorry,' came the reply. 'It's me, Mavis Patterson from the shop. I live around the corner, and wondered if you wanted to drop round for a cup of tea or something? It's only me and my old gran, but I know you haven't been here long, and thought you might want some company. Unless your bloke's coming back?'

Alex relaxed, hiding a grin. Mavis obviously scented a romance here. She must have been even more intrigued to discover that her new acquaintance was a PI, which wasn't someone you met every day of the week.

Her immediate instinct was to say thanks but no thanks. She was pretty tired from two heady and torrid nights with Nick, and then tramping halfway around Bristol yesterday. But she changed her mind. Mavis and her old gran might be just the kind of garrulous people she needed to meet. They knew the city. They knew people.

Nick would have called it using people. In his book, and in his business, he also considered it a perfectly legitimate thing to do. Alex preferred to call it networking.

'That would be lovely, Mavis,' she said into the intercom. 'I'll be right down.' To hell with tidying the flat. That could wait.

* * *

Mavis was waiting outside her door, a garish vision in a mottled fake fur jacket, skin-tight, loudly-patterned jeans and chunky boots. The snobby part of Alex wanted to screech at being seen with someone wearing such a mix-match of fabrics and colours, but the generous part of her warmed to the fact that this girl had bothered to contact a stranger at all.

'I never expected you to be one of them people,' Mavis greeted her at once, nodding towards the elegant sign printed on the office door. 'That was a bit of a surprise.'

'It's not immoral, Mavis,' Alex said with a laugh.

'Oh, I never thought it was,' the girl said hastily. 'Just that I never thought — well, you're not exactly Jonathan Creek, are you?'

'He's fiction,' Alex said, falling into step, 'and anyway, he's only half of the detection team, isn't he? It's Maddie who does most of the thinking.'

'Is it? Oh, I suppose so.' Mavis was clearly vague about that. Not a great thinker herself then, thought Alex. 'So do you have to go around looking for murderers and all that creepy stuff?'

She laughed as if she had said something terribly witty.

'Oh, all of that,' Alex said airily. 'I'm on a case right now.' And why the hell had she said that? *Showing off, Audrey*, her dad would have said.

'Really?' Mavis said, impressed. 'What's it all about then?'

'Sorry, can't tell you anything more. Client confidentiality, you see.'

It was a shame to tease her, but somehow she couldn't help it.

'Oh, I do see,' Mavis said, hanging on her every word. 'When I told my old gran who we had living on our doorstep, she said she was dying to meet you. She loves all those old murders on the telly, and real life ones too. Keeps scrap books on 'em, she does. Creepy, I call it. But she don't get out much.'

Creepy was clearly a favourite word. But Alex was no longer bothered by Mavis's quaint mannerisms. Her old gran kept scrap books, did she? Interesting. She realized she was falling into 'old gran' mode now, and maybe a little accent lapse would be all to the good too. This was a social call, after all, and what was called her posh voice could put some people off.

'You don't live with your parents, then, Mavis?' she asked next.

'Nah. They moved to Swindon with me dad's job, but I didn't fancy it, so I stayed with Gran. She could help you out with a few problems, I bet. You'll like her. She's a real card.'

'I'm sure I will,' Alex said, trying to keep a straight face.

They lived in a two up, two down little house, cosy and a bit stuffy in the winter, and probably boiling hot in summer, due to the coal fire that was kept stoked up day and night because of Gran's chest, Mavis told her.

Gran greeted her like an old friend.

'Now come and sit yourself down, my lover, and tell me all about yourself while our Mavis puts the kettle on,' she said, wheezing musically.

Alex laughed, easy in her company and the friendly atmosphere that reminded her of the farm back home, donkeys' years ago. Too many things were doing that lately, she thought uneasily.

'Oh dear. That's the sort of question that makes people clam up, Mrs — '

' 'Tis Gran, my lover. Everybody calls me Gran around here.'

My lover was clearly a local expression, Alex noted. 'Gran then. Well, I've just moved down to Bristol from London and — '

'And you're one of them lady detectives, I hear.'

'A private investigator, yes, and — '

'You'll be interested in my newsy bits and pieces, I'll bet. Our Mavis don't take no notice of them any more. She's got nothing but chasing boys in that head of hers, but I can see you're a young woman who's a thinker.'

Mavis poked her head round from the kitchen and called out cheerfully, before disappearing again.

'What's to think about, working in a poky little corner shop?'

'Are these newsy bits and pieces your scrap books, Mrs — Gran — ? Mavis mentioned them to me,' Alex said. She didn't want to appear too eager, but from the way the old lady's eyes sparkled, she realized she could be on to a winner here. She told herself cautiously not to get too excited, and that there might be nothing about the Leng case, but Gran was clearly overjoyed to have someone to share in her passion.

While Gran was rummaging in the sideboard for the scrap books, Alex couldn't keep silent any longer. She had to know, but she spoke casually, as if it was just a passing thought.

'I don't suppose you had any cuttings about that boy who was never found — except for his hand, I mean? It was a long time ago now, and it didn't happen around here, of course.'

'No, it was down Somerset way,' Gran said vaguely. 'It was big news at the time, but what really happened to the lad was a mystery. His mother still writes daft letters to the newspaper, swearing she's seen him somewhere. She's dotty, I reckon, but it makes interesting reading,' she added with a chuckle.

'I met her once,' Alex said.

'Did you? Then you'll know what she's like.'

She found her scrap books, and started turning the pages. Alex could see she would be here all day as Gran went through them, page by page, and she must have had cuttings of nearly every crime ever committed in the local area. She was better than an encyclopaedia. It was too much to hope that all the Leng cuttings were together, of course. They weren't. It had been front-page news at the time, but then the interest had waned, and only occasional, mostly gossipy, bits of information had caught Gran's eye.

Mavis brought in the tea, and Alex forced herself to remember that she was here to chat with her as well, and to make contact with people outside the narrow spectrum of her work. She asked Mavis about boyfriends, and what she did when she wasn't working, while still turning the pages of the scrap books and being mildly frustrated at the way Gran kept pointing out items of interest to herself, such as the fellow from down the road who was caught for shoplifting, and the flashy tart who turned out to be no better than she should be and ran off with the local vicar.

'Gran, I don't suppose you'd be kind enough to lend me some of these scrap books for a few days, would you?' she asked finally. 'I would take great care of them, but they might be very useful to me in my work. I — uh — like to know the kind of area I'm working in.'

Gran pursed her lips as if considering, and then nodded.

'I daresay 'tis all right. I can see you're a steady kind of person — not like our Mavis here, with her daft clothes. As long as you take good care of 'em you can keep 'em as long as you like. Well, for a week or two, anyway. Good-looking young woman like you can't have much time for reading — '

'I do when it's for my work,' Alex cut in before she went off into a long spiel again. 'But I won't take the wartime ones, thank you. I'm sure you like browsing through those yourself.' Old people did.

Gran gave a throaty chuckle that brought on a cough and a wheeze, and sent a florid hue to her cheeks.

'Oh ah, I could tell you a few things about them times, my lover — '

'Alexandra don't want to hear none of that old stuff, Gran,' Mavis put in, and then: 'Oh Lord, you don't mind if I call you Alexandra, do you?'

'I'd rather you called me Alex.'

'Oh, OK. And maybe we can go to the pictures sometimes.'

'That would be nice,' Alex said, already edging towards the door with the precious couple of scrap books in her hand, and itching to get back home and devour them properly. You never knew what nuggets you might find in the most unlikely sources.

'I'll see you around then,' Mavis called, as she got out of the house.

The blast of cold air hit Alex's cheeks with a welcome burst of oxygen. She hadn't realized quite how cloying it had been in the small house. No wonder Gran wheezed so much. A healthy dose of the outdoors would probably benefit her.

Then she forgot all about such thoughts as she closed the door of her flat behind her and prepared for a good long session with Gran's scrap books.

7

Jane Leng was perfectly aware that folk thought her completely barmy. Her doctor had warned her so many times that her nerves were at breaking point that she wondered why they just didn't snap and be done with it. She didn't have any truck with her London doctor, anyway. He talked with a plum in his mouth and she always expected him to wear white gloves every time he had to touch her.

He handed out pills as if they were sweets too. Anything to send a neurotic woman off with a Prozac prescription and get her out of his office. Oh yes, she knew. She never took them, anyway. She had quite a store of them now. She'd even toyed with the idea of putting them in Bob's tea now and then, just to shut him up when he bawled at her.

Jane much preferred their old family doctor in Chilworthy, who'd known her and Bob since long before their late baby Steven was born, a puny little thing who'd nearly torn her insides out at the birth, but thankfully had been the means of putting a stop to further torment. After Steven's birth, there should be no more babies, Doctor Davey had told her severely, much to Jane's huge relief.

Which had made it all the more reason for her to dote on Steven, of course, and all the more reason for her to totally disbelieve that he could be dead. Children didn't die before their parents. Not lovely boys who were only sixteen with all their life ahead of them. It was the wrong order of things . . .

Doctor Davey didn't believe in pills, either. He always said talking things out was the best medicine, and he'd always had time for a gossip, and to pass the time of day and discuss the price of bread.

'Are you going to stand about dreaming all day, woman?' she heard her husband's sarcastic voice. 'For God's sake, get that overall off and tidy yourself up. You look as if you're going out scrubbing instead of getting ready for my presentation this evening.'

She glared at him venomously. She hated him more than ever now, even though she had got her way and they were leaving London and going back where they belonged; where she could still feel the presence of Steven all around her, even if he couldn't — or wouldn't.

And this presentation, she thought scornfully. They'd brought it forward a couple of weeks because the Fire Chief was going on holiday on the day Bob retired, and they had to do things right according to protocol. It was a lot of fuss, according to Jane. Just a group of blokes dressing up in uniforms and slapping Bob on the back as if they liked him and were sorry to see him go, which was a laugh, since he'd managed to upset most of them in his time.

After the speeches, he'd be handed a medal or a clock or whatever it was they were giving him, and by the end of the week it was a sure bet that nobody would remember Bob Leng had ever existed.

Then there would be just the two of them . . . for a minute Jane felt the bleakness of the thought wash over her as usual. There would be only Bob and his hatefulness, and her and her memories. And the young woman with the posh voice who was going to help her, she remembered.

She felt slightly less frazzled at the thought. She had been totally disillusioned by the police who thought her nothing but a crank, and the stupid newspaper that still printed her letters, but didn't see the seriousness of what she was saying. She knew very well they only kept printing her letters when there was nothing else to fill the pages. She was a joke to them.

But all her hopes were pinned on

Alexandra Best now, and the minute she got out of this horrible place she was going to go and see her and find out what she had discovered. If the worst came to the worst, and it was proven beyond all reasonable doubt that Steven was dead, then at least she'd know someone had tried.

In her secret heart, Jane knew very well what the truth of it was, but it was something she would never admit, not even to herself, and certainly not out loud. If you didn't have hope to cling to, what did you have?

And while she could still look at all the photos of Steven that she surrounded herself with, he was still alive, still about to walk in the door at any minute and ask her what was for tea.

'Put that fucking thing down, will you? You disgust me with your stupid mooning about, and your tight-arsed face,' she heard Bob shout, and she hadn't realized she had picked up one of the framed photos and was running her fingers over the glass as sensuously as if she caressed a lover.

She flinched as if he had struck her, the way he had struck her a few nights ago. She clutched the photo to her chest, her eyes glittering with loathing. Even more so now, because he had defiled Steven's memory by using that horrible word.

'You won't stop me having the photos,' she screamed. 'I won't put them away, and I won't stop talking about him as long as there's breath in my body.'

As he lunged towards her, she wondered fearfully for a moment if she had gone too far with her dramatics. But this time it wasn't his wife he was after. He wrenched the framed photo of his son out of her hands, and hurled it at the stone fireplace, where it smashed into a thousand pieces.

'You bastard!' Jane howled. 'You rotten, stinking bastard. But you've only broken the glass. I've still got the photo — '

He strode over to the fireplace and ground the whole thing to pieces under his boot, while she let out an animal cry of anguish as she saw her son's image become twisted and torn. Her screams became more shrill.

'Well, that's finished it. You can go to your precious presentation alone, because I'm not leaving this house tonight — '

He turned on her at once, gripping her arm so tightly she was sure all the blood would drain out of it.

'You will come with me,' he grated. 'You'll behave yourself and you'll smile, if it's the last thing you do. Do you hear me, bitch?'

He overpowered her, the way he had always done. He threatened her, frightened her, and since she often wondered fearfully if he really would do for her one of these days, she caved in at once.

'All right, I'll go,' she said sullenly. She had often thought of going missing at such times, but she knew she'd never have the courage to go through with it. She always felt lumpy and unattractive alongside the other wives at functions. In this case, there might not be too many of them, Jane thought. Not like the Christmas do, when she had felt so out of place and nondescript.

'Go and wash yourself and do something with your hair,' Bob said freezingly, pushing her away from him. 'You stink of fish and chips.'

And you didn't fill your fat belly with them? Jane thought furiously. *God help me if I don't do for you one of these days.*

At least she was getting a bit of a reprieve for a little while. Tomorrow, Bob was going down to Chilworthy to sign the final papers for their new place, and to sort out the gas and electricity people, so she'd have a bit of time to herself. Thank God for small mercies.

* * *

Alex knew she had struck gold as soon as she settled down to study Gran's scrap books in more detail that evening. Gran had clearly been intrigued by the mystery of the lonesome hand and kept everything she could find about it. At least, the juicy bits, Alex noted with a smile, and there were plenty of photos. Gran was obviously hot on photos.

The newspaper cuttings were useful in their reports, but it was the photos which told her more than anything about the six boys who had intended going camping together.

There were single shots and many school groups, in which Gran had circled the relevant boys — good old Gran — and during the investigations there had been many character-witness accounts from anyone who knew any of the boys, including other school friends, teachers and neighbours.

It just went to show that people only saw what they wanted to see, thought Alex eventually. If you believed all you read, you'd deduce that Steven Leng had been a mummy's boy, easily led, though not averse to doing a bit of bullying himself, the way some mummys' boys were. Some called him a loner, which contrasted with the fact that he was supposedly popular. He was certainly a strange one though, and that came through loud and clear from every side.

'And what about you, John Barnett, killed on your motorbike six years after the event?'

she murmured over her third cup of coffee laced with vodka which was keeping her fully awake. That was her excuse, anyway.

She looked at his photo. He'd been a handsome lad, not like the Wilkins brothers, who were bruisers if ever she saw them. They were big and burly, and clearly destined for ownership of a family haulage firm, she guessed.

And there was Keith Martin, who had a hardware shop in Bath, and looked like an earnest type. A nervous type too. And finally Lennie Fry. Alex studied his photos with interest.

Lennie looked different from the rest. While the rest of them were tidily casual, he wore frayed jeans and a vest top, like some relic from an earlier hippy age. She could easily imagine him dossing down at the Glastonbury Festival, wreathed in clouds of smoke of the more suspicious kind, spaced out, stoned out of his head, happily incandescent . . .

'Are you clairvoyant now?' Alex asked herself out loud. 'Don't you know anything about not judging a book by its cover? And kids by their clothes? He was probably just your normal teenage rebel.'

She may not be clairvoyant, but she had always thought herself pretty shrewd when it came to sizing somebody up, until she had been proved wrong in the past, Alex remembered feelingly. *People are never what they seem* . . . that was one of Nick's reminders. But this boy certainly looked like one of the more interesting characters in the group. She flipped through Gran's scrap books to find out what people had said about him.

'Lennie was always a bit weird. He wanted to be a musician,' said a school friend. 'From the way he mutilated his guitar I don't think he'd have got anywhere. He and Steven had some wild idea of going to India, and then they got caught up in that other stuff, but they were always falling out about it.'

Alex sat up. So those two — Lennie and Steven — were caught up in the same thing, were they? Big ideas of going to India — and that other stuff, which she interpreted as being the link with the Followers. It was always interesting when groups fragmented for whatever reason. It may or may not lead to problems on either side. In this case, Steven Leng's death had ensued, which was some problem!

She spent the evening going through the scrap books, knowing she should put these findings into some kind of order, with half her mind on the arrival of Ray Smart, assistant, in the morning. Now that she had got him — on a temporary basis, no more — she had begun to wonder what the hell she was going to do with him.

He would have to act as dogsbody, though she wasn't sure that was what he had in mind. He'd want to do some detecting, seeing this as the first step to becoming a latterday Poirot — if he even knew who that was. She was still wondering if this had been such a good idea. At least it was only for a month. After that, she would know if she preferred to continue going it alone.

* * *

Ray arrived on the stroke of nine o'clock, not exactly as frisky as a Red Setter pup, but getting there, and she let him into the office with a bright smile and a mental query as to how she could shorten a month to a fortnight.

'Ready and eager then, Ray?'

'Oh yes — er — Alex.'

It was painful to watch the slow colour creep up his neck. For a moment she wondered just how he and the dynamic, sporty Philip Cordell had ever hit it off. They seemed like complete opposites.

'Right then. I'll show you around, and the

first job I want you to do today is to sort some old cuttings into date and character order and put them on to a computer file for me. I've put Post-its on the relevant pages in these old scrap books. There are masses of cross-references, mind. Think you can do that?'

The look on his face was almost one of glory. The enthusiasm for computers shone through, so at least Phil had got that right.

'Piece of cake,' Ray said, more breezily than he had spoken before.

'Good. And speaking of cake, which we weren't, I usually start the morning with coffee and a biscuit. OK with you?'

'Oh — yes, fine,' he said, fiddling with the scrap books Alex handed him.

'So before you get started I'll just show you how to work my coffee machine, then you can do it in future.' It was obviously going to take time to get Ray organized into office routine, including the pecking order of who did what, and she just hoped he was better with the computer files.

* * *

She was still making phone calls to various sources of information when he appeared at her desk with a number of printed pages later in the morning, and she revised everything she had ever thought about him.

'Ray, you're a genius!' she exclaimed. 'This is exactly what I wanted.'

He blushed at her praise.

'It was easy. What do I do next?'

'Well, first of all, let me remind you that what you've done here today is confidential. An elderly lady loaned these scrap books to me. I don't think I need to keep them any longer, so perhaps you could return them.'

She certainly needed space if he was going to spend every non-working moment hovering over her to see how she operated.

She scribbled a note of thanks to Gran before giving Ray the address.

'Oh, I know the place. There's a girl who lives there, isn't there? Works in the corner shop?'

'I can see you've been doing a bit of detective work on your own,' Alex said teasingly.

'Oh no. Not really. I just saw her, that's all.'

Oh God, he certainly wasn't a bundle of laughs. Mavis is right out of your league, kiddo, Alex thought, and she wasn't planning on acting as matchmaker. She put the scrap books and the note into a large envelope and handed it to him.

'Don't hurry back. In fact, it's nearly

lunchtime, so why don't we call this a short first day? When you've had your lunch and delivered the envelope to Mrs Patterson, go on home, and I'll see you in the morning, OK?'

It wasn't the way to conduct business, but he was starting to oppress her with his earnestness. She needed to get out of the office too, and upstairs in her flat was a delicious cheese and tomato pizza just waiting to be heated in the microwave.

'Don't I have to work this afternoon?' Ray said doubtfully.

'No, nor tomorrow, because I have things to do,' she lied. 'But on Friday we'll be doing some fieldwork. I have to interview some people, so I shall want you to accompany me as my backup, OK?'

'Sort of a minder?' Ray said.

'Sort of,' Alex said, finding it hard to keep a straight face. He evidently saw this operation as having Mafia overtones. And if this kid could successfully defend anybody, Alex thought, she was a Dutchman.

* * *

It was a relief to see him go, and she was halfway up the stairs to her flat when she heard the buzzer sound again. She was tempted to ignore it. It was probably Ray coming back with another query, but on the other hand, it just might be a new client, and she couldn't afford to ignore them. One case didn't make a career, and there were frequently smaller ones interspersed with the major one she was working on.

She went back downstairs and saw the shadow of the person outside her door. He was large and male, and she couldn't tell if she knew him or not.

'Can I help you?' she said into her intercom.

'I hope so. I need to speak to you on a personal matter,' the voice said.

Alex released the catch and told him to push the door. The next minute it had opened and then slammed shut behind the man, and he was lurching across the office towards her, his face dark with menace.

She felt her heart leap. Whoever he was, he was no ordinary client. They didn't usually approach her so aggressively before they told her why they were here. Unless he had just caught his wife in bed with his best friend . . . that would do it — not that this one looked as if he had a best friend.

He pressed both fists down on her desk and glared at her. He stunk of strong drink and body odour, and she recoiled a little.

'What is it you want? My assistant can take down any details — '

'If you mean the weedy brat who just walked out of here, lady, then he ain't coming back for a while, so don't give me none of your lip. I know you're on your own.'

Alex ran her tongue around her dry lips. 'So how can I help you?'

God, she sounded like somebody in a bad TV sitcom.

'For a start you can stop wasting my money, that's what you can do,' he snarled in her face, his eyes full of pent-up rage.

'I'm sorry, but I don't have the faintest idea who you are — '

Hadn't Nick Frobisher always told her she should have a switch beneath her desk to call out the local bobbies if ever she got into a sticky situation with a client? Why didn't she ever listen to him?

She edged open her desk drawer a little and fumbled into it as if to alert someone, not knowing if it would do any good or not. He didn't seem to notice, anyway.

'The name's Leng. Ring a bell, does it, lady?'

'Mr Bob Leng?' Alex said, just as if there could be any other.

'It sure as hell ain't Steven Leng,' he snapped. 'Are you getting there now?'

'Would you like to sit down, Mr Leng?'

'*No, I bloody wouldn't!* What I'd like to do is wring your fucking neck as well as hers. What's the crazy bitch been asking you to do?'

'I presume you're referring to the fact that your wife is my client,' Alex said frostily. 'And I never divulge my clients' business to anyone else.'

She had trained herself not to be shocked by whatever abuse she got from clients or villains, and she had got plenty of it in the past. But she had a job to stop her heart from hammering like fury, and she tried to keep as calm as possible.

She couldn't help remembering being told that Bob Leng was like a wild animal when roused, and from the way the veins were standing out on his head like purple ropes, she had ample proof of it now. She prayed he wouldn't hear the small whirr of the tape recorder in her drawer and spoke as quietly as possible.

'Mr Leng, if you want to know what your wife has instructed me to do, then I suggest that you ask her. That would seem to be the first logical step to take, wouldn't it? Other than that, I'm afraid I can't help you.'

He banged his fist down on her desk, making her flinch. She continued to stare him out. He might bully his wife, but he wasn't going to bully her.

'I can guess what she's up to, and she's driving me to drink with this madness. The boy's dead, and if anybody knows that, I do, God damn it.'

For a second, Alex saw the torment in his eyes, and remembered the horrendous discovery he had made, and the continuing nightmares Jane had spoken about. She had seemed genuinely concerned for him then, but by now Alex suspected it had all been a way to gain her attention and sympathy. There was little between these two now except spite.

'Mr Leng, I really am sorry about your son, and it must have been terrible for you — '

'I don't want your bloody pity,' he said, reverting to aggression at once. 'I want you to tell her to stop, before it's too late.'

'Too late for what?'

If she thought he was going to come out with some great revelation, she was mistaken. He turned and blundered towards the door, and she realized he had been drinking heavily already. She disliked him intensely, and any pity she felt for him was well and truly tempered by the tales she had heard from various sources of how these two were tearing one another apart.

Jane wasn't entirely blameless.

'Remember what I said,' he snarled as he reached the door, 'or my wife won't be the only one to be sorry.'

'Are you threatening me, Mr Leng?'

The only answer was the sound of her door slamming again, and then she wilted. But she thanked God she had had the nous to switch on the small tape recorder in her desk drawer. If anything happened to Jane Leng, or to herself, she had the evidence of this visit on tape, and she prayed it would never be necessary to produce it.

* * *

Her phone was ringing as she went upstairs to her flat and shut the door firmly behind her. If it wasn't the middle of the day a stiff drink would be in order, but that wasn't the way, and she knew it.

She grabbed the receiver and almost snapped into it.

'Alexandra Best.'

There was a small pause, and then she heard a touch of amusement in the male voice that answered. She couldn't tell what age it was. It sounded a bit throaty but in a fatherly, rather than a sexy way.

'My goodness. Nick said you were a bit of a

fiery one, and I can almost see the sparks coming out of my phone.'

Alex glared unseeingly at the wall. If this was some joker friend of Nick's, she could do without him right now. She was still flustered by the encounter with Bob Leng, and as her stomach rumbled in protest at being too long without food, she also needed sustenance.

'Look, I don't know what you want, but I'm afraid this is not a good time for me to listen to jokes, so goodbye — '

'Sorry, that was a pretty crass thing to say, wasn't it? Actually, I just wanted to welcome you to Bristol, Miss Best, and to suggest that we have a little talk. My name's Frank Gregory. DI Frank Gregory,' he added.

'Oh.' The wall came back into focus.

She heard him give a small chuckle.

'I really am an old friend of Nick Frobisher's, but you'll obviously want to check on that. When you've done so, call me back and perhaps we could go out for a drink one evening. Tonight, if you like, if you're not doing anything? It'll be good to know we're on the same side.'

The warning bells began to ring. This was not just a social call, and she knew the way the system worked. His 'little talk' meant that he wanted to suss out whether or not she was going to stir up a hornets' nest in the Steven

Leng case, which also meant he was seriously bothered that the whole thing was going to start up all over again, when it had died a satisfactory death years ago. Except in Jane Leng's mind, of course.

Alex's first impulse to tell DI Frank Gregory to go to hell subsided very quickly. For one thing, it was stupid to antagonize the local police, especially when you never knew when you might need them. She wasn't so invincible that she could always go it alone. She wasn't damned invincible at all, she reminded herself with a shiver, remembering how she had nearly been strangled by a very unsavoury character by meddling in what he saw as his affairs. *Affairs* being the operative word, as it happened.

'I need to speak to Nick anyway,' she said sweetly, dodging the issue.

His voice became coolly efficient now, confident that she would do exactly as he said.

'You do that, and then call me back on this number.'

He rattled it off, and she scribbled it down without thinking.

She was tempted to say 'I might', and then thought better of it, so she simply said goodbye and rang off.

As if in defiance of doing anything the guy

ordered her to do she went to her kitchen and prepared her enormous cheese and tomato pizza, liberally laced with Branston pickle, made herself a cup of strong black coffee, and spent a leisurely time over her lunch. She paid token attention to the television midday news until she got thoroughly bored with listening to pompous politicians slagging each other off, and watching the antics of overpaid footballers, and switched it off again.

And then she dialled Nick Frobisher's mobile number.

8

DI Frank Gregory was in his mid-fifties, with a receding hairline and a decided paunch. He arrived at Alex's flat at eight o'clock prompt, with a bunch of flowers in his hand, and an apologetic smile on his weathered face.

'Sorry we got off to an unfortunate start, Miss Best,' he greeted her, 'or may I call you Alexandra?'

'You can call me anything you like, but I prefer Alex,' she said, deciding to forgive him, and to stop making instant judgements. She had been wrong too often for comfort. Besides, he looked like the kind of homely old copper her father would have liked, and there was nothing of the predator in the way he looked her up and down as she invited him inside while she fetched her coat.

'Nick said you were a looker, and he wasn't wrong,' he said. 'So how do you like our fair city?'

He spoke with the air of one who took a civic pride in his surroundings. Alex approved of that, and after his big old rattletrap of a car had taken them to the Hole in the Wall pub, with its history of smugglers and press gangs, and he had told her some of Bristol's flamboyant history, and how he was living with his son and daughter-in-law since becoming a widower, she also decided that she liked him. She liked him a lot.

In the smoky atmosphere of the old pub she found it easy to relax in his company, easy to forget that he was a copper at all, and almost easy to imagine he could be her own father — except for the accent, of course. Her dad had been a Yorkshireman through and through, and this one had the more relaxed speech of the Bristolian.

'So what's Jane Leng been telling you?' he said casually. He had stuck strictly to his alcohol limit and was now on tonic water, while Alex was still pleasantly hazy on vodkas and lime, knowing that she didn't have to drive.

But she hadn't drunk so much that her senses were dulled to the importance of the question. No matter how softly it was asked, or how agreeable the company, or how relaxed the atmosphere was here, she knew a lead-in question when she heard it.

'What makes you think she's been telling me anything?'

'I don't think. I know,' Frank said, going straight into copper-mode.

It was amazing how, just seconds before,

the old eyes had been simply taking in the karaoke performers at the far end of the bar, and now they were copper-bright — in every way but colour . . . watching her, waiting for the slightest nuance in her voice, or shift of attitude.

'And I'm damn sure you already know far more than I do,' Alex said. 'All those police files can't have been cluttering up your nick for nothing all these years.'

Frank laughed. 'Frobisher said you were a clever one and he was right. And I gather he also told you to leave it alone.'

As the little warning note crept into his voice, she looked at him over the rim of her glass, giving him the full benefit of her green eyes.

'Are you going to tell me to leave it alone too? Is that what this little tête-à-tête is all about? And I thought you fancied me! How disappointing!'

He sighed. 'I'm bloody sure I'd fancy you if I was thirty years younger, Alex, *and* give the young studs a run for their money, but I'll leave all that to them now. So don't dodge the issue.'

She was immediately annoyed with herself for being so arch. It wasn't her style, and she didn't want him thinking it was. She spoke more crisply.

'The issue being that when I have an interesting case to follow up for a client who desperately needs my help, I'm supposed to leave it alone on a police say-so, is that it? That's not the way a PI works, Mr Gregory, and you must surely know that.'

He stared at her thoughtfully. 'The case was closed years ago, Miss Best — since we're being so formal — and my advice is to tell the lady quite firmly that there's nothing more you can do for her.'

'All she wants are answers about what happened to her son,' Alex protested. 'Is that so wrong? Without convincing evidence, it's all unfinished as far as she's concerned.'

'How much more evidence does the bloody woman want? Begging your pardon, but forensic teams don't make mistakes. The object that was found definitely belonged to Steven Leng.'

'And what about the rest of him? People can exist without a hand or a limb, and plenty of other bits, can't they? Or did the police discover something else about that incident in the woods that wasn't being made public?'

She felt a sudden surge of excitement at the thought. It wasn't unheard of for there to have been a cover-up. Families did it. Governments did it. And unless you were very naïve these days, it was a damn sure bet that the police did it when they thought it prudent to do so.

'Don't try to make mysteries where they don't exist, Alex,' Frank Gregory was saying now.

'But they do, at least as far as Mrs Leng is concerned.'

'Just don't make too many waves, that's all.'

'Good Lord, I wonder how many more threats I'm going to get today, Alex said without thinking.

'How many have you had already?' DI Gregory asked, on the ball at once.

She laughed, knowing she had better retrieve the situation fast. Or she could report Bob Leng . . . or simply hold on to the tape of their conversation until and if she ever needed it.

'Oh, I wasn't being serious. It was just a figure of speech, but I promise I'll heed your words, Frank. Now, can I buy you a last drink? Coffee would be good, wouldn't it?'

He'd know damn well she was changing the conversation, but he let her go to the bar and order the coffees, while she decided that the less the local constabulary knew about Bob Leng's visit the better. If she was to keep her investigations as private as possible, it wouldn't do for them to go warning him off, and making life doubly impossible for Jane.

* * *

Ray Smart had his own reasons for wanting to work for the glamorous PI who made him feel all fingers and thumbs and about as useless as a spare part at a wedding — except for his computer skills, of course, he thought, perking up. He could sort out anything the lovely Alex wanted. By now he had even spent a few hours showing her how to get on to the Internet and to use e-mail. And to prove his worth he could also report back to Mr Cordell whatever bits of information he could about the investigations into the Steven Leng affair.

Ray had been a small boy at the time, so he didn't remember any of it, but Mr Cordell was collating facts for a dossier on the whole business, and when he had spoken casually of his interest, Ray had had no hesitation in saying he would do what he could.

'I wouldn't want you to do anything deceitful, mind,' Phil Cordell had insisted. 'If anything emerges that is especially private, then you must decide whether you are able to divulge it or not. It would also be as well if Miss Best didn't know that we were collaborating on this, Ray. I admire her tremendously, and I wouldn't want to upset her in any way.'

'I understand perfectly,' Ray had said, blissfully blotting out the fact that in carrying out his hero's request, he was doing the very thing Alex had warned him against.

But this was different, and Ray had always had the knack of turning any dubious facts to something more savoury. He was helping Mr Cordell. He was *collaborating*, no less, which lifted his status no end. And since he'd never had any status to speak of, at least in the social sense, he was content to go along with his orders — without ever realizing that they were orders.

Today, they were going walkabout. That was the word Alex had used, which made it sound daring and bohemian at the same time.

* * *

Ray had obviously led a very narrow life, Alex reflected, when she saw how his eyes lit up at their task for today. He'd been OK in the more routine tasks she had set him, and he apparently had a brain, since he planned on going to university next year — though that didn't necessarily apply in all cases. But he seemed amazingly naïve when it came to real life. None of that mattered providing he did what she asked of him. But he did it in a puppy-like uncomplaining way, and she wasn't sure she could take this kind of adoration all the time.

'Right then,' she said now, studying the A to Z of Bristol. 'Today we're going to pay a call on Messrs Wilkins and Wilkins at their haulage yard.'

'And we're going incognito,' Ray said enthusiastically. 'That's why you're wearing a suitable change of clothes.'

He also had the knack of stating the obvious, which was starting to annoy her. In these few short weeks of having him around she already knew she had far too short a fuse as far as he was concerned.

She wasn't particularly flattered by the way he assessed her outfit, either. If Nick Frobisher — or the rampant Gary Hollis — had looked her over in her red check shirt, black cord jeans and brown fleece bomber jacket, with her hair coiled up inside a baseball cap, she'd have expected either some snide remark on going butch, or some crude lady lumberjack crack.

As it was, Ray simply approved of her disguise for the sake of going incognito. God, he was a drag.

'All we're going to do is ask a few

questions, Ray,' she said firmly. 'I'm an Australian cousin of Steven Leng and I'm here on vacation. I'm interested in meeting his old friends for an article I'm writing for a small local magazine. OK?'

'You don't sound Australian,' Ray said dubiously.

She put that right at once. 'Don't I, sport? I'll just have to do something about that then, won't I? Can't have the natives doubting my story, can I?'

He gaped at her accent, which, to his ears was as authentic as that of Rolf Harris. Ray was an avid viewer of *Animal Hospital*.

Alex laughed. 'Just one of my little skills,' she said lightly. 'You want I should be South Aaaaafricaaan in*stid*?' she added exaggeratedly. 'Or maybe Jam-ai-can, man!'

As he started to giggle in a very unmasculine way, she quickly tired of trying to impress him. Why bother, anyway? It was the Wilkins brothers who needed to believe she was who she said she was.

She didn't have to do it this way, of course. She could just go straight in there and tell them she was doing a little digging on Jane Leng's behalf. But caution stopped her. From what she had noted from Gran Patterson's scrap books, those burly, aggressive-looking young boys — she ignored the word thug

— were businessmen now, and might not take kindly to having their past investigated.

'By the way, have you seen Phil lately? Phil Cordell?' she asked Ray.

It was just a casual question, no more. Just to make conversation and to wipe that moon-struck expression from his face. But she hadn't expected the smile to slip or his perpetual blush to take on momentous proportions.

Christ, the two of them weren't *gay*, were they? Phil certainly didn't look that way, but that was the daftest assumption anyone could make. Gay people didn't come bar-coded like something in Sainsbury's, any more than anyone else did.

'I haven't spoken to him lately,' Ray stuttered.

'Oh well, it doesn't matter. It's just that I thought I might have heard from him by now. But you don't need to look so embarrassed, Ray. What you do in your own time is no concern of mine.'

His blank look was one of total incomprehension, and assured her that no, there was nothing going on between him and Phil Cordell of a sexual nature. She grinned at her own words. Actually, they weren't hers at all, but the kind of whispery 'Les Dawson' aside that her Aunt Harriet used whenever there had been something in the *Radio Times* she didn't approve of on TV that night.

'So let's go,' she said briskly to Ray now. 'Are you all set?'

'I think so. I'm just a friend of a friend, showing you around Bristol, and you're Steven Leng's Australian cousin. Is that right?'

'Ten out of ten,' Alex told him, pushing dark sunglasses on to her face.

He had proved his worth in the computer stakes again too, finding a map website on the Internet, zooming in and pin-pointing exactly where they had to go to find the Wilkins Haulage Company, before downloading it and printing it out.

Alex was sure she could have found it just as easily with the A to Z, but it didn't hurt to allow Ray the pleasure of proving what he could do with an Internet web-site. He didn't have much else going for him, and she doubted that the bouncy Mavis Patterson would have given him more than a second glance, if that.

* * *

Wilkins Haulage Company was some way out of the city on the road to Backwell, and then they had to drive some distance off the main road, through narrow country lanes to where they could look down on a huge water-filled quarry pit a little distance away from the main yard and some impressive office buildings.

No wonder it was well away from habitation, thought Alex, or there would surely be complaints from residents. Half a dozen lorries were parked in the yard or making their way to and from the quarry itself, and there was a general air of bustle and success. The noise of quarrying was deafening, and even looking down on the scene from the road above, dust rose everywhere, making Ray cough and wheeze like an octogenarian, and forcing him to take several undignified sucks on a blue asthma inhaler.

'Sorry,' he gasped. 'I'll be OK in a minute.'

'Take your time, Ray, and tell me if you'd rather stay in the car while I go and speak to these people. I don't want you expiring on me.'

For a moment he looked torn between longing to be in on the action, and dealing with the effects of the atmosphere on his lungs. Alex decided for him.

Besides, it was her show, she reminded herself, and if he wasn't feeling up to scratch, he might be more of a liability than an asset.

'It's going to be worse when we get down to the yard,' she said. 'So you stay in the car with the windows closed, Ray.'

'Are you sure you don't mind?' he wheezed.

'I'm sure,' she said.

But before she left him, she got out and took some pics of the whole area for reference. Then she got back in the car and cruised down to the yard, parking in the lane outside. There was no point in being too conspicuous before she knew the kind of reception she was going to get. God knows how those big lorries ever managed to manoeuvre their way through these lanes, but they obviously did. She'd found it hard enough not to scrape her precious Suzuki.

She left Ray still hunched up in the passenger seat, and only glanced back to see that he was all right as she reached the open gates of the haulage yard. By then, he was obviously feeling marginally recovered, well enough to be talking to somebody on his mobile phone, anyway. Probably his mum, Alex thought.

Then she forgot all about him, and remembered she was supposed to be Steven Leng's brash Australian cousin, who was interested in meeting his old friends for an article she was writing for a small local magazine. Pommie-based articles were always welcome for ex-pats and their descendants, she thought, throwing herself into the role and practising her line of patter.

'Are you looking for somebody, Miss?' a male voice asked her as she walked towards the office building.

She turned around and faced the man. He was dressed casually smart, and was obviously no lorry-driver or quarryman, and she didn't need to think twice to know that this was one of the Wilkins brothers. She had seen their photos, and recognized the aggressive, bull-headed looks at once.

'Gee, I hope so after coming all this way,' she said, with an ingenuous smile and lifting her voice on the last word. 'I'm looking for either David or Clifford Wilkins.'

'Well, you've found him. Clifford, that is. You're Australian, aren't you? I'm afraid we don't deliver that far,' he said, with a grin at his own joke.

Alex laughed back. 'No, that's not it. I was hoping you could give me a little background information on a cousin of mine. I never met him, as my folks emigrated to Australia just after I was born, but I gather he was an old mate of you and your brother's.'

'Really?' He gestured for her to walk alongside him, and they moved towards the office. 'Well, we're always ready to help a pretty lady, so what's your cousin's name?'

'Steven. Steven Leng.'

Cliff Wilkins stopped walking at once, and his eyes narrowed as he looked at Alex. 'That's a name I haven't heard of for years. What's your interest, Miss?'

'I told you. He's my cousin, and I'd like to know more about him for a sort of family history I'm compiling.' She quickly revised her intention of calling it an article for a small local magazine. This was far more plausible, she hoped.

'Didn't your parents ever tell you what happened to him? I find that a bit hard to believe.'

As suspicion came into Cliff Wilkins' eyes, she sensed that she was on dangerous ground. He might believe her accent, but he didn't trust her. And people who didn't trust someone who asked an innocent question usually had something to hide. You always had to think laterally in this business.

'My parents fell out with the rest of the family years ago, which was why they went overseas. They never kept in touch with any of them after that.'

Out of the corner of her eye she could see another man approaching them from the office. The brother, David Wilkins, was even tougher-looking than Clifford. She was thankful she didn't have Ray here as her so-called minder, she thought fleetingly. He'd have shrivelled at once.

'What's going on?' David Wilkins asked.

'The lady's looking for information on Steven Leng,' Clifford said baldly. 'Claims she's his cousin.'

After an imperceptible pause his brother spoke curtly.

'Steven never had any cousins. You know that.'

And why did she think he was deliberately directing his brother at that moment?

'I know it, but she doesn't,' Clifford replied. 'So just who are you, Miss, and what do you want?'

They could be calling her bluff on a double-bluff. Alex had no way of knowing, and nor had she had the foresight to check up on whether or not Steven Leng had any cousins, damn it. But she couldn't afford to back down now.

'Well, he'd hardly have mentioned me to you, since he didn't know I existed,' she said sarcastically. 'But look, I only wanted to meet some of his old mates and get to know a bit about him. If you can't tell me anything, I've obviously got a duff lead.'

'Yeah, I reckon you have,' David snapped,

not giving her an inch.

As they continued staring at her, Alex suddenly realized she hadn't thought this through properly. Any minute now they were going to ask her where she had got the information that they were friends of Steven Leng's. And how the hell could she answer that without giving the game away that she knew very well how Steven had disappeared on an abortive camping trip, in which these two were involved?

'Well, thanks for your time, anyway,' she said, edging away.

'Hey, just a minute — ' she heard one of them say aggressively.

Then there was a flurry of dust from one of their nearby lorries as the driver revved it up angrily, shouting that there was a bloody car with a bloody nerd sitting in it that was blocking the bloody lane and he couldn't get out for his bloody delivery.

'Sorry. It's mine. Shan't be a minute,' she called to him.

She just managed to resist saying she'd remove the bloody thing and get out of his bloody way quicker than bloody blinking, while thanking God for Ray's feeble presence inside the car.

The sooner she got away from here the better. Superficially she had got nowhere, but there was often more in negative responses than people ever realized. And she had got it all on the tape recorder tucked inside her fleece bomber jacket.

* * *

'Any good? Did you get anything out of them?' Ray asked, remarkably recovered from his wheezing attack, Alex noted.

'Not much. Maybe. I don't know yet.'

She was more concerned right now with backing up the car into a suitable passing space and turning it round, with the aggressive-looking Wilkins lorry bearing down on her and crowding her. She eventually managed it, and the lorry roared past, splattering her car with mud and dirt. *Bastard*.

'Are we going back to the office now then?' Ray persisted. 'And are you going to tell me what they said? I saw you talking to them down there — '

'Shut up, Ray, and let me think,' Alex snapped.

His inane chatter reinforced her preference for working alone. There had to be thinking time after any encounter, whether it was helpful or openly obstructive, and the best time to do it was immediately after meeting people like the Wilkins brothers.

'I'm only trying to take an interest,' Ray said, affronted. 'And if you want my opinion — '

'Well, sometimes it's best to just keep quiet . . . What opinion?'

'I'd say from the way they kept looking at one another, they definitely had something to hide,' he said importantly.

'Big deal,' Alex muttered beneath her breath, and then she spoke out loud.

'That's very observant of you, Ray. And where do you suppose they disposed of the body? In the quarry pit, perhaps? Maybe that's where they dump all their victims. Maybe they're mass murderers on the quiet and we're going to get the Queen's commendation for exposing them.'

And God knows why she was taking it all out on him. He was such a wimp, and she had hardly got started on this investigation yet, so there was no need to feel so frustrated. She did, though. She couldn't help the nagging feeling that this whole thing was a damn-good waste of Jane Leng's money.

Bob's too, she reminded herself. It was Jane's half of Bob's retirement money that was funding all this, and she wondered if he knew it yet — and what the reaction would be when he found out. Having had a sniff of his temper, she didn't hold out much hope for Jane's peace of mind when he did. She felt more than a brief unease on her behalf. She didn't like the woman any more than she liked her husband, but she didn't want to see any harm come to her either.

She realized Ray had said nothing for the last few minutes, and when she glanced at him she saw that his lips were clamped tight shut. From the side, he looked even more weaselly than usual, with his small hooked nose and his jutting chin. She had never noticed it so strongly before.

'Oh come on Ray, don't sulk,' she said. 'You know what my dad used to say? If you can't stand the heat, get out of the kitchen. In other words, don't expect me to be sugary sweet to you all the time, because I won't be. This isn't school now. This is the real world, and there are some bloody awful people in it.'

'I know. And my dad is already nagging at me to get out of it.'

Alex glanced at him in surprise now before giving all her attention to the road as another car's hooter screamed out at her.

'Up yours, fella,' she muttered. 'So what's up, Ray? Are you tired of the job already?'

She found herself praying that he'd say yes, giving her a way out. There was something about the little weasel that she didn't like, and if it wasn't for his computer skills and accessing the Internet . . . but, hell, she wasn't an idiot. She'd watched him do it, and he'd taken pride in instructing her. She could always take a course to improve herself. Or she could ask Nick down again, and get him to show her the finer points, which would be far preferable.

'Isn't the job all you expected it to be, then?' she asked Ray more gently.

'It's not that. It's my dad.'

'What about him?' They had reached the main road now, and she could breathe more easily.

'He says I'm nothing but a gofer, and he doesn't like the thought of me working for a lady snooper. That's his name for it, not mine,' he added hastily. 'But it makes things awkward at home. And now this thing's come up.'

'Like a wart, you mean?' Alex asked, trying to make the poor goof smile.

'No. A works experience vacancy in his office. He wants me to take it.'

'And what do you want?'

'I don't know. I always thought insurance would be a good job, with plenty of advancement. It was only when Mr Cordell told me about you, and he was so keen for me to try for it that I thought it was such a good idea.'

'I see.' Philip Cordell clearly had more influence over him than she had given him credit for. It was a shame to play on his adoration like that. And for what? So that Phil himself could get any information about her investigations through Ray? The idea was so absurd she didn't even bother to follow it up. Why on earth should he be interested in the Lengs, anyway?

'Ray, if it's causing ructions at home, then I think I should release you from our temporary arrangement. Providing it's what you want as well.'

'I think it would be best,' he said, not exactly unhappily.

'Then you can finish the day out, and we'll call it quits. When we get back to the office you can take my film to the camera shop to get it processed. Just bring me back the receipt and some doughnuts, and we'll have a cup of coffee and settle up and that will be that. And no hard feelings, OK?'

9

So now she was without an assistant — and so soon. But if Ray was getting aggro from home, the last thing Alex wanted was another irate father descending on her. Reluctantly, she knew it was time she called Philip Cordell and told him what had happened. She owed it to him, since he'd put Ray on to her in the first place.

She left it until that evening, and his reaction was affable enough.

'I'm sorry about that, Alex. Ray's a nice enough chap, but easily led, and his father's a big influence on him.'

Like you, she added silently.

'Well, never mind. It didn't work out, but thanks anyway, Phil.'

'But was he any help to you while he lasted?' Phil persisted with a laugh. 'I know he can be a bit intense, but he means well. And maybe I can find you somebody else — '

'No, please don't do that,' Alex said quickly. 'If I decide an assistant's necessary, I'll go about it in my own way. No offence, of course. And yes, Ray was very useful when it came to the computer.'

'That's all right then. So how about another date?'

'I'm really busy, Phil. Let's leave it for now, shall we?'

She couldn't really say why she didn't want to see him again. Perhaps it was because she had felt almost pressured into going out with him that first time, pressured into knowing him. Whatever it was, she didn't want to go out with him again. And when push came to shove — or even to pull back — she preferred to trust her instincts. They might not always be right, but they were all she had.

'Fair enough. Give me a call when you're less busy, Alex. And good luck with the case.'

She hung up, feeling unaccountably annoyed. And for no good reason she was also struck with doubts and a sudden fit of depression. What bloody case? So far it seemed to be leading her nowhere. Who the hell did she think she was, trying to solve a ten-year-old crime without even knowing if there was a crime involved at all? It was a tragic *incident*, to use the jargon of the fire service, and one that the police had handled satisfactorily all that time ago, and had now presumably wiped off their books.

What had she found so far? She had certainly learned that Bob Leng wanted her to stop meddling in his affairs and that his wife wanted her to carry on. She'd seen a lot of newspaper reports, including Jane's many aggressive letters to the press. She had seen a lot of character analyses of Steven's friends in Gran Patterson's scrap books, and she had discovered that one of those friends had died in an horrific accident. And she had visited two yobbish brothers who wouldn't give her the time of day.

Maybe her stupid disguise as a brash Australian long-lost cousin of Steven's hadn't been such a clever idea after all. Maybe she should have gone down to the haulage yard done up to the nines and dazzled one or both of the Wilkins brothers with her charms.

She shuddered. No thanks, matey. She certainly wouldn't have wanted to get in either of their clutches. Slimy gits.

She wondered how soon it would be before Jane Leng contacted her again, and decided that the least she could do would be to write up a detailed report of her meeting with the Wilkins brothers, and the information about John Barnett. It would be more detailed than the actual facts warranted, perhaps, but with the help of Ray's meticulous file on Gran's scrap books, she could do it justice. At least Jane could see that she hadn't been idle since coming here.

But not now. Not tonight. Tonight she was

going to take a leisurely bath and then curl up on the sofa with a drink and a box of chocolates — to hell with a few extra pounds on her thighs — and watch anything on the telly that would make her laugh. She'd had enough of morbid investigations for now.

* * *

She had just emerged from her bathroom, wreathed in the glorious scent of exotic oriental bath foam, when she realized her answer machine light was flashing. With her radio turned up full, she hadn't even heard the phone ring. She sometimes wished she could be the kind of person who could ignore doorbells and telephones and letters on the doormat, but she couldn't, and never had been.

There were two messages. One was from Jane Leng.

'I'm sorry to speak to you like this, Miss Best, and I don't really like these things, but I thought I should warn you that Bob's in Somerset for a few days, and I'm afraid he may come to see you. He knows all about you now, and he doesn't like it at all. He's becoming even more impossible to live with, and as soon as he gets back I'm coming down myself to see how the workmen are getting on with the house. It has to have some rewiring and pointing, so I'll be staying with my sister for a few days, and I'll come and see you then.'

She had hung up while Alex was still digesting the fact that Jane even had a sister. Why hadn't she told her before? It might have given her a different angle on the affair if she could have interviewed the sister. As it was, she didn't even know her name.

She tuned in to the second message. It was Charlie Adamson. For a few seconds Alex couldn't think who he was, and then she got a vision of him in the dungeons of the newspaper offices immersed in his beloved archives.

'Just thought you ought to know that we've had another letter from Jane Leng and it'll be in the paper tomorrow. Nothing different from the usual, except that she says she's now got you on the case. I presume you were aware of it.'

No, she bloody wasn't, Alex fumed as the message clicked off. What the hell was Jane playing at, brandishing her name about as if it was some kind of trophy? But that was it, of course. After years of getting nowhere with the police she'd got a tame monkey to do her dirty work for her now, and Alex was it.

Without stopping to think, she found

herself dialling Jane's London number. The woman answered cautiously.

'Oh, it's you, Miss Best.' The relief was obvious when she discovered who the caller was. 'Thank goodness. I thought it was going to be him.'

'Him?'

'Bob, of course. He may not be here in person, but he's still victimizing me over the phone every night.'

Alex ignored the pertinent word. 'Mrs Leng, am I to understand that you've sent another letter to the local newspaper here and named me in it?'

'That's right, dear — '

'Why on earth have you done that? How can I go about doing my job if everyone knows who I am and what I'm doing? I thought you understood the nature of my work.'

'Well, are you working for me or not? If I'm not paying you enough, then you must say so — ' she said, almost petulantly.

'That's got nothing to do with it.' She was beginning to dislike the woman more and more. As if payment counted for everything when she could manage very well without her kind.

But of course she couldn't, not entirely. To stay in business, you had to take on the clients you disliked along with the ones you desperately wanted to help. She tried again.

'Mrs Leng, I would appreciate it if you would withdraw that letter.'

'Oh, I couldn't do that, dear. Steven wouldn't like it.'

'Steven wouldn't know.'

As soon as she had said it she bit her lip, knowing it was heartless and insensitive, but she recognized a growing arrogance in the woman's attitude. In her eyes, she was right, and the whole world was wrong. It was more than a belief that her son was still alive. It was a blind ambition to be somebody in this affair, instead of being the little nonentity that she really was. And if that was demeaning to the woman, Alex didn't care.

She might have been a good wife and mother once, but she had turned into a harridan now. You had to see people for what they really were, and that was exactly the way Alex was seeing Jane Leng.

'I'm sorry if you think my letter will be a problem, dear, but I'm sure it won't harm you in any way.'

She was bland again, completely enclosed in her own little world, and she had hung up before Alex could say any more, proving to Alex that her assessment wasn't far off the mark.

Filled with frustration and anger that perhaps she was being taken for a ride, she drank more glasses of vodka and lime than was good for her, and ate a whole box of chocolates before she rolled into bed with a huge bout of indigestion that she knew she deserved.

First thing next morning she went down to the corner shop and bought a copy of the local newspaper.

'Hi, Alex, long time no see,' Mavis said delightedly, even though it had only been a few days since the last time she had been in there. She was as perky as usual, wearing a mauve sweater and matching eyeshadow, with silver and gold stars stuck haphazardly over her pale cheeks. Presumably the shopkeeper indulged these weird looks at nine o'clock in the morning. It might even attract customers, but the sight of her — young, bright, *thin* — depressed Alex.

'Hi yourself,' she croaked, her throat as dry as a husk.

'You look as if you've had a night on the tiles,' Mavis went on with a laugh. 'I see you're mentioned in dispatches, as Gran calls it.'

Alex groaned. She didn't need to ask what she meant. She just paid for the newspaper and some aspirins and went back to her office, with Mavis's shrill voice calling out behind her to let her know when she fancied a night out.

Right now all Alex fancied was another night in bed, in total silence, completely alone and in a darkened room. But the minute she got back to her office, she skimmed through the newspaper and found the letters page. And there it was, in all its glory.

It seemed as though Jane Leng was a virtuoso in letter-writing now, because hers was square-boxed with star billing at the top of the page. It said the usual stuff that Alex recognized. Her son had never been found and the police had never done their job properly, but now she had Alexandra Best looking into it, one of London's most successful private investigators, who had now moved to Bristol.

Christ Almighty. The woman was giving her top status as a PI, and inferring that she had come here especially to sort out the incompetent police force and solve the mystery of Steven Leng for once and all.

The phone rang even as she was counting the minutes until she heard from some eager newspaper reporter to get her reaction. She was surprised they hadn't done so before.

'Frank Gregory here, Alex. Have you seen the paper?'

'I'm reading it now. This was not my idea, Frank, and I'm furious. The last thing I wanted was to have my name blazoned all over the newspaper — '

'Yes, well as far as that goes, the damage is done. My advice now is to back off and issue a statement, playing down the whole thing.'

'I can't do that. Mrs Leng is still my client,' she protested.

'Well, I can't force you to do it, but I just hope you know what you're doing in dealing with this madwoman. I'll speak to you soon.'

Alex hung up slowly, not quite knowing what to make of that last sentence. What she did know was that the police didn't want this case reopened. They wouldn't be at all pleased to know that the Lengs were returning to their neck of the woods either. Sleeping dogs — and mutilated hands — should lie. *Lie* being the operative word, Alex thought, going off at a tangent.

Who was lying over what had happened to Steven Leng? Somebody must know something, and it all came back to his companions on the camping trip. John Barnett couldn't answer. The Wilkins brothers had clammed up the minute she mentioned Steven's name. She still had to track down the others — the chap who now had a hardware shop in Bath, and the elusive Lennie Fry, so-called rock musician and God knows what else — and that should be her next priority.

However, it would all have to wait until she had made some toast and taken some aspirins and black coffee to clear her head, and tried to stop her nerves from juddering so much. She had gone to the shop before doing any of it, and the throbbing in her head was a steady reminder.

By mid-morning she was feeling fractionally more alert, and getting down to some work. Though it wasn't proper work, she thought guiltily. Courtesy of Ray's help she now had an e-mail address and the facility to get on to the Internet, and she spent a considerable time looking at web-sites that may never be any use to her, but were interesting, anyway. One day soon she was going to send an e-mail to Nick and startle him out of his complacent belief in her inability to master anything so complex. Not that she could blame him. She had always been adamant in stating that she would never succumb to it — and now she had. *C'est la vie*.

Her buzzer made her jump and she spoke quickly into the intercom.

'I'd like to see Alexandra Best, please,' said a voice that was vaguely familiar. She couldn't readily place it, but since she was sure it wasn't Bob Leng she told its owner to push open the door.

And then she was face to face with Clifford Wilkins.

'*You!*' he said furiously, placing his fists on his hips aggressively.

'I'm afraid so,' Alex said, keeping as cool as possible. 'And what can I do for you, Mr Wilkins?'

'Well, you can drop the charade of being Steven Leng's Australian cousin, for a start. It was a hammy accent if ever I heard one.'

'It fooled you though, didn't it?' she said, deciding there was no point in not brazening it out.

'Not for one bloody minute.'

Oh yeah?

'Would you like to sit down?' Alex said, gesturing to a chair.

'No I bloody wouldn't. I want to know what you're playing at with that fool of a woman.'

'I take it you've seen the local paper then. And I do prefer it when people don't swear at me all the time, Mr Wilkins.'

She stared him out, knowing that her emerald green eyes and the sound of her cut-glass voice was often enough to quell the most irate client. And she was using every bit of her equipment to keep him in his place.

It didn't work with this one, though. He strode forward and thrust his face close to hers, in much the same way as Bob Leng had done.

'You're wasting your time. Steven's long gone and that mother of his wants putting away.'

'I do hope that's not a threat to Mrs Leng's safety.'

He continued to glare at her, and she gave a small sigh, forcing herself to speak more confidentially as she leaned forward, under cover of sliding open her desk drawer a fraction, and pressing the On switch of her tape recorder.

'Mr Wilkins — Clifford — I'm just doing what I've been retained to do. Mrs Leng only wants to know what happened to Steven, which is a perfectly natural thing for a mother's peace of mind, and if you can throw any light on the subject, it would be enormously helpful. You were there at the time of the incident, weren't you? You and the group of friends who were going on the camping trip?'

'Steven never came with us,' he snarled.

'I know that. So you just went off and continued with the trip without trying to find out if he'd been hurt in the explosion, I believe?'

God, it was hard to say it calmly and not to condemn. Even though she felt the utmost contempt that the others could have done such a thing, she made herself remember that at the time they were kids, and they were scared. They had been consorting with down-and-outs and winos, and God knows who else — maybe some of these Followers whose name cropped up from time to time — and they would have feared the consequences.

'Steven was already backing out of the trip. He was tied to his mother's apron strings and wishing he'd never agreed to come with us and was going home. It was no big deal when he did just that, as far as we knew, anyway. It was a bloody relief, if you must know,' he added.

'Why do you say that?' Alex enquired.

'He had some weird ideas. All that stuff about going to India and suchlike. *Finding* himself. Him and — well, it was all a load of tripe, anyway. He'd never have gone. His dad wouldn't have let him. A right bastard, his dad.'

He caught sight of Alex's raised eyebrow and scowled.

'Anyway, all I came to say is you're wasting your time, and if you want my advice, you'll lay off.'

'You know, I'm being offered so much advice on how to run my life lately, I wondered how I ever managed without you all. Even the local police are in on it now,' she said casually, watching him.

He stood up at once, his face dark and mutinous. 'Just keep out of things that don't concern you. They had their say when they got the chance, and a fat lot of use they were.'

She couldn't be sure, but she thought she heard a note of triumph in his voice. As if he — or the group — had somehow beaten the police at their own game.

'I may need to speak to you again sometime, Mr Wilkins,' she said, as he neared the door.

'You've already said enough as far as I'm concerned. Don't you ever know when to quit?' he snapped.

'Of course I do. When the case is over.'

He slammed the door on his way out, and Alex immediately got out the tape recorder and rewound the tape. She listened to it all over again, and towards the end there was one special bit that interested her.

'*All that stuff about going to India and suchlike. Finding himself. Him and —* '

Him and who? That was the question. Him and Lennie Fry, who was also a bit of a free spirit as they called them in the sixties, and didn't seem to fit in anywhere? And she was damn sure that the vague reference to Steven's weird ideas included his interest in the Followers.

It had been a revealing conversation though, and perhaps it wasn't all bad news that Jane Leng had mentioned her name in her newspaper letter after all. It had produced a reaction from Frank Gregory, and it had made Clifford Wilkins hotfoot it to her door. You might have expected friends of Steven to show an interest in what had happened to him, to want to know, even to have done a bit of detection work themselves. Instead of which . . . well, John Barnett might have shown an interest in his time, but he wasn't around to tell her anything now. And the Wilkins brothers were clearly going to clam up, closing ranks. Or covering up.

Her telephone rang, and she picked it up, going straight into professional mode. She relaxed as she heard Mavis Patterson's voice for the second time that day.

'Oh Alex, Gran just popped into the shop, and she wondered if you'd like to come and have supper with us tonight. She does a lovely shepherd's pie, and her special onion gravy to go with it. She thought you might like a bit of home cooking. Not that you can't cook yourself, of course, but she reckons it's never so much fun cooking just for one, is it? If you're busy, just say so, mind, but I know Gran would love to have a natter with you and find out how things are going — '

'Mavis, I'd love to come to supper tonight,' Alex broke in as soon as there was a pause for breath at the other end. 'What time?'

'Oh, about seven o'clock will be fine. Gran don't like to eat too late because of the wind — '

'That will be wonderful,' Alex said, before Mavis could expand on Gran's wind. 'I'll see you both then.'

She immediately forgot her need for an early night. Having seen the paper that morning, Gran would naturally have been impressed by the status of successful London Private Investigator that Jane Leng had bequeathed on her, but it was more than that. Gran Patterson was naturally interested in people, and especially in the kind of people who committed crimes. They had a lot in common.

Meanwhile she had to keep her mind on the job. Checking Ray's detailed instructions of how to get onto the Internet, she switched on her computer again and went through it step by step. It was still pretty much of a mystery to Alex, but if it worked, it worked. That was the best way to handle technology,

Nick always said: *If it ain't broke, don't fix it, and if it works, don't question it*.

After a considerable time of trial and error and getting nowhere except for being offered a million things to buy online that she didn't want, she clicked on to a line that said Find People, and typed in Followers.

She didn't really have much hope, and sure enough it was a non-starter. Then she had a tiny burst of inspiration, found one of the search engines Ray had listed, and looked for Religious Organizations or similar. If that didn't do it . . . but then up came 'Search For?'. Alex typed in Followers, and held her breath.

After an agonizing few minutes a whole page of information began to unroll as if by magic in front of her eyes. They were legit then. They existed. The sense of triumph Alex felt was almost orgasmic at that moment. Well, almost: it took more than a page of information about some freak cult that had captured Steven Leng's imagination, and possibly Lennie Fry's too . . .

She felt another surge of excitement as she saw several contact addresses scattered about the country. Not Bristol, though. The nearest one was Exeter. She didn't know the location or the area, but there was always somebody who would. She had contacts too. Ray Smart.

Or Phil Cordell. Or Charlie Adamson. Anyone but the local bobbies.

She clicked off, feeling as if she had climbed a mountain at even finding anything on the bloody Internet at all. Her pride in getting to grips with this alien thing was paramount, even though she knew she could simply have asked Nick Frobisher where the Followers operated from, but the less he knew how deeply she was going to get into this, the better.

* * *

She turned up at the Patterson house armed with a box of chocolates, since she guessed Gran wouldn't be into drinking wine. The minute she walked in the door, the aroma of cooking met her nostrils and alerted her taste buds. It smelled fantastic, and she was immediately transported back to a warm and steamy farmhouse with her mother's huge portions of comfort meals placed in front of her.

'Now then, my lover, I hope you've got a hearty appetite,' Gran said with a chuckle. 'We don't want no leftovers for tomorrow, and Mavis here sometimes eats no more than a sparrow.'

'I've got to think of my figure, Gran,' Mavis told her, but although she started off with a small amount on her plate it didn't stop her having second helpings, Alex noted, which rather defeated the object.

'So how are things going?' Gran asked, when they were all replete and sitting around the fire.

By then Alex and Mavis had done the washing-up and Gran was softly belching onion-breath at frequent intervals. As long as it stayed up top and didn't descend below, Alex thought.

'I wanted to ask you something,' she began without any messing around. From the look of her, Gran would be asleep soon, and she needed to know.

'Did you ever hear of a group called the Followers?'

'Oh ah, everybody knew about them. Oddballs, if you'll pardon my French.'

'Oh Gran, that ain't French!' Mavis said with a laugh.

'Well, Alex knows what I mean, don't you, lover?'

She said solemnly that she did.

'Funny folk, wore a lot of pale colours and did charity work, so 'twas said. Busking and that. They never stayed in one place for long, though I don't think the police were ever bothered by 'em. They had a place around here somewhere.'

Alex gave her a dazzling smile. She was a gem if she ever met one. This was a piece of information that wasn't on the Internet. Sometimes it paid to just ask people, she thought more humbly — and hadn't she always said as much? She smugly ignored her new-found expertise with the Internet.

'Did they? Do you know where it was? This place, I mean. Their headquarters, I suppose you'd call it.'

Gran shrugged. ''Tain't here no more. It was pulled down after they moved on. 'Twere ready to be condemned anyway. I dunno where they went after that.'

'When was that then?'

Gran leaned forward to give the fire a poke, and let out a gentle explosion of wind at the same time, and Mavis made wafting gestures behind her back.

'I dunno now. Must have been eight — mebbe ten years ago. They never did no harm, mind, but folk probably got tired of seeing 'em in the Centre and in Broadmead all the time, begging for money.'

She gave a huge yawn, which was marvellous timing, Alex thought, since a breather in the fresh night air was just what she needed. No offence to the old darling, but enough was enough.

'I've tired you out, and it's time I went, but

thank you again for a lovely evening, and a perfectly splendid meal,' she said. 'I really enjoyed it, Gran.'

'Good. Come again then,' she said vaguely, with a final rip-roarer that sent Alex scuttling to the door, with Mavis laughing her head off behind her.

'She can't help it, and half the time I don't think she knows she does it. See you around then, Alex.'

'See you, Mavis,' Alex answered in kind, thankful that the girl hadn't wanted to prolong the evening when she had to think very hard about whether to find Keith Martin of Bath first, or drive down to Exeter and suss out these Followers. But there was really no contest. She was as intrigued as the next person about these strange cults — and Keith Martin wasn't going to go away.

10

Since writing her letter to the press, naming Alex as her accomplice in the search for information about her son — which was the way Alex was viewing it now — Jane had stepped up her aggressive correspondence, and the letters now appeared every few days.

Bob Leng had stayed in Somerset longer than he had intended, if only to get away from his wife's acid tongue, and he was well aware of what was happening. Before he went back to London, he had stormed the newspaper offices in Bristol, demanding that they stopped printing his wife's letters or he'd have the law on them.

He had met with reasonableness from older members of staff who knew the whole story and his involvement in it, but pointed out that it was a free country and they were simply publishing one person's opinion, while stating that the newspaper didn't necessarily agree with the views of contributors — the usual editorial get-out clause.

He also had met with sniggering insults and mockery from several young cub reporters who were unaware that at the time of the incident, he had been the one to make the horrific discovery in the woods, and told him he didn't know his arse from his elbow if he didn't know that such letters made good copy, and they thought he'd be glad of the ongoing publicity.

Still incensed at the injustice of it all, he then went to the local nick and demanded that they put a stop to it. He bellowed at Frank Gregory that it was killing him, eating away at him like a bloody great cancer, since his wife made a great show of not only shoving a copy of what she had sent under his nose, but also having the relevant newspaper copy (which was regularly posted to her on subscription from Bristol) placed on his breakfast plate, with her letter heavily ringed in red.

'She couldn't even mark it in black. She has to do it in red, just like blood,' he raged to Frank Gregory, becoming irrational and close to hysteria now. 'The bitch is heartless, and she knows fucking well what she's doing to me. We lost our Steven years ago, so why can't she let him rest in peace? You've got to stop this campaign of hers. If you don't, I swear I will — '

'It's hardly a campaign, Mr Leng — '

'It fucking well is. It's a campaign of hate, and she knows it. She's picking away at me, bit by bit.'

'Have you seen a counsellor about this? Or a doctor? You obviously need to take things more calmly, Mr Leng, and to try to look at it from your wife's point of view — '

'*I don't need fucking counsellors and doctors. I just need to be rid of that blood-sucking vampire!*'

He blundered out of the office in a blazing rage just as the young WPC bringing in Frank's morning coffee came in. He knocked Frank's prized Queen Mother's 100th birthday commemoration mug flying out of her hand, splattering her brand new uniform as it smashed on the floor. She looked at Frank in dumb horror, expecting fireworks, but instead, he merely gave a deep sigh of resignation as she stuttered out her apologies.

'Not your fault, Carol. Just get a mop and bucket and clear it up, there's a good girl. And bring me some more coffee. I need it after dealing with that one. It's a toss-up whether it's him or his wife who ends up in the funny farm first.'

It wasn't a politically correct remark, and he'd have been howled at by the righteous for saying it, but Frank was beyond thinking politically-anything at that moment. He felt more like wringing Bob Leng's neck, and hoped the man's fury towards his wife didn't portend a murderous intent. It might be as well to give DCI Frobisher a call sometime and alert him to the current climate.

In Frank's opinion, and like most others, any sympathy for the Lengs had long gone because of their bloody dramatics. The temperamental old fool never knew when to leave well alone, and neither did his crazy wife. Between them, they were heading for a wonderful retirement together, I don't think, Frank mused sarcastically. And then he turned to calmer police matters and promptly forgot about the pair of them.

* * *

At that moment Bob was heading blindly for the Clifton Suspension Bridge. Anywhere to get away from his own thoughts, even though he knew that was an impossibility. Nobody was ever going to listen to his side of the story. It should be dead and buried, anyway, he thought savagely. He wanted shot of it. He had intended closing his eyes and ears to the whole affair years ago — and would have been able to do it but for Jane's obsession and his terrible nightmares. He blamed those on her too.

If she had any feelings for him at all, she'd stop sending these bastard letters to the press, and get rid of all the pictures of Steven, so that he wasn't constantly reminded of him wherever he looked. It wasn't that he hadn't loved his son, as far as he was capable of loving anyone, but couldn't she see that in all those bloody photos where the boy was holding a fishing-rod, or folding his arms with his school mates, or holding up a trophy for some sporting achievement — that all he could see was that festering, heaving, maggot-ridden hand?

There was only one sure way to rid himself of the horror of it all. He'd imagined himself free of her so many times, dreaming up the most elaborate ways to do bloody murder and get away with it. But he knew he wasn't clever enough. He didn't have the guts for it, either. He could bully her and strike her, but he knew he'd never be able to go through with the final act. So it had to be this way, and his last gleeful thought was that at least she wouldn't get his insurance money. They didn't pay out for suicides, did they?

* * *

Witnesses on the bridge swore that it was a tragic accident. One minute the man seemed to be walking purposefully from one side to the other, and then he paused as if he was intent on studying the shipping passing below on the full tide. He leaned further out, as if to see something in particular, and the next minute his feet had left the ground and he was hurtling over the side of the bridge and into the swollen river below.

* * *

'Oh no, he couldn't swim,' Jane Leng said complacently to the police officers who came to inform her a few hours later. 'Didn't see the need for it, you see, and he'd never go to anyone for lessons. He was as stubborn as a mule in that respect. Well, in everything, really. If he couldn't do something by his own efforts, he'd just heap scorn on anyone else who could. Our Steven was an excellent swimmer, of course.'

The two police officers glanced at one another. The WPC spoke gently, while the other officer continued to take notes.

'Mrs Leng, you do understand that your husband is dead, don't you?'

'Oh yes,' Jane said, more brightly. 'I understand perfectly.'

'And is Steven a relative? Where can we get hold of him?'

Jane looked at her pityingly. 'Steven's my son. I'm not sure where he is just now, but I'm sure he'll be in touch very soon.'

The second officer looked at her sharply as memory clicked into place. 'Mrs Leng, was your husband a fireman, and was there a terrible incident some years ago? I'm sorry if this is insensitive, but I didn't connect the name at first.'

'He *was* a fireman, just retired, so there shouldn't be any problem about his pension coming to me. Actually, I shall come into quite a nice little sum of money in insurances too. Enough to be comfortable and to make a nice home for when Steven comes home.'

The WPC stared at her in shock, clearly too new at the job to know what she was talking about. She just saw her as the coldest fish imaginable, she told her oppo later, to dismiss her husband's death like that, as if she was only interested in his pension and his insurance money.

'It's a long story,' he told her. 'But I'll fill you in when we get back to the nick. And I'm very sorry, Mrs Leng, but we have to ask you to identify your husband. A car will take you down to Bristol whenever you're ready.'

Her first instinct was to say she wouldn't go and she never wanted to see the fat oaf again. But then she realized there wouldn't be a death certificate without a positive identification, so she said she'd be ready in ten minutes, providing they would bring her back again, since she had things to see to.

'Probably suffering from shock,' the police officer confided to the WPC at her outraged look. 'It takes some of them that way sometimes.'

* * *

He might not have been so compassionate had he been able to read Jane's mind as she looked down at her husband's body on the marble slab. Like a great grey slug, was how she thought of him, and silent for one of the few times in his life. But it wasn't his life now, was it? It was his death.

She kept her eyes lowered so that the police officer and mortuary attendants wouldn't see the gleam of pleasure in her eyes, and nodded quickly.

'That's him. That's my husband,' she said in a muffled voice.

Once the car had taken her swiftly back to London again, as she insisted that was what she wanted until she had time to think, she lost no time in calling Alex Best.

'Fished him up out of the river, like the drowned rat he always was,' Jane said viciously. 'So now I don't have to bother about him any more, do I?'

'Mrs Leng, I don't know what to say,' Alex

began, appalled at this callousness. She knew there was no love lost between them, but Jesus, there were limits. 'Does this change your plans for moving to Somerset at all?'

Please say that it does. Please say that I need have nothing more to do with you.

The hell of it was, though, she was already caught up in the mystery of Steven Leng's whereabouts, and knew she would have to carry on.

'Oh, it doesn't change my plans at all. I'll have to be there for the funeral, anyway, though I'm sure my sister will see to that side of it. I was never any good at all that. So I'll see you quite soon.'

She was unbelievable, thought Alex. Hateful, and unbelievable. She spoke as if she was obliged to attend a social function she didn't much care about, and a far more important occasion would be meeting Alex again.

'I have to be away on business for a week or so,' Alex said quickly, having no intention of waiting around to watch her crow. 'In fact you only just caught me before I leave town, but you can always contact me on my mobile phone.'

She hung up before there was any reply, hating the woman, hating the job, hating the whole rotten human race that could tear one another apart.

Her phone rang again, and she was tempted to leave it. But if she did, her answer machine would only kick in, and she'd have to check it out later. She snatched up the receiver again, and heard Nick's crisp voice.

'Alex, have you heard?'

'If you mean have I heard that Bob Leng's jumped off the Clifton Suspension Bridge, then yes, Jane has just told me very charmingly.'

It was a relief to hear his voice, and yet it brought her to the edge of tears, reminding her again of how sweet life could be, and yet how destructive people could be to one another.

'Jumped? The witnesses are adamant that he fell.'

'Well, I'm sure that's what Jane will want to hear, so she can claim all his insurance money.'

'Since when did you become so cynical?'

'That's my prerogative,' he said, clearly intending to jolly her along despite the seriousness of the call.

'Not any more,' Alex retorted.

'Do you want company this weekend?'

God, that was so tempting. It was exactly what she wanted, and needed. But there was also the thought that Jane Leng might be descending on her, twittering about her new-found widow's wealth, and she couldn't bear that. If it seemed like running away, so be it.

'Nick, can we leave it a while? I'd love to see you, but I'd planned on going away for a few days.'

'Hardly the time of year for holidays, is it?'

'It's business, and don't ask any more, because I'm not telling you.'

But he knew her too well. 'Don't be an idiot, darling. If you're still at the Leng woman's beck and call, she'll never leave you alone if she's coming into money. Haven't you worked that out yet?'

'Nick, I have to go. I've got an appointment. Sorry. I'll call you, OK?'

Her voice always became jerky when she was nervous or upset, and right now she was both.

But she was already mentally planning which clothes she was going to throw together before she drove down to Exeter and looked for the Followers, though she didn't have a clue what she was going to say to them. One thing was for sure: there was no way she was going to apply for membership, if that was what you did, and no way she was going to let herself get into their clutches.

* * *

She switched off her mobile while she was getting ready, unwilling to answer any more calls, and didn't turn on her answer machine until the last minute before locking up the flat and the office. By now she was dressed as an ordinary tourist. There was no sense in trying to make a fashion statement when checking into a B & B for a couple of nights, especially as she needed to merge into the wallpaper, so to speak.

You could never do that, doll, she seemed to hear one Gary Hollis's sexy voice drawl. She ignored it, twisting her hair up into a large clip and pulling on her brown fleece bomber jacket over her check shirt and jeans.

Then she bundled everything she needed into her car, making a mental checklist as she did so: tote bag, notebook, laptop, camera, tape recorder, mobile phone, route maps and AA town maps. She had no idea how long she was going to be away, but she needed to be prepared for everything. Then she headed out of Bristol, and didn't start breathing easily until she reached the M5 motorway and cruised towards the south-west. Only then did she start to think seriously about the implications of Bob Leng's death.

⋆ ⋆ ⋆

'It's suicide, but we'll never prove it, not with these bloody witnesses adamant that Leng looked perfectly normal just before he fell,' DI Frank Gregory said in answer to Nick Frobisher's latest call.

He held the phone away from his head as he heard Nick's response.

'*Normal*? Christ Almighty, the day anybody calls that bugger normal is the day I hang up my boots.'

Frank was tetchy. 'You don't need to tell me that. I was probably the last one he spoke to — or rather, the last one he verbally abused. How's the wife taking it?'

'How do you think? She's probably out on a spending spree right now with all the loot she's about to get. It was no accident, Frank.'

'You know it and I know it, but we'll never prove it, so it looks as if she'll be doing the merry widow act from now on.'

'And paying Alex Best anything she wants to do her bidding,' Nick said grimly. 'Anyway, have you seen her or heard from her? I can't get hold of her.'

'Sorry. We're not her keepers down here, Frobisher. We do have other things to deal with as well as wet-nursing your bit of fluff.'

Nick heard the edge in his voice, and backed off. But he was less than happy about the fact that Alex seemed to have gone to ground. He was bloody uneasy about her, if the truth were told.

Where the hell are you, Alex? He fumed. *And whatever else you do, keep out of the way of the black widow.*

* * *

At that moment Jane Leng was creating her latest newspaper letter and preparing to fax it off that afternoon from the little printing office she had discovered that did it so cheaply. Not that cheapness mattered to her any more, or wouldn't as soon as she got the insurance policies in motion.

For such a nondescript little woman, who never seemed to have much gumption about her, she had done a surprising amount of personal business since hearing about Bob's demise that morning.

She had phoned her sister and brother-in-law, and listened to their shocked reactions, and then asked them crisply to get in touch with the undertaker's for her and arrange the funeral to their convenience and then let her know when it would be. There was no point in pretending a grief she didn't feel, and all she wanted was to get it over and done with, without having to go through all the messy business of dealing with these people.

She had dug out the insurance policies and telephoned the company with the news, promising to send copies of the death certificate as soon as possible. She had had the foresight to discuss it with the police doctor who had accompanied her to the mortuary and pronounced Bob dead. There would have to be an inquest, but he assured her it would be a formality, since there was little doubt that the cause of death was drowning by accident.

Then the death certificate would be issued and she could get copies. Bob was dead and drowned, she reminded herself again, with a jubilation bordering on euphoria. It gave her a sweet sense of satisfaction to know the way it had happened. *She* knew, and *he* would have known that it was no accident, even though he had always hated the water. God only knew why he had done it this way, but there was no doubt in her mind that he *had* done it, of course. Saving her the trouble, anyway, she thought callously.

Steven would want to know. Steven would want to see his father planted. She revised her words on his account. Steven would want to see his father decently buried. Steven would finally turn up once he had seen her letter in the newspaper, which was why she had to get it off straight away and not wait for the post to deliver it.

She read it once more before she faxed it, to make certain she had got everything right. This time it was addressed directly to Steven Leng, via the newspaper letters page.

'Steven, your father is dead, so now you must come home, and we can live very comfortably in the new house in Chilworthy. We can do anything we want. We can travel to India like you always wanted, or go all around the world. We'll have such times together now, Steven. So I want you to contact your Auntie Grace and Uncle Joe for details of the funeral, and I'll look forward to seeing you there.'

She paused, and then signed it, 'Your loving mother, Jane Leng.'

She smiled as she pushed it through the fax machine and imagined the look on the editor's face when he received it. She had no doubt it would be printed. They always used her letters, and this was an added bit of news as well. She had no intention of sending in an obituary notice to the paper, but no doubt her sister would feel it necessary. Grace was a stickler for convention, even though she knew as well as Jane that Bob had always been a bastard. Grace wouldn't have used such a word, but she knew it all the same.

Once the fax had gone through and she had reclaimed her original letter, all she had to do was to sit back and wait for Steven to get in touch. She knew he was somewhere near. She felt it as surely as if he was smiling benignly at her now, approving that her life of misery with Bob was over.

And if he wasn't, Jane thought, with a vicious little aside to whatever gods were listening, then she hoped he'd take his revenge in the Great Upstairs on his ungrateful father for all the torment he'd put his wife through all these years. They'd probably never meet though, since Steven would be Up There, of course, while Bob would assuredly have gone to hell.

⋆ ⋆ ⋆

Alex reached Exeter without any problem — straight down the M5 until junction 30 and then parking in the nearest car-park while she got her bearings. There were two things she needed to do — three, if you counted finding a loo, which she needed pretty fast, she reminded herself. She also needed to find a reasonable B & B, and the local nick.

Thankfully there were toilets at the car-park, and once that essential little visit was over, she was glad to leave the car after the long drive, and take a walk around to stretch her legs. There was a town map in a glass frame at the exit of the car-park, with a large red arrow telling her You Are Here. There was also a list of local points of interest detailed below, including a nearby Tourist Information Office.

Twenty minutes later, she was armed with a small list of B & Bs and several phototcopied routes for finding them. She decided that was her next priority, as it was getting late in the afternoon and she needed to find her base. And she wasn't going to spend the rest of the day searching. The first one that looked decent would do, even it was called Dun Roamin'.

The landlady, just as quaintly named Mrs Dunstable, welcomed her inside, quoted her terms and asked how long she would be staying.

'Two nights, maybe more. I'm not exactly sure. Is that a problem?'

'Not at this time of year, my dear,' the landlady said expansively. 'You're welcome to stay as long as you like. You'll find the beds as comfy as if you were in your own, and you'll just need to give me a few hours' notice if you're staying on longer than a couple of days, so I can prepare a nice evening dinner for you.'

'Are there any other guests?' Alex said, hoping she wasn't the only one to get all this treatment.

'Just my regulars who like to stay for the winter weeks, dear, but they won't bother you, so you just come and go as you please.'

Alex fully intended to.

'On holiday, are you?' Mrs Dunstable said next, eyeing her holdall and the tote bag with all her working gear in it.

'Sort of a working holiday. I shall have notes to write up for my job, so I may sometimes have to spend time in my room. I hope that's not a problem.'

'Bless you, no. We have lots of working folk down here, students as well. I could tell you were a business person, soon as I saw you.'

She beamed approvingly at her, and Alex was thankful when she left. Landladies were a breed of their own, she reflected: chatty, well-meaning, and sometimes too inquisitive for comfort, but this one seemed well used to students and business persons, so that was all right.

She began to unpack, and the next minute there was a tap on her door. Mrs Dunstable called through it to remind her that dinner was at seven, and she hoped Alex was partial to beef stew and dumplings, as all her regulars liked homely fare.

Her mouth watered, and the thought of tramping around the city looking for the police station was something that could be delayed until tomorrow. There was no need to hurry, and Jane Leng couldn't get at her here. She called out that the meal sounded wonderful, decided she had done enough rushing around for one day, and spent a luxurious half-hour in a steaming hot bath before lying full-length on the bed in her red kimono and closing her eyes blissfully.

However, she was unable to keep out the thought of work indefinitely, and by the time she had changed into something casually smart to wear to dinner, she had switched on her mobile phone again. It beeped immediately, telling her there was a text message waiting. She smiled, guessing it would be from Nick, and then the smile faded as she saw that it came from DI Frank Gregory.

'Wherever you are, Alex, I thought you should know that your mad woman has contacted tonight's paper. Call me for more details.'

Alex chewed her lip. Why should she care? What was it — some kind of weird obituary for her husband to salve Jane's conscience or something?

Annoyed at the thought, she punched in Frank's number and waited for him to respond.

'Alex Best here, Frank. Sorry I was unavailable earlier.'

'Never mind. I'm sure you'll want to know what the crazy Leng woman's done now.'

'I gather it's something that doesn't please you,' she said mildly.

'She's asking for trouble, that's what she's doing. I'll fax you through her latest letter if you'll give me a number — '

'Sorry. Not possible. You'll have to read it out to me if you think it's that important.'

He wasn't getting at her whereabouts that way, either. But when she heard the contents of Jane's letter, she could see exactly why it was so very important — and so very dangerous. It was more than the letter of a deranged woman. It was an open invitation to every crook in the vicinity to help himself to some of her new-found wealth.

'I knew she was crazy, but this is sheer stupidity,' Alex said when he had finished. 'Is she going to be put under police surveillance?'

'What for? For shooting off her mouth as if she's the lady of the manor now? It's her problem, but I thought you'd want to know.'

'Thanks. And I'm glad you told me, though there's not much I can do now, is there? The damage is already done.'

She ended the call as soon as she could,

not wanting to prolong it. Jane was a fool, and Frank's remark about her being the lady of the manor now probably wasn't far short of the mark. She'd be preening herself at having got all of Bob's money without having to lift a finger to do it. And writing that impassioned letter to Steven was enough to get all the cranks in the area posing as her long-lost son. It was something Alex hadn't thought about before, but now that she had, she knew she had to warn Jane about it.

She dialled her number, and Jane's eager voice answered at once, then immediately lost some of its warmth when she knew who the caller was.

'Did you think I was going to be somebody else, Jane?' Alex said.

'Perhaps,' she said cautiously.

'Jane, I know about the letter you've put in tonight's newspaper, and I wanted to warn you,' Alex went on directly.

'What about?'

Alex knew she had to go carefully. The woman's nerves were fragile. She was just as likely to suffer a heart attack if her long-lost son ever turned up, as if she accepted positive proof that he was never going to do so.

'Jane, it's possible that someone who isn't Steven might pretend that he is. You've implied that you're going to have a great deal of money very soon, and there are a lot of villains out there who would dearly like to get their hands on it.'

'Do you think I won't know my own son when I see him?' The voice was decidedly shriller now.

'Yes, but all your memories are of a young boy from ten years ago, Jane. He would — will — be very different now. Young boys change considerably between the ages of sixteen and twenty-six. Please remember that, and be very careful if someone contacts you, and especially who you arrange to meet.'

She realized she was talking to thin air. The bloody stupid woman had put the phone down on her, and there wasn't a damn thing she could do about it . . . except to call Nick and tell him she had warned Jane, and the response she had got. Dinner must wait.

11

After a leisurely breakfast the next morning, during which she was very much the interesting newcomer to the elderly regulars at the B & B, Alex found her way to the local police station.

This one was no different from any other, she thought, as she entered the front door. Even the smell was the same. Police stations were either buzzing with activity or there was a bored sergeant at the front desk and a couple of minions behind him fiddling with some paperwork or staring at a computer screen trying to look busy. This morning it was the latter scenario.

‘’Morning, love. Can I help you?’ the desk sergeant said, giving her a fatherly smile.

‘I hope so. Can you give me any information about a group called the Followers? I understand they have a base somewhere in Exeter.’

The guy’s eyes flickered for a moment, and Alex guessed it probably wasn’t a request he heard every day. She could have enquired at the Tourist Office, she thought suddenly, but this seemed the most likely place, especially if the Followers weren't exactly *infra dig* in the town.

'Thinking of joining them, are you, Miss?' he said next.

Alex laughed. 'Not really, but I'm trying to trace a relative. Nothing heavy, you understand, it's just that he's required at home for personal reasons.'

Why did she get the uncomfortable feeling that this guy didn't believe a word of it? She thought it sounded feasible enough, and it was better than saying she was a PI going to check them out on account of an old crime that may not even be a crime at all.

'Those people don't like us to give out information unless it's for a genuine reason, so I can't really do that, Miss, unless I know exactly what the problem is. In any case, they don't welcome strangers except by personal recommendation,' he went on, his gaze never leaving her face.

'But you don't object to them being in the town, do you?' Alex said, chancing her luck. 'I was told I could find them here.'

'They do no harm,' he said without expression. 'But if you're really keen to get in touch with them, I could contact them on your behalf, if you'll just give me your name and phone number.'

Before Alex could respond negatively to

this, one of the police constables behind him spoke up.

'The young lady could always find a group of them busking in the town and see if one of them could help, couldn't she, Sarge? They're always around at lunchtime and in the afternoons, and some of them will talk to you.'

'Thank you, Stavely,' the sergeant turned on him freezingly. 'When I want your help, I'll ask for it.'

Alex gave the younger man a winning smile. *Thank you*, she said silently.

'Well, I think I'll leave it for now, anyway. I only called in here on the off-chance. I have some things to do in town, so if I see them, I'll give one of them a message for my relative. That will save me the bother. Thanks for your help.'

She could almost feel the sergeant's gaze following her out of the door. But she wasn't born yesterday. Cult groups had a bad name even if they were totally harmless. As yet, she didn't know which category the Followers came into. They were obviously tolerated here, but she guessed that any enquiries about them would be noted — and she had no intention of having her name and phone number logged into any police file.

* * *

'Pretty girl, Sarge,' the constable commented nervously, knowing he'd made a boob without really knowing why.

The desk sergeant rounded on him at once, his eyes flashing. 'If you thought with your brains instead of your bollocks you'd know when to keep your mouth shut, Stavely,' he snapped. 'Stop gawping like a wet fish and find me the memo that came in from that London DCI asking to be informed if anyone started asking questions about the Followers. And then get me his number.'

* * *

Exeter was an interesting city, Alex decided. Nice and compact, with a beautiful cathedral with plenty of grassy space all around it, and a great shopping centre. She decided to make the most of it, and be a tourist for the morning. If the buskers didn't come out until the afternoons — presumably starting at lunchtime when there were more shoppers about — then she might as well enjoy herself and forget about work for a short while.

She did the cathedral and the maritime museum, and spent more than she would normally have done on a couple of glittery black tops and leather trousers in an exclusive little boutique.

But what the hell? Jane Leng was paying for it. At the thought, Alex remembered what she was here to do, sobering a little as she went into a small coffee shop in the main shopping street to take a breather, and a cream doughnut to go with her coffee. She was the only customer just now, and the waitress was happy to chat.

'Not bad weather for the time of year, is it?' the girl said, nodding to where the breeze just rattled the leaves of the trees in the pavement outside. 'Haven't seen you around before.'

'I'm just here for a few days,' Alex told her. 'Looking for a relative, as a mater of fact,' she added, deciding to continue her alibi.

'Oh yes?' the waitress said. 'Living here, is she?'

'I'm not sure. It's a young man, actually, and I think he may have got caught up in some group. I don't really have much to go on at all.'

She made it sound very vague. It was often a better way to extract information than by going in like a bull at a gate.

'What, like those twits who stroll around the town busking every afternoon? My mum always puts something in their charity box, but I'd like to know what they do with it!'

Bingo! Before Alex could ask any more, an older woman came out from the kitchen area of the coffee shop, exuding a variety of cooking smells. The girl spoke to her.

'The lady's asking about them buskers, Mum. I say they're only after your money, but you quite like 'em, don't you?'

This was obviously something about which her Mum was quite passionate, and on which she disagreed.

'Oh, you always get uppity about 'em, but they're all right, I reckon.'

She turned to Alex. 'They bring in business, see Miss,' she said. 'Folk stop to look at them and listen to them, and then they come in here for a coffee or a snack. They're always friendly and smiling too, which is more than can be said for some.'

This was said with a glare at her daughter, and then she spoke more sharply. 'Don't forget they paid to send a child to the deaf school and helped to pay for repairs to one of the old buildings that got damaged in last year's storms, so they're not all bad, my girl.'

She disappeared again, and the waitress sniffed. 'Mum's got a bee in her bonnet about them twits, and she likes it when young men smile at her. Nothing funny about it, mind,' she added hastily, just in case Alex thought there was.

'Well, I must say these people don't sound too bad if they do these good works in the town — er — Tracey,' she said, noting the girl's name badge. 'I shall have to take a look at them myself.'

'We've got a bigger dining-room upstairs, and if you're in for lunch, I'll reserve you a window table, and you can get a good look at 'em from there. You might spot your young man.'

'Who? Oh, yes. Well, reserve me a window table for one o'clock then.'

She beamed at the girl, thinking it was fate that sent her here. It always felt good when that happened. With an upstairs window seat, she could probably take a few camera shots of the group, as well as mingling with the shoppers later on and getting some at street level. Instinct and common sense told her they wouldn't be exactly happy at posing for a camera, but a few unobtrusive shots could produce wonders.

'How many buskers do you usually get around here?' she asked Tracey casually.

'Oh, quite a few. There are the singles, of course, and a guy who does a kind of one-man band thing. The police usually move him on after a bit, but the yellow twits are always here. They're a bit of a tourist attraction now.'

Alex remembered being told that they always wore pale yellow colours, which was presumably why Tracey called them yellow twits. It was descriptive, if nothing else. She finished her coffee and cream doughnut and decided she had probed for long enough. Any more, and her curiosity would be too noticeable.

'I'll see you later then, Tracey,' she said, leaving a generous tip, ensuring that she would get the best window table going.

She eventually found the library and spent an hour browsing among the shelves and assimilating a bit of local culture. She knew it would be a long shot to expect any books about religious or other cults, let alone one that was specifically about the Followers. There was no point in having a secret or closed-shop society if you were going to tell the world about it.

* * *

She was back at the coffee shop before one o'clock, and there was already a small clientele inside. It was clearly a popular eating-place, and she was glad she had booked a table in the upstairs dining area. From here she realized she could see the cathedral, which gave her a good excuse for taking some photos before she concentrated on the arrival of some of the Followers.

She felt a growing excitement. If Lennie Fry was among these buskers, she would surely recognize him from the photos she had seen in Gran Patterson's scrap books. Just as quickly, she remembered that it was ten years on, and she had already told Jane Leng that Steven would have physically changed. But the Wilkins brothers hadn't changed that much, and with any luck, there was no reason to think that Lennie Fry would have done, either.

'What can I get you?' she heard Tracey say beside her, tapping the menu deliberately, and reminding her that she wasn't here just to admire the view.

'I'll have the lasagne, please,' she said.

'Good choice,' Tracey told her. 'And chips?'

'And chips,' Alex said weakly, knowing she shouldn't.

Even before it was ready, she heard the sound of music from the street below. It was a tinny sound, mostly penny whistles and drums and a guy on the banjo. But right then, Alex was more interested in the group themselves than in the music they were playing. She leaned forward to get a better look, and began shooting off her camera as they came nearer.

There were eight of them: five smiling young men and three equally smiling young girls. They all wore long robes in pale lemon or cream, made out of some cheap cotton stuff, as far as Alex could make out. It was presumably to add to the effect of suffering for their art, sackcloth-and-ashes-style, she thought cynically. It looked pretty cold for this time of year, but she'd bet a pound to a pinch of snuff that they all wore thick sweaters underneath.

What intrigued her even more was the colour of their hair. They were all bleached to the colour of corn, tending towards a yellowy-blonde, which gave them all a cherubic, youthfully uniform appearance. They were certainly striking enough to make heads turn, and so similar that it would be hard to differentiate between them. And Lennie Fry, one-time hippy rebel of Steven Leng's group, if appearances were to be believed, had been dark.

'Here you are then,' came Tracey's cheerful voice. 'A plate of Mum's finest, and she's put a few extra chips on for you.'

'Thanks,' Alex said. 'That's just what I need!'

In fact, if the smell of her lunch hadn't been so inviting, she would have left it all and gone down to the street to watch and listen to the group of buskers. But since they would presumably be there most of the afternoon, there seemed little point in wasting a good meal. As it was, the lasagne was so steaming hot it burned her tongue with the first mouthful, and she had to treat the rest of it with caution.

By the time she had finished, with liberal quantities of iced water to help her through, the buskers had moved on a few hundred yards, which was presumably their *modus operandi*. They had a small crowd around them now, and one of the young girls was weaving in amongst them with a collecting tin in her hand. It had a large label on it announcing that all money went to charitable causes.

Alex studied the faces of the young men. It was too much to hope that he could be one of these five — except for the fact that he had been a one-time wannabe musician, she remembered. So why not? But as far as she remembered, not one of them resembled the Lennie Fry in Gran's scrap book photos. Or rather, all of them did. That was the hell of it. They were all clones of one another.

The Mormons toured housing estates dressed in smart black suits looking like businessmen while they tried to convert you, Alex thought. And there was another lot who did the same thing done up like elderly housewives with shopping bags on their arms, and often a younger woman with a child in a pushchair in tow, all chattering nineteen to the dozen while they thrust their tracts under your nose and asked if you believed in Jesus.

Just like them, these Followers were all an identical set. So how the hell was she going to separate any one of them to ask any pertinent questions?

She hovered in a shop doorway, ostensibly taking photos of the street, and occasionally centring her gaze on the cathedral, but in reality zooming in on one or another of the smiling faces until she realized the girl with the collecting tin was rattling it under her nose, and smiling right into hers.

'Oh yes, hang on a minute,' she said quickly, and fumbled in her small change purse for some coins.

'Peace and harmony,' the girl said in a soft, melodious voice, and moved on to the next person.

She could only have been about seventeen, Alex thought, and she wondered instantly if her parents knew where she was, or if she had been listed as a MisPer as the police called them. In the pale persona of the Followers, any missing person who wanted to disappear for whatever reason would have an ample disguise. It was an intriguing thought.

'Beautiful, aren't they?' she heard someone say close by. An elderly gentleman with a military bearing was smiling benignly on the group as they moved on, resembling a cloud of yellow butterflies as their robes fluttered in a small gust of wind.

'I suppose they are. People don't resent them then? Forgive me if I seem inquisitive, but I'm new to the area, and I've never seen these people before.'

'They brighten up a dull day,' the man went on. 'And they're properly licensed for the busking, of course.'

'Oh well, you can't say fairer than that then, can you?' Alex said.

'Do I take it that you don't approve, young lady?' he asked her. 'I assure you that we in the civic society have had cause to thank them in the past for their charitable efforts.'

'Then I think that's admirable,' she said. 'Please excuse me.'

It was just her luck to run into a member of the civic society. But perhaps it wasn't *bad* luck, because it had told her that the Followers knew how to keep their noses clean. What better way to cover up any less than legal activities than to keep in with the civic fathers and help the town? She was becoming as cynical as any hard-nosed copper, since she had no idea at all what their activities were, other than what she had already seen.

Without warning it started to rain, with what began as a shower quickly becoming a downpour, and the streets emptied just as quickly as people scuttled inside the shops. It was enough to curtail the Followers' busking for the day, anyway, and since the rain had brought a decided late-January chill to the air it was time for her to call it a day too. The thought of Mrs Dunstable's warm and cosy B & B, with-afternoon-tea-if-required, was a temptation she couldn't resist.

Once she arrived back at Dun Roamin' she told Mrs Dunstable she'd be down to join the regulars at half past three, and then went to her room to pull on a sweater. She got out her sketch pad and did a few skilful sketches of the buskers while she could still remember the way they had looked, and then took notes of all the conversations she had had that day.

It hadn't been entirely wasted, even though it might not be as easy to check out Lennie Fry as she had hoped. Short of marching right up to the front door of the headquarters — whose address she hadn't been given, she remembered — the only way would be to speak to one of the buskers and ask outright. It was hardly the simplest way to go about tracking down someone who had chosen to hide his real identity, especially since she had no idea whether or not she was barking up the wrong tree. There was no definite evidence that said Lennie Fry had gone to join the Followers, only her own instinct.

She closed the notebook as she heard the distant sound of a bell from the bowels of the B & B. Mrs Dunstable was calling her troops to order, she thought with a grin, and even though she seemed to have been eating and drinking all day, she was more than ready for afternoon tea and home-made cakes. At this rate she'd end up looking like a beached whale so, tomorrow, she made a firm resolve to walk into town and leave the car behind.

She joined the regulars and spent a jolly touristy hour telling them where she had been that day, and hearing about the history of the town and its people. She was tempted to ask them if they knew anything about the Followers, but decided better of it. The fewer people who knew her real reason for being here, the better. She finally left them in the afternoon lounge, with the excuse that she had a phone call to make.

Actually, she liked talking to them. They were all pretty long in the tooth, but they were still with-it and interesting, and they reminded her of her own family when they got to reminiscing. But she wanted to check her answer machine to see if there were any messages. Thankfully, there weren't, and she let out a long breath of relief, realizing she had been half-expecting Jane Leng to call and tell her the errant Steven had finally turned up. Not that it would have been him, of course, just some bogus guy on the make, reasoning that there was a packet to be made from a doting mother and non-grieving widow.

So now all there was to do was watch TV in her room, take a shower and get ready for the evening meal. *More food?* asked a little disapproving voice inside. The answer was that she needed all her energy, and she was going to be no good for anything if she fainted away from lack of sustenance.

But when the time came, she couldn't face another gargantuan meal after all, and she felt all the nobler for leaving half of it. She left the dining-room after coffee and went back upstairs to loosen off a few things, and turned on the TV again. The local news might be interesting.

Her mobile rang before she could find the right channel, and she answered it quickly. Her heart jumped at the sound of Nick Frobisher's voice.

'Hi, Alex, just thought I'd give you a call,' he said easily. 'And how's the big city? Living it up, are you?'

'Not exactly,' she said cautiously. 'I'm just

about to watch TV, actually.'

'Good God, that's no way for a babe to spend an evening,' he said with a laugh. 'Not that I mind if you're pining for me. Are all the studs in Bristol spoken for or something?'

'As far as I know. I haven't seen one yet to tempt me away from my fireside, anyway.'

Why did she have the sudden feeling that he might be testing her? Checking up on her whereabouts? But he couldn't know, could he? She had told nobody she was coming here.

'Well, I wanted to be sure you were all right,' he said, more seriously now. 'You had a shock, and I daresay the black widow got on to you pretty quickly, didn't she?'

For a few seconds Alex didn't connect his words. What shock had she had? And then it flooded back. Bob Leng's death, of course. How could she have forgotten for an instant?

'Oh yes. And she's convinced it will bring Steven out of the woodwork now. You've heard about the latest letter she sent to the paper, I suppose? I know news travels fast between you lot.'

The minute she said it, Alex knew. There had been something in the penetrating looks that desk sergeant had given her when she asked about the Followers. She ground her teeth, furious with herself for not thinking that one out. Knowing she was hot on the trail (tepid to ice-cold was more like it), she wouldn't put it past Nick to have put the word out to alert him if anyone started asking questions about the Followers. Anyone with a certain striking description.

Too late, Alex knew she should have gone to the Tourist Info place instead. They might even have given her the address of the Followers' headquarters instead of being so bloody cagey. It would have to be her first port of call tomorrow now.

She realized Nick hadn't said anything in the few seconds when the wheels were turning around in her head, and she gave a deep sigh.

'All right, so what do you really want, Nick?'

'I want what I've always wanted.'

'As well as that.'

'I want you to give up this pointless case before you get hurt.'

'What makes you think I'll get hurt? From what I've seen of the Followers, which is very little, and only from a distance,' she amended hastily, 'they look like a harmless bunch. They do good works, so I've been told. And since I take it you know where I am, you'll know that the local police tolerate them.' She paused for breath. 'So stop bloody tracking me, will you?

Are you my keeper now?'

'You know the reason for that,' he said shortly.

'Good night, Nick,' Alex said, and switched off her mobile.

* * *

She felt angry and uptight for the remainder of the evening. He was her best friend, and she loved him, but he had no right to treat her like an imbecile who couldn't do her job. She didn't need police backup for everything she did, for God's sake, and the more she thought about that, the angrier she got. Having him track her every move was worse than being a criminal.

The bed was unfamiliar, and nothing like as comfortable as Mrs Dunstable had intimated. Alex spent a restless night, her brain still too active for sleep. By morning she had a thumping headache, and after breakfast she found the nearest chemist and bought some super-strength painkillers to ward it off. She needed her wits about her if she was going to approach one of the Followers later that day.

She had noted that the soft-spoken girl with the collecting tin went into several of the shops after the busking group moved a little way down the street, so presumably that was also allowed. She found her way to the same coffee shop as yesterday and asked Tracey casually if any of them ever came in here. They must get dry throats singing their awful chants, which were never going to get in the charts, nor the Eurovision —

'Sometimes a couple of them pop in for a cuppa,' Tracey reminded her.

'Do your customers object to the collecting tin?'

'Nah,' said Tracey. 'The girl who usually does it is a nice enough kid. Calls herself Zelena, but I bet that's not her real name. More like the yellow peril, if you ask me. They've probably all got made-up names, though I've never heard any of the others.'

She left Alex to serve several shoppers taking a breather. This was a useful bit of information, thought Alex, but it was hardly going to help if she wanted to trace a young man called Lennie Fry. She reserved the same upstairs table again for lunch, and just hoped that Zelena would pop in with her collecting tin.

She heard them long before she saw them. They had quite a distinctive sound, she thought with a grin, though the guy on the banjo wasn't bad, and she wondered if he could possibly be Lennie Fry. The trouble was, he didn't look in the least bit like Lennie Fry, or the way she imagined him to be.

Halfway through her chicken salad she caught a glimpse of yellow cotton out of the corner of her eye, and she saw Zelena come smilingly towards her.

'Hello again. I saw you yesterday, didn't I?' the girl said, recognizing her. 'I don't want to bother you, so I'll leave you in peace — '

'No, don't go,' Alex said. 'I'm always willing to contribute to a worthy cause.' Especially if it was a cause of her own that was going to produce results, she thought, pushing a note into the collecting tin, and seeing the girl's eyes widen a little at this generosity.

'That's very kind,' she murmured. 'Peace and harmony — '

'I wonder if you can help me,' Alex said.

'Do you want to join us?' Zelena said at once.

Alex didn't hesitate. 'I'm not sure yet, but in any case, I wouldn't know how to go about it. I don't know where your headquarters are, or who to ask for.'

'You will find us at the Old Mission building on Mistral Street, and you ask for Lord. Just Lord.'

'Well, thank you,' Alex said, memorizing it. 'And tell me, do you have a member by the name of Lennie? Lennie Fry?'

'I don't know that name. I'm sorry.'

She moved on, her mouth still smiling, her eyes still bland. There was no sign of recognition in them as Alex mentioned Lennie's name. If she knew it, she was brilliant at hiding the fact. And if she didn't, then either he wasn't here at all, or like her, he had ditched his old identity for a new one.

Either way, it might be a dead end, Alex thought, with a swift sense of disappointment. Except that she now knew where they hung out, and she knew the name of the boss man. Lord. How corny — and how arrogant — could you get?

12

Alex watched the girl move about the few customers having lunch, and then she lost sight of her until the group of buskers came back down the street again. From her window seat she saw Zelena speaking to the guy with the banjo, and they both looked up at the coffee shop window.

Alex felt her heart beat faster. Of course, whatever she said to him might be no more than to comment that someone had been asking about the Followers, and seemed interested in joining them. Or it could have been something else.

As the group broke up into smaller twos and threes, she realized that Zelena and the banjo player were coming this way, and a few minutes later they appeared in the upstairs dining-room. By then, Alex had her tape recorder switched on in the open tote bag on the floor by her side, and she looked up enquiringly as they approached her table.

'You were asking about someone, I believe,' the banjo player said, his voice almost as soft and bland as the girl's.

Did they programme their people to speak

this way, Alex wondered? Did this softness go along with the 'peace and harmony' message that seemed to be the order of the day?

'Yes. Someone called Lennie Fry,' she said, her eyes never leaving his face. She almost said *someone I used to know*, but that would be fatal if this guy turned out to be the real McCoy.

'We have no use for surnames here,' he went on. 'My friend is Zelena, and my name is Drew. If that was your query, I'm afraid we can't help you.'

As they turned to go, Alex spoke again. It was now or never. 'What about Steven Leng?'

As Drew's body tensed, she sensed his antagonism as he turned back to her. His eyes had lost their blandness now. They were cold and full of anger, but his voice still held that flat quality. It was as if he was holding himself very much in check from the way a normal person would explode at being confronted with something from his past that he'd much rather keep hidden.

'I believe you are here under false pretences. If you have no wish to join us, please do not try to make contact with us again.'

'But you do know the name, don't you? In case you've forgotten it already, let me repeat it. *Steven Leng*. He'd be about your age now.'

'I can't help you,' Drew repeated. 'Peace and harmony go with you.'

As Alex watched him and Zelena go, she felt unaccountably chilled. There was such an air of finality about the way they spoke, and all that peace and harmony crap was only words. Brainwashing came to mind, and she wondered just how much of an influence this Lord person had. But she wasn't feeling brave enough just yet to go and find out. She needed to think — and to play back the tape.

'Everything all right?' she heard Tracey's voice say close by. 'I saw you talking to them yellow twits. I hope you didn't let them screw you for a tidy sum?'

'Good Lord no. We were just passing the time of day.'

'You want to watch them,' Tracey advised. 'They're all sweetness and light, and the girl's all right, I suppose, but I wouldn't trust them further than I could throw them.'

And there speaks an instinctive philosopher, thought Alex as she paid for her meal and again gave Tracey a bigger tip than was necessary. At this rate, she'd be seen as a big spender, she thought feebly, or a soft touch.

She went back to the B & B to play back the tape, trying to read between the lines of everything the couple had said to her, and finding nothing. Everything they said was crystal clear. Drew professed not to know Lennie Fry and couldn't help her; and if it hadn't been for the tension in his body and the quickly suppressed anger in his eyes, she would have believed him.

She realized she still had the headache that had plagued her that morning, and any thought of going to the Old Mission building on Mistral Street and demanding an audience with Lord was farthest from her mind. But she couldn't stay indoors either. It was claustrophobically hot, presumably for the benefit of the elderly regulars, and she needed fresh air.

It was definitely wrapping-up-warm weather though, as her dad used to say, and she put on an extra pair of socks inside her boots, and wrapped a scarf around her neck. At this time of year, whatever sun there was soon sank below the horizon, and it was definitely more wintry than anything else. As it had a perfect right to be in January, Alex reminded herself.

The B & B wasn't far from the river, and she took a brisk walk along the waterfront, past the Maritime Museum again, to where the various smells of fish and bustling shipping activity permeated the air. She hadn't realized before that the River Exe, from where the city got its name, was so close to the sea, but that was because she was a north-country girl who had known nothing about London or the south-west before coming here.

But she liked everything about this place, from the old buildings close to the confines of the Cathedral and the little cobbled streets nearby, to the tales of the old Underground passages that the regulars had told her about, some of which had collapsed during the Blitz in the second world war. You could take a tour in the passages that still survived, the regulars had assured her. No thanks, Alex thought with a shiver. She had never been too keen on going underground, except for the London railway system that is, and she wasn't too sure about that either. Her dad always said there was time enough for that when you were six feet under.

She looked at her watch, knowing she had done enough wandering about, and that her feet were cold despite the extra pair of socks. By now the thought of afternoon tea at Mrs Dunstable's was becoming ever more attractive. Besides which, she had neglected to put all her latest findings on her laptop, and there wasn't much point in bringing it if she didn't use it. Tapes could be wiped and accidentally rewound, and she needed to write it all up as a backup. That was her next job.

She reached the B & B, glad to be

assaulted by the welcome warmth as she went inside, together with the smell of fresh baking that made her mouth water at once. As she went towards the small lift to change out of her outdoor clothes, the landlady called out to her from behind her grandly-named reception desk.

'I think you've got an admirer, dear. This arrived for you a little while ago.'

From the archness in her voice, Alex could almost read the possibilities running around the woman's brain. Perhaps there was a broken love affair somewhere in the background . . . and Miss Best was pining for him, waiting for him to make amends . . . and the reunion would happen right here, under Mrs Dunstable's romantic novelish nose . . .

'Oh, I don't think so!' Alex began crisply. 'I'm here on private business, and none of my friends know where to contact me — '

Except Nick Frobisher, of course, she thought angrily.

She didn't really need to tell the woman anything, she thought, annoyed at her own reaction, and then her voice died away as Mrs Dunstable reached down behind the desk and handed her a florist's sheaf containing a single white lily.

'Lovely, isn't it, dear?' she said with a small sigh. 'I had some of them in my bridal bouquet. Of course, we went in for such things in my day. Nowadays young girls don't bother with all that fuss, if they bother at all, do they? Don't forget your gift, dear,' she called out, as Alex made for the lift, intending to ignore the whole bloody thing.

She quickly changed her mind, knowing it would look more than odd if she did so. And while the Mrs Dunstables of this world might think it a lovely flower, to Alex — *and* she suspected, to whoever had sent it — it was the flower of death. She grabbed the tissue-wrapped lily and mumbled a word of thanks before heading straight for her room, aware that the landlady was gazing after her, clearly thinking her touched by the unexpected gift.

As she was. Touched, and alarmed, and unnerved. She was perfectly sure there would be no card or message with the flower, but there didn't need to be. It was message enough. She was being warned off.

It took a few minutes for her heart to stop hammering, and then her sleuthing brain came into gear and she told herself not to be such a wimp. What else did she expect? When you started meddling into dark activities, you expected to be warned off in one way or another. This was mild. Next time it might not be.

It was a pity Lennie Fry and the rest of Steven's friends hadn't been old enough to be into criminal activities before Steven's disappearance, instead of the usual teenage stuff. If they had, there would be fingerprint records, and she could have checked if Lennie Fry's fingerprints were on the wrapping paper.

It was such a long shot she dismissed the likelihood at once. But she was damn sure it had been the banjo-playing Drew, or Zelena, his sidekick, who had had the flower sent here. Which meant they were worried about something. Which meant she was on to something. Every cloud, etc. etc. she thought next. She should have asked Mrs Dunstable who delivered the gift, but she was just as sure it wouldn't have been either of the pair she had met. The landlady would certainly have said so. They would have sent some lackey with the flower. But she should have asked, and if she hadn't been so panicked, she would have done.

When she went down to the dining-room where the regulars were already congregating, she asked the question casually.

'That was the mysterious thing, dear,' Mrs Dunstable said with a smile. 'I'd left reception for a short while and since nobody rang the bell I wasn't aware that anyone had been in. When I returned, the gift was on the desk, with a short note saying it was for the lady with the lovely red hair.'

One of the old boys chuckled.

'Oh ah, 'tis a secret admirer, me dear, and I can't say I blame 'im. If I was twenty years younger — '

'More like forty, you old fool,' his counterpart commented, and Alex laughed, though it just confirmed what she thought.

Her questions hadn't been welcome. Someone had been watching her and found out where she was staying, and had delivered the flower as a warning. They weren't called Followers for nothing then, she thought, trying to keep it all in perspective. But they weren't chasing her away, either — now she knew she had got them ruffled. And if she was ever going to tackle this Lord, whoever he was, it might as well be now. She resolved to do it now, tonight. Or maybe tomorrow.

After she was sated with tea and cakes, and an hour of jolly conversation with the regulars, she went back to her room, took a leisurely bath before dinner, and lingered in the dining-room with the old codgers again. She knew what she was doing, of course: putting off the evil moment . . .

But it Would Not Do, Audrey, as her old history teacher used to tell her severely every time her attention wandered from the boring lists of dates they used to have to memorize by rote. Not that meeting up with this Lord person could be even remotely compared with Henry the Eighth or the mad King George — as far as she knew. She finally switched on her mobile and gave her voice check to her answer machine for any messages, well aware that indecision was becoming her middle name. There was only one message.

She didn't recognize the voice, but the minute she heard the caller's name and got the gist of the message, she sat up straight.

'Miss Best, my name is Roger Fry. I saw your name in the local newspaper recently in connection with the Steven Leng case. It was in one of those letters the mother keeps sending in. And now she's lost her husband as well, poor woman. If you're still investigating, I may have some information for you, but I prefer not to discuss it through a machine. It may not be relevant to your case, but something rather odd has happened and I would very much like to talk to you, so perhaps you would call on me at your convenience. As I said, my name is Fry, and Leonard is my son. You'll want my address, of course — '

Alex was already scrabbling for pen and paper, unable to believe her luck. She had met with so much opposition from all sides, and this was the first real piece of luck to come her way. The Fry parent's information may mean anything or nothing, but it was something that had to be followed up. He hadn't left a telephone number, but if he hadn't wanted to discuss things over the phone, he probably wouldn't have wanted an anonymous phone call either. In any case, she needed to speak to him face to face.

There was no way, now, that she was going to tackle the Followers at their headquarters that evening. It could wait — and there was nothing cowardly about that, either, she reminded the little dig of her conscience. It was always better to follow up a real lead rather than a vague one — especially one that was almost certainly going to be obstructive. Leonard — Lennie — Fry's father would have something informative to tell her.

'Don't get your hopes up, girl,' she told herself, already mentally packing as she ran back downstairs, ignoring the lift, to tell Mrs Dunstable that she would be leaving first thing tomorrow morning.

'Oh, what a shame — or is it something to do with that lovely flower you were sent, dear?' the woman said, clearly scenting a secret liaison.

'Sort of,' Alex said, trying to keep her face

straight. The woman should definitely be writing romances, she thought. 'So if you would prepare my bill, I'll pay it first thing as I shall want to get away right after breakfast.'

'It shall be done,' Mrs Dunstable said, reverting to efficiency-mode. 'But we'll be sorry to see you go,' she added. 'You've cheered up my regulars no end.'

That said a lot for the mundane life they led, Alex thought, then pushed them out of her mind as her mobile rang. She turned away from Mrs Dunstable and answered it quickly, preferring not to see the expectant look on the other woman's face. In her mind it would be the lovelorn swain, naturally.

'Alex. How are tricks?' said Nick's voice.

'Wonderful, darling,' Alex said in a sexy voice, mischievously giving Mrs Dunstable all the material she could want for her next romantic disclosure. 'And it's so lovely to hear from you. I've been thinking about you all day.'

In the small pause that followed, she had to stop herself from laughing out loud, knowing Nick would be digesting all this with a copper's suspicion.

'OK, so what's going on? Who have you got with you?'

'Why would I have anybody with me when the only person I want is you? I can't wait to see you again, darling, and I'm coming home tomorrow.'

She was playing a stupid game and she knew it, but she couldn't resist the landlady's pop-eyed look — and since Nick knew very well where she was, and he was safely miles away in London, there was no point in pretending she was anywhere else.

'That's perfect timing then,' she heard him say in the smooth, sly way he sometimes used to disarm his victims. 'I have to be in Bristol on business, so I'll be at your flat tomorrow evening. Keep the champagne on ice, and the bed warm and especially your beautiful body — *darling*.'

'Oh, but Nick — '

It was too late. He had gone, and she had only herself to blame. And from the bemused look on Mrs Dunstable's face, she had probably been applying her own colourful dialogue to the phone call — turning herself on in the process.

'Your young man?' she couldn't resist asking.

'Yes,' Alex said in a strangled voice, unable to think of any other way of deterring her, and disappearing to her room as soon as she could.

Damn Nick, she thought savagely. She didn't want him hanging around right now, when she thought she might finally be getting somewhere. It would only complicate things.

Though she couldn't deny that there was another part of her — a very erogenous, hormonal and essentially female part of her — already insisting how very much she wanted to see him, and how much she missed having him around. There was a lot of truth in the old saying that you never knew how much you missed something, or someone, until they were no longer around.

'Stuff that,' she said out loud. 'I don't need a crutch.'

She laughed out loud at the innuendo she hadn't intended, and caught sight of herself in the bedroom mirror, her face flushed, her eyes bright and sparkling like emeralds, her whole attitude oozing adrenalin because of the message on her answer machine — and not only that. OK, it was also because she'd be seeing Nick again too. And by the time she did, she might have some new information at her disposal that she was damn sure she wasn't going to share with the police, whether or not they came well-filled with the special brand of libido that made it difficult to say no. It was highly unlikely that she would, anyway.

* * *

She drove back to Bristol at a fair speed the following morning, and went straight to the address Lennie Fry's father had given her before even going back to her flat. A quick tidy up on the nearest motorway services was enough to tell her she looked respectable enough for anybody.

The impressively large house was in the elegant Clifton area of the city, from which she deduced that the Frys were pretty well-heeled. Whatever the elder Fry did, he wasn't short of a few quid, which meant he could surely have hired a private detective years ago to try to find his son. But she realized she was jumping fences. She had no reason to believe Lennie Fry had gone missing, or that his father hadn't known exactly where he was all this time. Nor if banjo-playing Drew was his son at all.

A sudden sense of uncertainty swept through her, knowing it was fatal to make assumptions. In this business, you had to pick through the evidence like a dog picking at bones until you had uncovered everything there was to see.

'Mr Fry?' she said to the neatly-dressed and well-preserved man who answered the door. He was in his late fifties to early sixties, she guessed, which would make him about the right age to have a twenty-seven year old son. 'I'm Alexandra Best,' she added, handing him her card. 'You contacted me on my answer machine.'

'Ah yes, Miss Best. Please come in.'

She was shown into a light and airy living-room that, in estate agent's jargon, had all the appointments of the affluent businessman. Her feet made no sound on the plush Persian carpet; the gilt-framed paintings surely had to be genuine, as did the highly-polished antique furniture and a glass-fronted case full of what looked like valuable Japanese netsuke. The quantity alone must make it a pretty expensive collection, Alex noted.

Why the hell would any kid want to walk away from all this? But she didn't need a crystal ball to answer that. Teenagers did. It was the nature of the breed not to be satisfied with anything their parents had. Hadn't she been the very same?

'Please sit down, Miss Best, and I'll ring for tea. Unless you prefer coffee?'

'Tea would be fine,' she said, presuming from his words and his attitude that there was no Mrs Fry. By the time they had discussed the weather and the view over the city from this high vantage point, the appearance of a housekeeper and then a tray of tea and biscuits confirmed her thoughts.

'You'll be wondering why I contacted you,' Roger Fry said finally.

'I believe it has something to do with your son,' Alex said.

He gave a small smile. 'Of course. In such charming company I was forgetting for a moment that you are a private investigator.'

Alex hid a smile as his gaze quickly flashed over her. The old rogue. He'd clearly forgotten how much he'd already told her in his message. It hadn't been that much, but it was enough to tell her he was agitated about something. And that Lennie — Leonard — had something to do with it.

'Mr Fry, does your son still live at home?' she asked, deciding on the direct approach. She saw his mouth tighten at once.

'He does not. We had a serious falling-out some years ago, soon after his mother died. It pains me to tell a stranger, Miss Best, but I did not approve of my son's lifestyle. It was not what his mother and I wanted for him, you see. We didn't approve of the company he kept, the living rough and taking miserable little jobs as a small-time rock musician when he could have done so much better. There was a lot of nonsense of wanting to go to India and find himself that never came to anything. And then there were the drugs that you always associate with these people, though I never had any real evidence of Leonard's involvement with them, I assure you.'

And if you had, you'd simply have closed your eyes to it, Alex thought shrewdly. She'd met parents like this before. Pretend it didn't exist and it would go away. Unfortunately, it rarely did.

'So where is Leonard now?' she persisted gently. 'Are you asking me to find him for you? Forgive me, but unless you tell me what this meeting is all about, Mr Fry, I am unable to help you — '

'He's contacted me,' the man said abruptly. 'Well, in a manner of speaking.'

'Yes? You won't mind if I take a few notes, by the way?' she spoke easily, hoping to disarm him for a moment. 'Just so that I get all the facts correctly.'

'Oh no, of course not.'

'So how did he contact you? By telephone or letter? Fax? E-mail?'

Or even by perishing carrier-pigeon, she thought, wondering if he was ever going to come out with it. In his ordered and preciously narrow-minded world, she could just imagine how disruptive a tearaway son could be, even though he would seem pretty harmless to anyone else.

'There was just a card enclosed with a

twenty-pound note to pay for the flowers,' Roger Fry said.

'Flowers?' Alex echoed, a creepy feeling in her bones.

Fry handed her the plain white card with no distinguishing marks on it. Alex read it quickly.

'Please use the money to pay for flowers for Steven Leng's father,' it said. 'Lilies for preference, for peace and harmony in the afterlife.'

Her heart jolted. The words 'peace and harmony' shrieked out at her — it was the motto of the Followers. And the sender wanted lilies for preference, just like the one that had been delivered to her in Exeter, when she was damn sure there had been no suggestion of peace and harmony in that.

She had always thought of it as the flower of death, which would seem to be confirmed in Lennie's request for lilies for Bob Leng's funeral corsage. If it *was* Lennie Fry.

'Was there a postmark on the envelope, Mr Fry?' she asked carefully.

'I didn't think to look. I'm afraid I just threw it away.'

Typical. 'Well, are you sure this is your son's handwriting?'

Roger Fry seemed to slump suddenly. 'I couldn't be absolutely sure, though it certainly looks like it. It's been a long time since I've seen it. I don't really know why I thought this might have been of interest to you, but it was just so odd coming after all this time, you see.'

What Alex could see was that he was clutching at straws. He still missed his son. He wanted contact with him, but he still couldn't forgive him for not being all that his parents wanted him to be. It was sad, and a far more common state of affairs than he might think.

'Mr Fry, I presume you realize that I'm trying to trace all Steven Leng's old friends,' she said more briskly. 'Do I take it that you also want me to try to trace your son? If so I need to have as many details about him as I can, including the latest photograph you have of him.'

It was almost agonizing to see the conflicting emotions on the man's face. Oh yes, he wanted to know that Lennie was all right, Alex guessed, but the barrier between them was probably too wide now for it ever to be breached. She spoke more gently.

'You don't have to do anything about it, you know. If I found out where he was, I would merely give you the information, and the rest would be up to you.'

The man took a deep breath and gave a

small nod. 'Of course. And all I want is to know that he's safe. His full name is Leonard Andrew Fry — '

'Andrew?' Alex said, her hand pausing over her notebook.

'That's right,' Roger Fry said, turning to a drawer and bringing out several small photographs. Hidden away as if he couldn't bear to look at them, thought Alex, which was even sadder.

She looked into the soft brown eyes of the young man smiling out at her from the photographs. She had seen his photos before, in Gran Patterson's scrap books, but he had been younger then. This young man was a few years older and more mature. His hair was still long, but in one of the photos he had it tied back, probably in a ponytail. He was holding a guitar, standing nonchalantly beside a tree, and the strong summer sunlight was dappling through the leaves and lightening the darkness of his hair. Turning it almost blond — blond enough for Alex to know instantly that Leonard Andrew Fry and Lennie Fry were one and the same, and that they were also the banjo-playing Drew, who needed no other name.

'Mr Fry, I believe I know exactly where your son is,' she said quietly.

13

'I'm not really sure what he wanted of me,' Alex reported to Nick that evening. There seemed no point in not telling him of her meeting with Roger Fry, since he already seemed far too aware of her movements for comfort.

'To get his son back, maybe?' Nick said lazily, his arm around her as they sat cosily on her sofa.

'I don't think he wants him back. He just wanted to know where he was, and to be able to say so if people asked. It's a pride thing. Though I doubt that he'd admit that his precious Leonard was a busker with the Followers. In his eyes it would be begging. But I still think it's just passing the buck, and shelving his parental responsibilities.'

'He's hardly got any responsibility towards him if the bloke's twenty-six or seven years old, for God's sake.'

'Once a parent, always a parent,' Alex said doggedly. 'At least, that's what my dad used to say. But Roger Fry seemed a pretty cold fish — the complete opposite to Jane Leng, who still wants to smother Steven with motherly love. Whether he's alive or dead.'

She gave a shiver. Obsessive love was harmful to the giver and the receiver, in her opinion, and that was how she saw Jane Leng's feelings for her son. It was hardly incestuous, but it was unhealthy all the same. It was like one of those creepers that wound its way around a house and finally choked it.

'Come back, darling,' she heard Nick's voice say. 'I can think of better ways to spend an evening than thinking about the parents Leng and Fry.'

'A better double-act, you mean?' Alex said with a grin.

'Precisely,' Nick said.

* * *

Over breakfast the next morning, he asked her casually if she was dropping the case now. Not that there had ever been a case, he reminded her.

'I can't do that. Mrs Leng's still paying me. Just because her husband's dead doesn't mean my involvement has ended.'

Nick sighed. 'Well, it should. Anyway, now she's got no opposition she'll probably be glad enough to let things lie. Be satisfied with what you've done, Alex, and tell her there's an end to it.'

'How can you say that? She still thinks her son's alive. I don't believe it for a minute, but she's not going to change her mind about that just because her husband fell off the Clifton Suspension Bridge.'

'*If* he fell.'

'He wasn't pushed, if that's what you mean. There were witnesses. It was an accident.'

'Or suicide. If that were proven, his pension money may well come under scrutiny, and Jane won't get a penny out of his insurances. And neither will you, my sweet.'

Alex pushed back her chair. 'You're not going to put me off with all that guff, Nick. I happen to know they're satisfied it was an accident, and Jane's laughing all the way to the building society.'

He nodded. 'Unfortunately, yes.'

She glared at him. 'You've got a damn nerve. You were just trying it on, weren't you? You really don't want me to continue with this, do you?'

'I want you to come back to London,' he said flatly. 'I miss you.'

'I miss you too. But I'm not a wife or a hanger-on, and I have my own life to lead. I'm quite willing to share it with you on a part-time basis, mind — '

She stopped, appalled at herself. God, she

was sounding so pompous, and so *blokey* . . . and she realized Nick was laughing at her.

'Well, thank you Ma'am, I'll just go and get my pinny,' he said solemnly. 'Anyway, are you aware that Jane's already moved down to Somerset? She didn't waste much time, and she got Bob planted pretty soon too.'

'You mean he's already been buried?'

'Last week, as fast as it could be arranged. I came down to represent our mob. We felt it was the decent thing to see the old boy safely put underground and it was a pretty weird occasion, I can tell you.'

'Don't talk to me about weird funerals. I attended Leanora Wolstenholme's, remember? You'd have thought you were going to a fancy-dress affair.'

She shuddered, remembering the kooks she had met there during her last big case, and angrier still with Nick for stirring her memory.

'Anyway, I thought Jane would have told me. I thought she'd have wanted me there.'

Why the hell was she feeling so resentful about it? Hadn't she considered herself Jane's prop in all this? Jane's last hope? So much for loyalty.

'She's the important one now,' Nick was saying. 'She doesn't have to be Bob's whingeing wife any longer. She's a woman of property, at least in her eyes, and Christ, wasn't she throwing her weight about and letting everybody know it. She was done up to the nines too, in an expensive black outfit. All for show, of course. It was pretty sickening, if you must know, so just be glad you weren't there in the thick of it.'

Alex stared at him, her resentment fading away as quickly as it had come. This was throwing a whole new light on Jane Leng's character. It was as if she were metaphorically ditching her dull crimplene image and emerging as the glossy black widow — in more ways than one.

'I'm sure she'll be in touch soon,' she said, intending to call her just as soon as she could get Nick out of here. 'So when do you have to get back to London?'

Nick laughed. 'OK, I can take a hint. Now you've had your wicked way with me — and bloody fantastic it was too — you're chucking me out. But I trust I can come again soon?'

His eyes challenged her boldly and she laughed back.

'Oh, I'm sure you will.'

* * *

Alex decided against calling Jane Leng, and instead drove down to Chilworthy near the Chew Valley where Jane was now ensconced.

It didn't take her long to get resettled, Alex thought resentfully, and despite what she knew about both the Lengs it appalled her that two people who had once presumably been in love and had a child, had been so full of venom towards one another.

Jane smiled delightedly at her visitor.

'How lovely to see you, Alex. Come in and take a look around.'

Confidence oozed out of her. Indoors, she still wore her crimplene frock, and probably nothing would change that, but her hair was now waved and tinted in a hideous shade of mauve. She patted it continually, as if to draw attention to it, when Alex thought she would do far better to hide in beneath a scarf.

'I thought we should get in touch,' Alex said, feeling oddly out of place, when she should be in charge. 'I didn't expect you to have moved yet, either.'

'There didn't seem any point in delaying. The sale had already gone through, and since Bob was no longer around to fuss me and get on my nerves, I just did as I wanted. Tea, dear?'

'I won't, thank you,' Alex said mechanically. 'I just wanted to report on my findings so far. And I have to go back to Exeter later today.'

She didn't, but now that she was here she

couldn't wait to get out. There was something so damn unwholesome about Jane's attitude. She was almost *jubilant* thought Alex, as if she had suddenly seen the promised land because Bob wasn't here to fuss her or get on her nerves.

'I know you'll find my Steven soon,' she was saying confidentially now.

'Mrs Leng — Jane — please don't be too hopeful. Nothing's changed, and I'm still tracking down his old friends — '

'Oh, I know. I've sent another letter to the paper praising your efforts, and now that I can afford to pay whatever you ask, I shall leave no stone unturned.'

God, she should be in amateur dramatics. 'You didn't put all that in your letter, did you? About being able to afford to pay — '

'Of course. Why not? Here, I'll show you.'

Alex hadn't seen the local paper for a few days, but she quickly scanned Jane's latest piece, confirming what she had just said and leaving the way wide open for any unscrupulous thug to come down here and take what he could from a silly old woman.

'Have you got locks on these doors, Jane? And a proper security system?'

She laughed. 'Bless you, no! Nobody ever locks their doors in these villages. We used to live here, and we know everybody. Why would

I want to have locks and security systems?'

Alex was reluctant to tell her, but in all honesty she could hardly do otherwise. It only resulted in more laughter.

'Goodness, who'd want to rob a widow-woman like me! No, you don't need to worry about me, dear. Besides, my sister lives nearby. I can always call her on the telephone if I'm feeling nervous. But to tell the truth, I'm enjoying being on my own so much, I don't even want her around!'

She beamed, pressing Alex's arm. It was a job not to jerk it away from this unfeeling madwoman who'd just lost her husband, for God's sake, and was so enjoying being on her own. Alex's dad would have said '*there's nowt so queer as folk*,' and this was one of the queerest.

She gave Jane her printed report and was pushed into accepting a bonus cheque which she didn't want and didn't need, since she didn't feel she had done much to deserve it. It was clear that Jane was euphoric with her new-found wealth and intended to make the most of it. And when the window cleaner arrived at the cottage and was given a much bigger tip than was reasonable, Alex knew that however uneasy she felt about it, there wasn't anything she could do to stop her.

She drove back to Bristol in a fury. She was

furious with Jane's callousness and stupidity; furious with Bob for topping himself; furious with herself for ever getting involved in the first place, when Nick had warned her off so vocally. But she still had a job to do and she was going to see it through as far as possible.

She remembered her visit to Roger Fry, and knew she must go back to Exeter to interview Lord, and ascertain once and for all that Drew was in reality Lennie Fry. She could easily go there and back in a day, but she decided to take a couple of days away from here to try to make sense of it all. Maybe the time really had come to tell Jane Leng she had come to the end; that she had to accept that her son was dead, and there was nothing more she could do for her. If only she didn't have this nagging little doubt in her mind that too many people were covering up what really happened all those years ago . . .

* * *

Her answer machine was flashing when she got back to her flat.

'I was going to call you on your mobile,' she heard a familiar voice say. 'But I've tried once or twice before and you've had it switched off, so this seemed the best way to get hold of you. Seems ages since I saw you, Alex, so how about a night out on the town? I'm free tomorrow night, so I could call round about eight o'clock if you like. If that's not convenient, let's fix another date. Nothing heavy. Just a few drinks, perhaps, so call me when you can. You know my number.'

She did indeed. And why not? Why the hell not? Exeter wasn't going to go away, and tomorrow was another day, she thought in best Scarlett O'Hara style — as she so often did. She dialled his number at once.

'Phil. Nice to hear from you. I've been away for a few days, and in fact I'm off again soon, so you just caught me between trips. But a night out would be great, so if the offer still stands, I'll see you tomorrow evening.'

'Fantastic,' he said enthusiastically. 'And you can tell me all about where you've been and your latest case.'

She laughed. 'Oh, you wouldn't want to know, and I don't particularly want to talk shop. Let's just have a good night out.'

'That's fine by me,' he said, as cheery as ever.

She hung up, still smiling. Odd that he should have called her right now when she hadn't heard from him in weeks. But he was good company, and if she spent too much time alone she'd just carry on brooding about

Jane Leng being a sitting target for a mugging . . . or wishing Nick was still here.

Before that thought took too much of a hold, she called Mrs Dunstable and booked her room again, fully aware from the cautious note in the landlady's voice that she clearly thought the big romance had fallen through again, and that Exeter was proving a refuge for a broken heart. Oh well. Better that, than having her know what the real purpose of the visit was.

* * *

Phil Cordell arrived sharp on time the following evening, looking dapper and smelling of aftershave, his fair hair salon-sleek. He was probably a wow with his female students, Alex thought briefly. Shame he did absolutely nothing for her. Or maybe it wasn't such a shame. It saved any complications.

'You look terrific,' he said, holding her hands and assessing her. 'You certainly know what colour to wear to greatest effect with that gorgeous hair and those stunning green eyes, Alex.'

'Black isn't really a colour, is it?'

She really didn't know why his compliments made her squirm, unless it was because they were just too perfect, too calculated.

Nick would have said in a sexy voice: '*Hey babe, you look far too luscious for me to share you with the outside world. What say we forget all about going out, and just hit the sack?*'

'Black is *your* colour,' Phil said solemnly, sliding his arm around her waist and giving her a peck on the cheek. 'And you know it.'

'OK, and you look good too, so now that we've done with the flattery, where are you taking me?' she said lightly.

'I thought we'd go to the Roadway. You'll like it and they do a great pizza. You look like a woman who likes her food — nothing personal intended, mind.'

It was a stupid remark if she ever heard one. How else was she supposed to take it if not personally? But when she realized she was starting to analyse everything he said, she made herself laugh.

'You're right, I like my food, and pizzas are OK.'

'Nice OK or just OK?

'Edible OK,' Alex said, wondering if he was always this tedious, or if it was just her mood. She followed him out to his car and found herself hoping it wasn't going to be a long evening in more ways than one.

The Roadway was a pleasant enough pub with plenty of mock-oak beams, the added gimmick of a covered wishing-well in the middle of the stone-flagged floor, and a landlord who resembled Mr Pickwick. It was noisy and brash, with a darts match going on in one corner and a group of students at the other end, and a cross-section of all ages in the middle.

'So how's the investigating going?' Phil said easily, when he had brought her a large vodka and lime and a pint of beer for himself.

'As well as can be expected,' Alex said, telling him nothing.

He took a long draught of beer before wiping the foam from his top lip before it resembled a moustache. Not good for his image, Alex thought swiftly.

'As good as that, huh?' he said. 'So have you found out anything to keep the widow-woman happy? I must say her letters to the press have become a bit less waspish recently.'

'I daresay it's because she's glad to be rid of her husband, which isn't a nice thing to say, but unfortunately true.'

'And you're not answering the question,' he said with a smile.

'I'm not, am I?' Alex said, smiling back. And why should I, she thought, when it's none of your damn business?

'So where have you been for the last few days?' he went on casually. 'Hot on the trail, or on holiday? I suppose a successful operator like you can afford a winter holiday any time it suits you.'

Alex suddenly sensed that he was fishing. He really did want to know where she had been, and her intuition told her it was more than just casual conversation. She didn't know why, but she decided to play his game.

'I've been to France for a few days. I've got friends there.'

She kept her eyes fixed on his as she spoke, and she had the satisfaction of seeing them flicker. He didn't believe her, and she didn't know why he shouldn't. It was almost as if he knew exactly where she had been — but even if he did, he couldn't know why. And how could he possibly know? She would do better to keep her wild imagination under control.

'Taking a break from the case then?'

'Perhaps. Or perhaps I was checking up on a possible sighting of Steven Leng. How about that for headline news?'

'That's impossible!' Phil said quickly. 'Everyone knows he's dead, and it's only his pathetic mother who perpetuates the myth that he's still alive.'

'You seem very sure about that.'

His attitude went from tense to relaxed in a split second. If she hadn't been so sure of the former, Alex would have said she imagined it. But she hadn't, and she knew it. Curiouser and curiouser.

'I only know that you've got to be wasting your time.'

'Well, since Mrs Leng is happy enough to pay me for wasting my time, I see no reason for not continuing to do it. Now can we please talk about something else, or I shall think you only asked me out to find out what I've discovered? Which is precisely nil, as a matter of fact,' she added for good measure.

He leaned towards her, wafting the concentrated scent of the aftershave she wasn't sure she liked, and looked deep into her eyes.

'I asked you out because I like your company a lot, and for no other reason. And I suppose the boyfriend's still on the horizon?'

'Very much so,' Alex told him firmly.

* * *

Long after he left her that night, she couldn't put her finger on why she didn't altogether trust him. He was almost too smooth, too upright a citizen. There seemed to be no flaws about him, and nobody was that perfect.

Everybody had hang-ups and a darker side to their nature, but by all accounts everybody liked and looked up to Philip Cordell.

She finally gave up thinking about him, and thought about her proposed meeting with Lord tomorrow. Providing he agreed to see one of the common herd . . . and thinking like that annoyed her even more. As if he really *was* Lord God Almighty. She wasn't overly religious, and rarely went to church. She ignored the unexpected stab of guilt, but she had been brought up in a Christian household, and there were some things you didn't do — like calling yourself Lord, and fancying yourself as the Saviour of all Mankind, when there was only one of those.

At the thought, she decided she was possibly more religious than she gave herself credit for, and that God would surely forgive a poor sinner the delights of so much flesh whenever she could get it — if he didn't ostracize her altogether for such blasphemous wicked ways. Still smiling at the thought of Nick Frobisher's sinfully rampant flesh, she drifted into a dreamless sleep.

* * *

She awoke with a start around four in the morning, her duvet on the floor and her limbs cold and shivering. She was sure it was nothing physical that had woken her, no intruders in the night, or the scrawny neighbourhood cats fighting in the darkness like a couple of banshees. It was a feeling of unease, of something she should have considered or missed. Whatever it was, it continued to elude her, but it finished her sleeping for the rest of the night — or morning, she conceded, seeing the signs of dawn through her bedroom curtains.

It was far too early to start the day, but it was also far too cold to stay in bed. She wrapped herself in her duvet, made herself a cup of coffee and curled up on her sofa with the gas fire full on to watch some early-morning TV. Thank God for cartoons, she thought weakly, as the antics of Tom and Jerry assailed her senses. At least their fights were all fantasy, and you didn't need to concentrate too hard.

But the heat from the fire was soporific and she came to with a jerk as the empty coffee mug dropped from her hands on to the carpet. She realized that the programme had changed, and there was now a news bulletin telling her about some inevitable new crisis in the Middle-East. And it was daylight. The rattle of the postman's delivery sounded below, and she went downstairs to pick up the handful of letters to shake herself out of her lethargy.

The only thing of interest was an invitation to a party thrown by one of the tenants in her old building in London. Charmaine was celebrating a successful conclusion to her advertising stint, and it would be shown on TV at the end of the month. Partygoers were invited to her flat in order to watch the inaugural event.

'I'm sure you'll want to be here if you can, Alex,' Charmaine had written excitedly. 'Bring a bottle and a friend — oh, and that old boyfriend of yours will probably be coming too. Just thought I should warn you. Gary Hollis, remember?'

Of course she remembered hormone-packed Gary Hollis, Alex thought with a stab of something half-pleasure, half-lustful. But she doubted that he'd remember her any more. She hadn't seen him in months, and 'pastures new' was Gary's motto. She wouldn't go, anyway. It was easy enough to pretend another engagement and promise to watch the ad, or tape the whole evening, so she wouldn't miss it. Charmaine's début would be something to see. Stick-thin and twittery was how she remembered her — and then she remembered too, how kind she had been when Alex had got flu, and unexpectedly produced cooking like mother used to make. Which just went to prove the old saying: you should never judge a book by its cover — or the persona that people showed you.

She was wide awake now, and she threw off the duvet and took a shower before having a scrappy breakfast and throwing some things into an overnight bag once more. If she was on the road by nine o'clock she could be in Exeter by mid-morning. However, a fine sprinkling of snow had begun to whiten the roads by the time she left, and it made the surface more slippery than expected, with the result that all the traffic was slowing down long before she turned off the M5 and headed towards Dun Roamin'.

'Come inside and get warm, dear,' Mrs Dunstable said, fussing over her at once. 'It's really not the kind of weather for travelling, and you're looking quite pinched. Are you quite well?'

'Perfectly, thank you.' And I'm not pining away for anyone, either, though she had to admit there was a little devil inside her that was tempted to play up to the landlady's romantic soul. But it wasn't fair, and besides, she didn't want it spread around the regulars that she was only here because of a broken heart.

'Actually, I'm celebrating,' she went on determinedly. 'I've got a new business plan going through, and it looks like being very successful.'

'Oh well, I suppose that makes you young people happy nowadays,' Mrs Dunstable said, clearly mystified that any such thing could put a glow on a young lady's face. 'You're in the same room, by the way, dear, so you know the way.'

She was virtually dismissed, Alex thought with a grin, and clearly a huge disappointment after such a promising beginning. But she couldn't spend time on providing Mrs Dunstable with a fictitious romance. She was here for a purpose, and there was no better time than now, before she lost her nerve, because there was nothing in the rules to say that a PI shouldn't have nerves. There were no rules at all.

She unwrapped the pre-packed tuna and cucumber sandwiches she'd bought at the last motorway service area and made herself some tea before going out into the cold of the January afternoon and finding her way to Mistral Street. The Old Mission Building, Zelena had told her. It shouldn't be too hard to find. And then she was going to confront Lord — even though she hadn't yet decided exactly what she was going to say to him. But now she had the added input of Roger Fry's query about his son. Far better that she should be making enquiries on his behalf than on Jane Leng's.

* * *

The Old Mission was a run down, shabby looking building badly in need of repair. The paint on the front door was peeling, the windows were dirty with net curtains that may once have been white, and there was a general air of neglect about the whole place. Only the soft sprinkling of snow gave the place a habitable look. It certainly didn't inspire Alex to go boldly where no man had gone before . . . though plenty of people had, she reminded herself, and mostly young kids, from the look of the buskers in the main shopping area.

But the general shabbiness of the building contrasted sharply with the appearance of the Followers she had seen. Despite the way Tracey had referred to them so scathingly as the yellow twits, they had certainly seemed to shine with health and cleanliness. As she hesitated outside the building, the door opened, and a young girl appeared in the familiar Followers garb.

'Can I help you?' she said, in the same soft monotone Alex was becoming accustomed to hearing now.

'I hope so. I'd like to speak to Lord,' she said, feeling totally idiotic and wondering if she should cross herself — though it wasn't the gesture that readily came to mind.

'Please step inside, and I'll see if he'll grant you an audience,' the girl said.

Oh God . . . but the girl had gone away as silently as if she had glided. *Nuns on wheels*, Alex thought irreverently, but since it was the only way she could stop a mild hysteria threatening to take over, she knew she had to cut this situation down to size, or she would have fled.

Just imagine all suspects and villains wearing red flannel underpants, Nick always advised her.

The young girl reappeared. 'Lord will see you now. Please follow me.'

They were all so excruciatingly polite, Alex reflected. It was unreal. Then she stopped her meandering thoughts as she was shown into a large room with plain white walls and basic white furniture. MFI's best?

She sat nervously on the edge of a long white bench. A door opened at the far end and a tall man in white robes edged with lemon came in smilingly, holding out both hands as he approached her.

'Peace and harmony, my young friend. In time-honoured hospitality, may I offer you a glass of iced lemon tea? Or something warmer on this cold day, perhaps?'

'Iced lemon tea will be fine, thank you,'

Alex stuttered, wondering for a moment if she had stepped straight back into the Bible.

She didn't know what she had expected. Some rampant sex-god, perhaps, intent on ravishing all the young girls who fawned over him. But this man was older than she had expected, his hands and face showing the lines and marks of age. His fingernails were excessively long and his well-groomed but sparse hair was pure white, reaching well below his shoulders.

She was obliged to touch his hands with her own, and as she did so a shudder of pure abhorrence swept through her, if only for the blasphemy of using God's name. His presence was so awe-inspiring that she hadn't noticed the young girl still hovering behind him, but at the soft flick of his fingers she disappeared at once to fetch the refreshments. Then he turned to face Alex with an enigmatic expression.

'Now, what can I do for you? If you wish to join us — '

'No. Oh *no*,' she said quickly, before she could stop herself.

At which he smiled almost benevolently, with a come-into-my-parlour-said-the-spider-to-the-fly kind of smile.

14

Lord waited patiently, as if he had all the time in world, which unnerved Alex even more. She took a sip of the iced lemon tea the young girl handed her before moving silently from the room, and wondered briefly if it contained anything other than the normal ingredients.

'I'm trying to find someone,' Alex said, telling herself to stop being paranoid, and placing the glass on the small white table in front of the bench.

'And you think this person may be here among our devotees?' he asked.

'I have reason to believe so. Or perhaps I should say, I think it's possible,' she added quickly. 'I thought I saw him in the town the other day, and his description was somewhat like the photos his father showed me.'

'Ah,' said Lord. 'Then you're searching for this person on behalf of his family?'

Alex wished she had dared to have her tape recorder switched on so that she could have played it back later and noted any small change or nuance in the voice. But she hadn't dared, and she was too jittery to have truly said whether or not Lord's voice became slightly more relaxed when the word family was mentioned.

'Yes,' she replied. 'I'm a friend of the family — or more accurately, an acquaintance of the young man's father.'

She nearly slipped up there. If Lennie Fry and Drew were one and the same, then he would know she wasn't a family friend. But since he had been away from home for so long, she could easily be a newer acquaintance of Roger Fry. She looked at Lord more boldly, pulling all her acting ability into action. If this guy assumed she was Roger's bit of fluff, so be it. If he had any such thoughts at all, she amended. From imagining him to be something of a sex-god, she now assessed him as being probably asexual. A nothing. A eunuch, maybe. Wasn't there some cult in America — it had to be America! — where blokes voluntarily had their testicles cut off for some weird reason no sane person could fathom? That wasn't the case here, was it?

She dragged her thoughts away from the unwelcome imagery and spoke as calmly as she could.

'His father's name is Roger Fry, and the young man's name is Leonard, usually known as Lennie.'

'We have no one of that name here.'

'But you do have a young man named Drew. I spoke briefly with him a few days ago. Lennie Fry's full name is Leonard Andrew Fry, so I was wondering if he could be one and the same. It would reassure his father so much to know that he was safe and well, you see — ' Her voice fell away lamely as Lord continued to stare at her without expression.

She hadn't noticed how strange his eyes were until now. They seemed almost devoid of colour at all, blind and penetrating at the same time. If there wasn't some other bloody substance in this iced lemon tea then she was in danger of hallucinating out of sheer terror. The room was large and not particularly warm, but its very starkness had a claustrophobic effect, and she was starting to sweat uncomfortably.

'Perhaps I've made a mistake,' she said in a panic, knowing she was backing down, being Audrey Barnes, farm girl, desperate to get out of here alive before something unspeakable sucked her in.

'Perhaps you would like to speak to Drew,' Lord said placidly.

Alex blinked. The room settled down into an ordinary room with four white walls that stayed in one place, and she cursed herself for her momentary panic.

'Is that possible?' she asked.

'All things are possible in this world and in any other.'

He flicked his fingers again, and a door opened at once. Alex's nerves were razor-sharp now, and so was her brain. There was no way anyone outside could have heard the tiny click of his fingers, which meant that the room had to be wired, so that someone in another part of the building could overhear every word.

She guessed this was only the case when Lord wanted his conversation with an outsider to be overheard. Perhaps to warn someone that they were being sought so they could be prepared for any questioning. It figured.

'Drew's presence is requested,' Lord said pleasantly to the young girl who had admitted Alex.

When she had left them Alex asked if she could see him alone.

'Of course. Everyone is at liberty here and they come to us voluntarily. We do not chain our people, Miss Best. Please remain here, and Drew will join you in a very few moments. Peace and harmony go with you always.'

'Thank you,' she said in a strangled voice.

He left the room and she was so very

tempted to get up and flee. But she couldn't be sure exactly where she had entered the building, and besides, now she had got this far, she had to see it through. She had to be sure whether or not Drew was really Lennie Fry, and discover what he could tell her about the events surrounding the disappearance of Steven Leng. She had to remember who she was and why she was here. Without warning, she went cold and rigid, but before she could formulate the thought that screamed through her head, the door opened, and Drew came inside. His eyes were dark and resentful, his whole body full of suppressed angst as he sat on the edge of a wooden chair. She spoke quickly.

'You know why I'm here, don't you? I'm looking for Lennie Fry, and I suspect that you may be him, and that you were one of Steven Leng's friends. And your father would rather like to know where you are,' she added sarcastically.

If Lord, or anyone else was listening in to this conversation it hardly made any difference now. She was here to do a job and she had to do it. Jane Leng depended on her. She saw Drew's face tighten, but his voice was mechanical.

'We are all here out of choice, and we don't have to answer to anyone for that choice.'

'I'm not asking you to leave the Followers, and nor is your father. You do remember him, do you, Lennie? He lives in a big house in Clifton — '

'My name is Drew,' he said, almost in a chant. 'I have no father outside the fraternity of the Followers. I have no need of worldly goods and chattels, and my philosophy is to bring peace and harmony wherever I go — '

'*Christ*, the old Jesus freak really does have you under his thumb,' Alex said recklessly. 'I'd say there's not much difference between his demands and the way any normal father would chastise his teenage son for dabbling in drugs and wanting to go to India with some nonsense idea of finding himself. But you're no longer a child. So tell me. Have you found yourself here, Lennie?'

She saw the flash of anger in his eyes and knew she was on dangerous ground, but if she hoped that goading him would produce some wild response she was disappointed. Or perhaps it was because he was aware that Lord was listening, and maybe even watching.

That was an even creepier thought. When he didn't answer, but just stared at her in the same way Lord had, she tried another tack.

'If Roger Fry is your father, then all he wants to do is know that you're well. Any son owes his father that much, wouldn't you say?' She had the satisfaction of seeing his eyes flicker, and he gave the smallest nod. 'And all *I'm* after, is to know if you ever saw Steven Leng after the incident in the woods, or if he ever made contact with you again. His mother believes he's still alive, you see, even after all these years. She's my friend, and I want to help her, especially now that her husband has just died.'

She watched him carefully, but again he didn't respond. Did he know Bob Leng had jumped from the bridge, or was he so indoctrinated in the Followers' code that it meant nothing to him? But he couldn't know, could he? So if that was the case, how come he had sent money for flowers for Bob Leng's funeral? If he'd done that, he had to know Bob had topped himself. So who had told him?

He stood up. 'Our time is up.'

'Yes,' Alex said, keeping her voice as steady as possible while her heart raced. 'Well, thank you for talking to me, Drew. I can see I have nothing to report to either Lennie Fry's father, or Mrs Leng.'

'Peace and harmony,' he said mechanically.

Alex held out her hand to shake his, and after a few seconds' hesitation he took it briefly, and she felt the tiniest pressure of his fingers. He was Lennie Fry all right, and something had scared the hell out of him. Whether or not it was Lord or something more sinister, she didn't know. But she recognized dilated eyes when she saw them, and it sure as hell wasn't love that produced them. It was fear. Lennie or Drew or whatever the hell he called himself, was shit-scared.

As he turned to leave the room the young girl entered as silently as before, and gestured to Alex to follow her. She went gladly. This place might be full of peace and harmony to those who chose to be here, but to Alex it was as dead as a morgue, and she couldn't wait to get out.

'Peace and — ' the girl began at the door.

'Crap,' Alex said. 'Same to you.'

She stepped out into the daylight, annoyed with herself for reacting that way, and needing to take long deep breaths to rid herself of an atmosphere that had been stifling in its deadness. In the street, doing their busking, smiling and sweet-natured, they all seemed so happy and content. Such a close-knit family, with a father — an overlord — who was as dictatorial in his own insidious way as any ranting father of wayward teenagers. Alex knew which she preferred.

She had been so intent on catching her

breath and feeling relieved to have got out of there alive, however bizarre the thought, that she hadn't noticed the white world in which she was now standing. During the time she had been inside the Old Mission building, the snow had come down with a vengeance, the streets were slippery and treacherous, and for a moment she felt completely disorientated.

There was very little traffic moving around this part of the city, and in any case, Alex had decided to walk, rather than make her presence too obvious by driving up in a car. She was glad now that she had left it at the B & B, and she had also been wary enough not to want the make and number of her car noted by any inmates of the Old Mission for future reference. You couldn't be too careful in this business.

These boots weren't meant for walking, she thought feelingly a while later. At least, not for walking in snow. They were long black fashion boots into which she had tucked her black jeans, with the idea of keeping out the cold from her legs. But they also let in the wet, and she was chilled and shivering by the time she neared the main part of the city. That would be all she needed, she thought, angry with herself: to be landed — and stranded — down here with a dose of flu. But if she was, she wouldn't damn well give in to it. The only place to deal with that was in your own home and your own bed and beside your own fireplace.

She knew very well that the only reason she was giving in to these inane thoughts was to keep out the one she should have remembered earlier. It wasn't even the fact that Lennie/Drew had known about Bob Leng's death, although that contributed to the other thing. It was the thing that should have alerted her the minute she heard it. The fact that Lord had addressed her by her name — and she had never given it.

⋆ ⋆ ⋆

She tottered into Dun Roamin', wet and miserable, hoping to reach her room unseen while she considered this and decided what to do about it. But it was too much to hope. Mrs Dunstable materialized almost at once, her face horrified at Alex's bedraggled appearance.

'My dear girl, where ever have you been in this weather? My regulars always hibernate the minute we get snow, and it looks as if you should have done the same.'

Maybe she would if she was ninety years old, like some of them. She managed not to say it out loud and suppressed a sneeze with difficulty, guessing that the landlady wouldn't be too pleased if she infected the entire establishment.

'I'll be fine when I've had a hot bath and a hot drink,' she assured her.

And entered everything on her laptop and made a few phone calls, she thought.

'You go on upstairs and get out of those wet things and I'll bring you a drop of whisky, dear. On the house, of course,' Mrs Dunstable said, and Alex couldn't argue with that. And besides, one threatened sneeze didn't mean the flu, she told herself determinedly. She wouldn't even think about it.

'Thank you, Mrs Dunstable,' she said. 'You're very kind.'

'Oh well, I've got nieces who are just as scatty as all you young things, and I'd like to think somebody was taking care of them too.'

Then God bless Mrs D's scatty nieces, Alex thought silently.

'What is it you do exactly, dear?' she said, following Alex to the lift as if to make sure she was doing as she was told.

'I'm in public relations,' she answered, knowing of old that this was a description that covered a multitude of possibilities. People assumed what they liked, and few of them questioned it. As the lift doors enclosed her she saw the landlady give a nod, and she leaned weakly against the back wall, eyeing her appearance in the lift mirror and realizing what a sight she looked.

Before leaving for the Old Mission she had arranged her hair in a thick plait for neatness. It made her face look thinner, and by now her fringe and eyebrows were edged with snow. She looked ancient, she thought irrationally. Old Father Time in drag. Once in her room, her boots seeped on to the carpet, and she tugged them off hastily, shivering as her sodden trousers clung to her legs. She should have taken the car — but the sight of some of them sliding on the roads had made her revise that idea. Why were the British never prepared for bad weather?

When she answered the knock on her door the landlady handed her a tray with a selection of spirits in small bottles — the type you got on aeroplanes. There was whisky, brandy, vodka, rum and gin. A secret tippler, possibly . . .

'Take these, dear, and let me have what you don't use. Some of my regulars bring them back for me from their travels, and I keep them for emergencies. There's no hurry.'

'Thank you,' Alex said, trying not to laugh. It was all so twee, but she had to admit the woman was all heart, even if she did want the unused bottles back. No wonder her regulars were so — well, regular.

She decided on the whisky, even though she didn't like the taste of it much, and grimaced as it went down and hit her stomach like fire. But as long as it killed off any germs it would be worth it. For good measure she decided to lace her tea with the other bottle when she had had her bath as hot as she could bear it, and washed the snow out of her hair.

By the time it was all done and her hair was moderately dry, she was snug in a sweatshirt and jeans, with her feet in thick woolly socks, and she curled up on the bed with the tea and hot toddy. And then she reminded herself that she must record all that had happened while she still had Lord and Lennie's conversations fresh in her mind. At least, they *had* been fresh before the whisky . . .

* * *

She awoke a couple of hours later, aghast to find that she could have fallen off to sleep so soundly. There was obviously more punch to that whisky than she had bargained for — and she didn't usually indulge in the middle of the afternoon, either. But at least she had no sense of impending flu, and she wasn't so muzzy that she didn't instantly recall where she had been earlier that afternoon.

She sat up quickly and fetched her laptop, typing in every single thing she could remember. It didn't amount to much, really. Except for the two things that bothered her the most.

One was the fact that Drew was definitely Lennie Fry, who had sent money to pay for Bob Leng's funeral flowers, and yet wouldn't identify himself, either to his father, or to her. And the second was the fact that Lord had known who she was — or at least, had known her name. Which meant that somebody had told him. She dismissed the thought of Mrs Dunstable at once. Why would she, when neither had any connection as far as she knew? The person who had delivered the lily to her had just left it for the lady with the lovely red hair.

Tracey at the coffee shop? She hadn't told her her name either. She hadn't given Zelena her card, and certainly not Drew. She liked mysteries herself, but not those of a personally threatening kind.

The sound of the dinner bell startled her. Had she really been up here for so long? She looked towards the window, and the lightness she had assumed was still daylight she now realized was attributed to snow.

'It's what we call a mini-blizzard,' one of the regulars in the dining-room told her with the superior satisfaction of the local. 'You won't be driving away from 'ere for a few days now, me dear.'

'I shall have to,' Alex said with a smile. 'I've got business to attend to — '

He gave a bucolic laugh, as if business was a foreign word to him. It probably had been for twenty years or more, Alex thought shrewdly.

'When you get to my age, you'll realize that business can always wait, miss. 'Tis better to be safe than sorry on these roads.'

'Mr Horsey's right, dear,' the landlady said, fussing around the tables to see that everyone had everything they wanted in the way of mountains of potatoes and sprouts and lashings of steak and kidney pie. 'The weather forecast is bad and they're advising people not to travel unless they have to.'

'I see,' Alex said. It had never stopped her before, and she would make up her own mind, even though for the rest of the evening until she escaped back to her bedroom she had to listen to the regulars yarning about their own personal weather disasters, and the times they had been cut off by floods or snow — and to listen to them, you'd think no other place in the whole of England had ever experienced such weather conditions before.

But when she turned on the TV in her room and saw the news pictures, she had to admit that it didn't look too good. Mrs Dunstable had been right, and people were being urged not to travel unless it was absolutely necessary. So now she had to ask herself — would a day or so longer matter a damn? She was cosy and warm here, and Jane Leng's money was paying for it, so why not do as she was told and hole up here for tomorrow, anyway?

Perhaps it would all be gone in the morning. Tales of treacherous slush, broken limbs and crashed vehicles in swollen rivers had been part of the regulars' stories as each tried to outdo the other. She wanted none of that!

* * *

The mini-blizzard lasted for six days. Mrs Dunstable reported that nothing was moving in or out of the city, and the delivery men were struggling to provide food and essential services. But to reassure her guests and to prove her good landladyship, or whatever it was called, thought Alex, it was lucky that she had such a vast deep freezer to provide for them all.

There wasn't a damn thing Alex could do about it, and there was no point in calling Jane Leng to report no progress. She did feel morally obliged to call Roger Fry, to let him know that she thought his son was with the Followers, as he had suspected, but that he seemed very well, and that Roger wasn't to worry.

She made it sound as if Lennie himself had asked her to pass on the message, thinking that a little white lie never hurt anybody. Kids never had the remotest idea how much their parents worried over them.

'Then if that's his choice, I must abide by it,' she heard cold-fish Fry say in a voice barely tinged with relief. 'But I thank you for contacting me, Miss Best, and of course you must send me your bill.'

'There's no need. I was in the area anyway, and I didn't have to do very much,' she said, crossing her fingers as she spoke.

The less she had to do with him, the better. All he wanted was to know that his son was still alive and kicking, if anybody asked. He didn't really want to know him, whether he was still a hippy-freak or India-bound. She wondered how he would react if he could see him now — blond and beautiful and banjo-playing in a public street. For one second she was tempted to send him a photo, and decided it would be too cruel. Let him keep his image of his son, whatever it was.

She called Nick several times, just to hear a normal voice and talk about normal things. It didn't matter that he knew she'd found Lennie Fry, since it was no concern of his, anyway, but she played it down, realizing she had played a very bad hand in asking Lennie so little about Steven Leng.

Somehow she hadn't felt able to, with the thought of Big Brother Lord listening or watching. But she knew she hadn't done her job properly, and that annoyed her. If the snow hadn't been so thick now, drifting and piling up against doors and virtually covering her car, she would have accosted Lennie in the street, and forced him to answer some questions, but the weather had put paid to that. She doubted that even the saintly Followers would be busking in these temperatures.

'I'd come down and keep you company if I could, babe,' Nick told her. 'I could just fancy a few days — and nights — holed up in a little hotel together. But I couldn't get away at the moment, though the weather's not as bad in London or anywhere else as it sounds down there. But you know I'll be with you in spirit, babe, even though I'd much rather be with you in body.'

'Yeah, I know all about that,' Alex said with a grin. 'Goodnight, Nick.'

She called him every night, knowing she was using his friendship unfairly to stop her being lonely, when he wanted far more than friendship. So did she — often — but on her terms.

* * *

'Thaw's coming,' the old boy called Mr Horsey informed her knowledgeably on the sixth night. 'My rheumatics are a sure sign of a change in the weather. You mark my words, me dear, tomorrow morning they'll be sending out for plumbers to mend burst pipes and sending out for sandbags to stop the sewers overflowing and sending rivers of muck through the streets — '

'Stop that talk now, Mr Horsey,' Mrs Dunstable told him. 'You'll be worrying Miss Best. It won't be anything like that.'

'Well, if it means I can get back to Bristol, I shall be thankful,' Alex said.

'Will you, dear? Oh well, I suppose you will. There's no place like home, of course, but it's nice having you here. You brighten up the place, and I know we all think the same,'

Mrs Dunstable told her.

Maybe they did, but Alex felt the need to get back to her office and start putting everything together she had done so far. After six days of suffocating small talk and assessing what information she had gleaned for Jane Leng, she was at the point of telling her she wasn't sure she could logically do anything else.

Ten years ago the police had been satisfied that there was no crime to answer. Steven Leng had been the victim of accidental death, and the ferocity of the fire at the old hut in the woods and the desperation with which the firemen had fought to put it out and prevent it from spreading, had almost certainly dispersed any possible evidence of a body. Except for the horrific discovery of the disembodied hand that the unfortunate Bob Leng had found some weeks later.

Gran Patterson had even made the gruesome comment that maybe the reputed beast of Exmoor had mutilated and eaten any remains that there were — even though the woods were nowhere near Exmoor, and that was merely the boys' camping destination. Gran was a glutton for embellishing the dramatics, thought Alex with a shudder, and the bloodier the better.

But despite her longing to finish with the

whole affair now, there was still one more of Steven's friends she hadn't interviewed yet. She still had to go to Bath to see Keith Martin, and in all conscience she couldn't leave it half-done before she gave Jane her final report. But once that was done, perhaps it really was time to call it a day.

The thaw came just as Mr Horsey had predicted from the ache in his bones, sheeting with rain, and sending rivers of slush through the streets.

'You're never driving back in this, are you, dear?' Mrs Dunstable asked her. 'At least wait until the streets have sorted themselves out,' she added, as if they chattered among themselves and had physical properties.

'I really must,' she said, but then came the news of an horrific accident on the M5 that stopped the traffic in both directions with a colossal tailback, and made her decide otherwise.

* * *

'It's bloody fate,' she fumed to Nick, when she answered his call on her mobile that evening. 'First it was the blizzard and then the thaw, and now this terrible accident. They still haven't opened the motorway, and heaven knows how many people have been killed and injured. I know I've got to be thankful I wasn't on it at the time, but I've had it up to here with the old darlings at Dun Roamin', and I just want to get back home now — '

'Alex, will you shut up for a minute?' he broke in almost savagely. 'I'm not calling you just to get a bloody accident report.'

She was suddenly aware of the tension in his voice, and it wasn't like him to be so dismissive of an RTA. She could usually tell when something was wrong, but she hadn't picked it up until now.

'What's happened?'

'Brace yourself, kid,' he said brutally. 'We got the news late this afternoon. Jane Leng's been shot.'

She couldn't take in his words for a moment, and she sat down heavily on her bed, every nerve-end prickling.

'*What*? How? Where? Is she badly hurt?'

'In her cottage. The police doctor says it must have happened last night, and she probably disturbed the intruder after he had ransacked the place. Unfortunately nobody identified the noise as a shot at the time, and neighbours thought it was a car backfiring. Her brother-in-law discovered the body — '

'The *body*? Are you telling me she's dead?' Alex said, her skin beginning to crawl.

'I'm afraid so.'

15

'It can't be true,' she stuttered, her head whirling with the news.

'Believe it, Alex. And sit down, for God's sake.'

'I am sitting down,' she snapped. 'Is that supposed to make it easier to take in? If so, the bloody shrinks have got it all wrong, and you can tell them that from me.' She was starting to babble now, and she clamped her lips together to stop them shaking. But this was definitely *not* on the agenda, she thought wildly.

'Stop talking, Alex. Do as I tell you and take some long, deep breaths,' Nick ordered. 'And then drink a glass of water, unless you've got some of your favourite vodka handy.'

'Funny you should say that — all right, I'll stop talking,' she said quickly, hearing him give an impatient sigh. She made him wait while she did exactly as she was told. Took some long, deep breaths, and then drank a glass of water.

'Right, I've done all that,' she said to Nick. 'And Jane Leng's still dead. Right again?'

'That's right, darling,' he said more gently.

She gave a great swallow, still finding it hard to take in. 'Do they know who did it?' Oh God, not one of Steven's friends?

But if it was, then maybe that proved something after all — that Jane was on to something, via Alex Best, PI, and that they wanted to silence her and her stupid letter-writing . . . and maybe Alex would be next. Before that thought could take hold, she heard Nick's voice again.

'Oh yes. they've got him all right. It was a bogus window cleaner.'

'*Oh*.'

'What do you mean, *oh*?'

'I mean she had a window cleaner there when I went to her cottage. He must have been looking the place over' — she just managed to resist saying *casing the joint* like some pseudo-American TV cop — 'if it was the same one, that is.'

'Apparently, the regular one in the village is somewhere in Ibiza on his annual holiday. The suspect reckoned he was a temp, but they found the gun with his fingerprints all over it, and some of Jane Leng's property in his possession. There's no doubt at all who it was, but since you saw him at the cottage you may still be called to identify him, Alex.'

She realized he had swung straight into

copper mode now, and she stared resentfully at a peeling patch of wallpaper on her bedroom wall, as if she personally had it in for the flaw in Mrs Dunstable's immaculate B & B.

'Why should I, if the police have already got him?'

'Just for confirmation. You know that. I'll have to get on to DI Gregory about it. You know that too. He's got your number, hasn't he?'

'Oh yes, he's got my number all right,' she said bitterly, wondering how the hell she had let herself in for this.

'Don't let all this upset you, sweetheart. As soon as I can get some time off, I'll get down to Bristol. I'll certainly try to join you for the funeral, anyway.'

'You think I'll be going to it?'

'Well, won't you?'

Of course she would. He knew it and she knew it. If anything was guaranteed to bring Steven Leng out of the woodwork it would surely be the news of his devoted mother's death. But of course, in reality, it wouldn't do any such thing. Alex knew that too.

When they finished the call, Alex helped herself to the miniature vodka the landlady had left with her. What the hell? She needed it. And although she would even have preferred the oldies downstairs for company right now, she stayed where she was, awaiting the inevitable call from DI Frank Gregory once Nick had informed him that Alex Best could identify the bogus window cleaner. Just her bloody luck.

'You've heard the news, I take it, Miss Best?'

'Yes thank you,' she said, as graciously as if it was some spectacular event.

'So when can you get back here? I gather you're in a water-logged Exeter right now, but the motorway should be open tomorrow, and if not, there are other roads.' And he was taking no prisoners, she thought sarcastically.

'I'll be back tomorrow,' she said in a clipped voice.

Bastard, she thought as she switched off her mobile. She had hardly been fond of Jane Leng, but he must know that she'd be shaken by what had happened to her. He was as unfeeling as they all were, despite his fatherly appearance.

When she could start to think more clearly, she reasoned that Jane's death almost certainly had nothing to do with her obsessive belief in her son's survival. It was an isolated incident made possible because Jane herself had sent all those wild letters to the press, and then practically broadcast her subsequent pleasure in coming into Bob's money.

A fat lot of good it had done her, Alex thought, suddenly guilty that it was the first stab of compassion she had felt since hearing the news.

She was becoming harder and more cynical than ever — but if she didn't keep those feelings intact, she knew she would just crumple up and die right now. Like people in the medical profession, you couldn't afford to get personally involved with your clients, even the likeable ones. Jane had hardly been that, and Alex wasn't hypocritical enough to pretend that she was, just because she had been shot dead. But even so, she had known the woman, and now the woman was dead.

She ran down to reception, ignoring the slow-moving lift, and told Mrs Dunstable that whatever the weather, she had to get back to Bristol tomorrow — even if she had to walk.

'Are you sure, dear? It's such a gloomy start to February, and I'm sure a few days more wouldn't do you any harm. You look very flushed now, if I may say so.'

It's the vodka, Alex told her silently. She was tempted to say her imminent return home was for a funeral, but that would invite questions and sympathy she didn't want. Aloud she said:

'I'm perfectly well. Actually, I've heard

from my young man, and I really do have to get back to see him.'

'Oh well, that's understandable then,' Mrs Dunstable said, beaming, and went back to her sitting-room and the romantic tear-jerker she was watching on TV, well satisfied.

* * *

The local TV news didn't cover the same area as Bristol here, so there was no report of Jane Leng's death. It was just another statistic on a police murder file, which was a terrible way to look at it, but sadly true in these violent days. There was no solemn-voiced comment that it was an unrelated incident to the woman's obsession about her son; no identification of the killer; no face flashed on the screen for Alex to remember as that of the bogus window cleaner, who had looked like any other window cleaner as far as she could remember. Just an ordinary bloke doing an ordinary job.

She shivered, thinking that perhaps if she hadn't been there that day, Jane would have been killed all the sooner. It may have been her presence that had deterred him from his intention that same day. Instead of that, he had gone back. It was a sobering thought. He may not have had killing in mind, of course.

He might have just had the gun as a frightener, only it had all gone wrong. Maybe Jane had braved it out. Maybe she had taunted him, threatened to call the police, pretended a caller due at any minute. Whatever the circumstances, it hadn't changed the outcome.

She tried to push the thoughts out of her mind while getting her things ready for an early start tomorrow morning. She couldn't wait to get out of here now. She needed the familiarity of her own things around her. She needed her own space. She needed Nick.

'Don't be a wimp,' she told her reflection in the dressing-table mirror as she emptied the drawers of her stuff and flung it in her tote bag. 'You started this thing against his advice, and now you've got to see it through.'

She paused because, of course, she didn't. Her involvement with Jane Leng was now at an end, apart from attending her funeral and identifying her killer, and seeing the sister and brother-in-law, who would presumably be distraught. She prayed the sister wasn't as mad as Jane, and wanted her to carry on as some kind of memorial to her. *God*, what a thought.

Her next thought was to consider whether to call round to the Old Mission building and inform Lennie or Drew or whatever he called himself about Jane's death, and see what reaction she got. She quickly decided against it. She might get in touch with Roger Fry though, and ask him to let her know if any other communication came through to him because of this latest development. If it did, if Lennie sent more money for more flowers, then she'd know that somebody else was well aware of where he was, and was keeping him informed.

In the end, she couldn't resist doing it, assuming that Roger Fry would have heard the news about Jane. It would assuredly be in the local evening paper.

The housekeeper answered her call.

'I'm sorry, but Mr Fry has gone away for the winter. He left for the Bahamas yesterday. If you want to leave a message I will see that he receives it in due course.'

'No. No message,' Alex said, and switched off.

So much for his need to know about his son. She doubted that his plans had been made instantaneously, which meant that whatever she had found out, the parent Fry would have gone off for his winter sunshine, and wouldn't have waited for news if she hadn't responded so promptly. She had been repelled by Lennie, but she realized she hated his father with a passion.

* * *

Next morning she was on the road early, having said her goodbyes to the regulars and promising to call on them if she was ever this way again. The motorway had been cleared by now, but traffic was moving more carefully than usual, with memories still fresh with all that had happened here, and the fact that a blinding drizzle of rain was impairing visibility.

By the time Alex got back to Bristol she felt as if she had been wrung out through her Aunt Harriet's wringer. She stumbled over the small pile of letters inside the door and ignored the flashing answer machine until she had made a good strong cup of black tea, since she hadn't milked the cow, she thought facetiously, and laced it with sugar for once.

Nerves were funny things, she reflected. You could go for weeks or months blithely thinking you didn't have any, and then one single thing, or a sequence of things, could set them prickling through your body like needle-points.

She jumped again when her phone rang. She picked it up quickly, and heard the annoying sound of her voice message as the answer machine kicked in before she switched it off.

'Sorry about that — '

'Just a reminder, Miss Best,' came DI Gregory's voice. 'Shall we say about three o'clock this afternoon?'

'You don't mind if I get in the door, do you?' she snapped back, biting her lip and knowing she was sounding petty and shrewish. And sure as eggs made omelettes he'd be putting it down as PMT.

'Don't worry, I'll be there,' she said coldly, and put down the phone before he could say anything more.

It wasn't something she relished, even though she knew it had to be a formality. Identifying someone, even a villain, always felt like a betrayal. But the guy had shot Jane Leng and had to pay for it.

In any case, when she saw the man later that day, there was no doubt that it was the bogus window cleaner she had seen at Jane's cottage. And once she had affirmed it, the police let her go.

When she thankfully returned home and turned the central heating up high to ward off the frozen feeling, she discovered a letter from Jane's sister, Grace, among the pile of mail she hadn't read.

'I know Jane would appreciate you being at the funeral, Miss Best. She always spoke so highly of you, and me and hubby know you did your best for my sister. We never thought Steven was still alive, but we couldn't ever say so, for fear of sending her right over the edge. It was all she had to hold on to, especially with Bob the way he was. He was always a trial to her. Me and Jane were never close, mind, and those newspaper letters of hers were an awful embarrassment. Anyway, this is just to say that we don't expect you to carry on looking for clues now she's no longer with us. It's far better that it's all laid to rest now.'

And so say all of us, thought Alex. Except that there was still Keith Martin to interview, and she had promised Jane to check out the list of boys. Just that, and no more, she vowed. But since he'd have no idea that she was on his trail he was hardly going to go away, and it could wait until after Jane's funeral, which she noted from the rest of Grace's letter, was to take place at the end of the week. And reading between the lines, she got the feeling that Grace wouldn't be too sorry that the troublesome relatives were no longer around.

⋆ ⋆ ⋆

Nick couldn't get away for the funeral after all, which was a major disappointment, since Alex knew no one there. There were a few locals who had known the Lengs in the past, and one of the local newspaper juniors had been sent along to cover it, presumably because in life Jane had provided some colourful copy for them, and they might as well finish off her story in style. Eerily, Alex discovered that Jane's sister was her clone in dress and manner, while the brother-in-law was a meek little man who scurried about, hardly speaking to anyone.

'We never had any other relations,' Grace confided to her, clearly seeing the presence of the tall and glamorous Alexandra Best as her claim to fame of a kind. 'Me and hubby live a simple life, and I don't know who'll want to buy the cottage now. It's a shame Jane wasn't able to stay there very long after all, especially as she never liked London. She never fitted in, and it was Bob's wish, not hers.'

Alex murmured the usual platitudes, thinking the sale of the cottage was probably going to be a trial to Grace too, and wondering how soon she could decently leave without causing offence. There wasn't going to be a proper reception afterwards, Grace told her, grandly elevating the post-funeral bun-fight to something of an occasion, but Alex was very welcome to come back to her and hubby's cottage for a cup of tea and a chat.

She wondered briefly if hubby had a christian name at all. For a few seconds she wondered if she should agree to go back with them, in case there was any additional information she might pick up about Steven, but decided against it. If Jane and Grace had never been close, it was unlikely Steven would have figured very much in this relationship either.

She drove back to Bristol, feeling almost savage at the way people could pick and tear one another apart, and vowing to be nicer to people and to phone her Yorkshire relatives more often. She was met on her doorstep almost immediately by Mavis Patterson. She shrieked out a greeting, and Alex's *bonhomie* vanished at once.

'Where've you been lately, Alex? Me and Gran have missed seeing you about. We thought you'd deserted us. You've heard about your lady, I suppose?'

'My lady? Oh, you mean Jane Leng. Yes, as a matter of fact — '

'Bit of a turn-up, innit? Gran says it was her own fault, for bragging about her money and all that after her old man popped it.'

'It doesn't mean somebody has to go to your house and shoot you, does it?'

She aggressively defended Jane. She had been a foolish, pathetic woman, but nobody deserved to be shot in the head and having their brains splattered all over their own furniture — which was the way DI Gregory had described it to her.

Mavis clearly took her attitude personally. 'Well, I was only trying to be friendly and making conversation. I know we ain't been seeing much of one another lately, but I thought we were friends!'

'Oh Mavis, we *are* friends. It's just that — well, I've just got back from Mrs Leng's funeral, if you must know, so I'm feeling a bit down in the dumps. But if you want to come in and have some coffee with me, I'd love a chat.'

It was really the last thing she wanted, but Mavis had been her first real friend since coming to Bristol, if you didn't count Phil Cordell, and there was no point in seeming too stand-offish to talk to her.

'All right, but I'd rather have tea.'

'Tea then.' Anything to stop standing on the doorstep while the wind blew up and down the street, and made her shiver even more than the chilly atmosphere of a country churchyard.

'So how did it go?' Mavis asked, once they were upstairs in the flat, her eyes taking in everything about it to report to Gran later.

'What? Oh, well, the same as any of them do. There's not much fun at a funeral, is there?'

'There will be at Gran's. She wants jazz music playing. Acker Bilk for preference. He was always her favourite. Local man, see?'

For a minute Alex didn't take in what she was saying. When she did, she started laughing for the first time in what seemed like ages. It was so like Gran Patterson to want jazz music at her funeral, Acker Bilk for preference, and so like Mavis to be damn sure that she got it!

'What have I said?' Mavis asked, mystified.

'Nothing, but you do me good.'

'Gran wondered if any of the blokes were going to turn up. You know, Steven Leng's old friends.'

'I don't think so. There was hardly anybody there, really. It's sad when nobody remembers you, isn't it?'

Mavis shrugged. 'Yes, well, that's not going to happen to Gran neither. She's made out a list of all her old mates for me to contact when she snuffs it. She wants to make sure she gets a good turn-out and a proper booze-up.'

* * *

Long after Mavis had gone home, Alex found herself wondering who in the world was really right. Was it the likes of Gran, who wanted jazz music playing, and a good turn-out and a proper booze-up at her funeral? And the likes of her one-time clairvoyant client, Leanora Wolstenholme, whose weird friends had turned up in garish clothes and spent the night swopping stories about the dear deceased and ended up as cheerful as if they'd been to a wedding?

Maybe they all had the right idea after all, and Jane's sister Grace and her crocodile tears were just a display of hypocrisy. Whatever. She felt more relaxed now, anyway, and if the emotionless Grace and hubby wanted to play it that way, it was nothing to do with her. She could forget the lot of them. Almost.

All except for her obligation to Jane, which didn't end with a shooting in a Chilworthy cottage, no matter how much she longed to think that it could.

'You know what, Dad?' she muttered, raising her eyes to some vague heavenly plane. 'You left me with a conscience, that's what you did, and now I have to see this through.'

The sound of her phone ringing sent her heart racing again. No, it *wasn't* her father coming through on some ethereal mobile, she told herself angrily. It was Nick.

'Are you all right? Was it harrowing?'

'I'm fine and no it wasn't. It was all very emotionless. I came away hoping that people care more about me than those two seemed to care about Jane Leng.'

She hadn't meant to say anything like that, but now she realized it had been nagging away at her, and she should have known he'd pick up on it.

'You know how much I care about you, Alex, and so do your family. But you're not an easy person to make friends with, are you, darling?'

'What makes you say that?'

He gave a small laugh. 'Don't get on your high horse, but you do put people off with that delicious voice of yours. Mind you, it's a turn-on as far as I'm concerned, but not everybody sees it that way. You're very self-contained, Alex.'

'Well, thanks for the character analysis — '

'There you go, up in a minute. So I rest my case.'

She clenched her teeth at his smugness, but he was probably right, she thought, wilting, and she didn't feel like arguing with him, anyway.

'What should I do then, adapt to the

natives? And don't think I can't,' she added, smiling now, because he knew it was one of her stock-in-trades.

'It might not be a bad thing. You can try it out on me next weekend.'

'You're coming down?'

'All the way, babe.'

When she hung up, she admitted that he could always cheer her up. He was good for her, and she, apparently, was good for him. Her spirits lifted, and maybe by the time she saw him she would have done with the Lengs once and for all. During the next week she would have interviewed Keith Martin, made her final assessment of all Steven Leng's friends, and that would be that.

There was nothing more she could do, and no one else she could report her findings to, since Grace obviously didn't want to have anything to do with it. If Nick or anyone in the local police force was interested in seeing her final report, they would be welcome to it. It probably only confirmed what they already knew, and what Jane had known in her heart. Steven had been a long time dead, and the only two people who had cared for him in their separate ways, were also dead.

* * *

On Monday she made a determined effort to call on Gran Patterson and give her the lowdown on the funeral proceedings, and compare notes over funerals of old and Gran's determination to make hers a memorable one. Though not like that clairvoyant woman's, she told Alex firmly, after she had listened to all of that. She wanted no such nonsense at hers. Alex was invited to supper again that evening, and didn't feel able to refuse, although the combination of Mrs Dunstable's cooking and now Gran's hefty portions of steak and kidney pudding made her wonder if she would ever get into half her clothes again.

And where was that local gym she had fully intended joining, she asked herself when she finally got back to the flat that evening, thankful to slip into something less constricting than her black trousers and sweater. You didn't dress up for Gran's. You left that to Mavis, with her red and yellow striped top and her blue shiny jeans, and this week's cerise hair colour.

Tomorrow she was going to Bath to find Keith Martin, and she still toyed over whether or not to be Alex Best, PI, or someone asking a few questions on behalf of an old friend of Steven Leng's parents. The Aussie accent she had adopted with the

Wilkins brothers might have been useful, but there was always a faint chance that they would have contacted Keith Martin and warned him to be on his guard if someone like that came snooping around. In the end she decided to be herself, but to dress casually in a blue sweater and jeans and a dark jacket, and to tie her hair back in a ponytail. No point in frightening him off.

She was on the road to Bath before ten o'clock the following morning, after routing the way by means of an internet web-site and printout. It had taken a damn sight longer than finding the roads in an A to Z, but now that Ray had taught her some of the skills, she felt duty-bound to use them. And by all accounts, Bath was a nightmare city for driving and finding your way around.

Thankfully, Keith Martin's hardware shop wasn't too hard to find. It was on the outskirts of the city and had his name emblazoned in large letters over the shop front. Even so, she had to park some distance from it and walk the rest of the way. All to the good of the promised exercise regime, Alex told herself, and put on a bright smile as she entered the shop.

The man sorting through a box of nuts and bolts behind the counter was about her age, which put him right in the frame for Steven's friend. But he didn't resemble Alex's image of him by one iota. The fresh-faced boy in the school photos had been thin but fairly wiry. This man's skin was as pasty as if he rarely saw the light of day. His hair was thinning and fast-receding, he wore unflattering rimless glasses and he was weedy to the point of gauntness.

'Can I help you?' he said, in very nasal tones.

Not exactly the most attractive male of the species Alex had ever come across, she thought.

'I hope you can,' she said, putting as much warmth into her voice as she could, and broadening her accent to that of a Bristolian. 'I don't want to buy anything, but I think you once knew a boy called Steven Leng.'

The box of nuts and bolts slid out of Keith Martin's hands, and the contents clattered on to the counter. If his face could have gone any whiter it would have resembled parchment. As it was, it had the effect of making his sharp nose stand out more than ever, and his eyes darkened behind the rimless glasses.

'Oh dear, can I help you pick those up?' Alex said conversationally, but determined to push on now. 'I'm so sorry if I startled you, but perhaps you didn't know that Steven's father died recently. You remember that he was a fireman, I'm sure. Well, of course you would remember that in the circumstances. Anyway, Mr Leng fell from the Clifton Suspension Bridge, and ten days ago poor Mrs Leng was shot and killed in her cottage. Terrible, wasn't it?'

She chattered on as if it was no more than local gossip, not giving him time to think as she bombarded him with everything at once. Sometimes it was the best way to get results. And of all of them — the aggressive Wilkins brothers, John Barnett who couldn't answer anything, the slimy Lennie Fry — Alex had the sure feeling that if she was ever going to get at the truth, *this* was the one who was going to crack.

'What do you want with me?' he said in a noticeably higher voice than before. 'I never met Steven's parents. I never knew anything about them.'

'But you know about Steven, don't you?'

16

Someone else came into the shop then, and with a muttered 'excuse me' Keith turned away to serve him, but Alex could see that his hands were shaking. He knew something all right, and the last thing he had expected was to be reminded of something that happened ten years ago. It might not be a bad thing to let him mull it over for a few minutes, she thought, as she saw how he fumbled over the customer's change. He was definitely disturbed.

'I'll be back later,' she called out, moving towards the door.

There weren't many shops around here, but there was a snack bar, and she could do with a cup of coffee. It was nearly lunchtime, and she could offer to buy him lunch, but she didn't see why she should, even to get the truth out of him. She doubted that a slice of pizza or a tired-looking meat pie, which was all the place seemed to offer, would do much to loosen his tongue. Better by far to ply him with drinks and see what developed.

She didn't know Bath, but she was a great one for making instant decisions — mostly.

The one that was forming in her mind now didn't take much thinking about. She finished her coffee and went back to the hardware shop, where Keith looked at her apprehensively now.

'I can't tell you anything about Steven,' he said at once. 'I'd just about forgotten his name until you mentioned it.'

Oh yes? The small tic at the corner of his mouth told Alex otherwise.

'It's only some family business I want to clear up,' she said, 'and I'll make it worth your while.'

'You're not a reporter, are you?'

'Why would you think that?'

'Well, you said Steven's parents were both dead, so I thought it might all get stirred up again.' He gave a convulsive swallow.

Alex glanced at her watch as if she had somewhere to go.

'Look, Mr Martin — Keith — I've got things to do this afternoon, but perhaps we could meet later when you've closed the shop. I'd be glad to buy you dinner anywhere of your choosing, and we can talk in a more relaxed atmosphere.'

She could see that he didn't want to talk to her at all, and yet her instincts told her he didn't find the chance to get it all off his chest exactly unwelcome, whatever it was. He was clearly a weak character, possibly the weakest link in the chain, and from the look of him a good meal wouldn't go amiss. Now that she had a good chance to look at the shop it was pretty seedy and she wondered how he ever made a living in an elegant and prosperous city that assuredly had high taxes. He wasn't the affluent businessman she had expected him to be — which was all to the good for her purposes.

'I'm not sure — ' he went on lamely.

She made up his mind for him. 'Keith, I'll come clean with you. Mrs Leng was convinced that Steven was still alive, even though the case was closed years ago. She just wanted someone to look into it for her, since she kept thinking she saw him, in crowds, at football matches — '

'Steven never went to football matches!' he broke in, his face redder now.

'But she couldn't stop worrying that it might have been him. Now that she's dead I can't report my findings to her, but it would still be satisfying to know the truth. I thought you might have an inkling about that. Shall we say that I'll pick you up here around half past six and we'll have an early dinner and talk about it?'

She still didn't give him time to think, and for a moment she thought she had already gone too far. He could so easily bluster it out and tell her to get lost. But he didn't. He gave a grudging nod.

'I don't know anything more than I already told the police years ago, but if you just want to talk about it — '

'That's all I want to do, Keith. Just to get the story straight in my mind.'

He wasn't too bright, Alex thought, as she went off to do the tourist bit in the city. Jane was dead, and any report that she made could only be for her own satisfaction — or someone else's. She couldn't deny that the thought of getting one over on the police findings was always an attractive one, knowing their opinion of PIs, especially young female ones with an accent as plummy as *Thunderbirds*' Lady Penelope, and a reasonable record of successful cases behind her.

Sometimes she had to remind herself of that, to offset the doubts that still beset her at times, wondering what the hell she was doing in this business at all, when she could have a cushy little number as a secretary, or working behind the checkout at Sainsbury's . . . and at the thought, she knew why.

But now that she had a few hours to kill, she may as well make the most of it. She did all the tourist spots in Bath, from the glorious cathedral to the art gallery and costume collections, and the lovely riverside pubs. Back in the shopping centre there was the irresistible purchase of a slithery black cocktail dress, and then the obligatory visit to the Roman Baths and springs and taking afternoon tea in the Pump Room. If you missed that, you were a philistine, according to one of the natives who pointed out the way.

Altogether it was an enjoyable, refreshing afternoon, Alex decided, and even though she ended up metaphorically kicking her heels in a car-park listening to music on her cassette player and hoping it wouldn't strain her car battery too much, she knew she had to spin out the time until she called back at Keith Martin's shop. Half past six was about the limit she could stretch to, though she wondered how much wine she could get him to drink at such an early hour to get him to unwind. It all depended on his state of mind, and what he was used to. He didn't look like a tippler, but you could never tell.

He was already outside his shop when she got there, standing nervously as if he had been waiting hours for a bus that never came. She was glad she had made him nervous. Nervous people usually said more than they realized, and she fully intended getting every bit of their conversation on tape.

'So where do you want to go, Keith?' she said easily, as if this was just an ordinary date. 'This is on me, remember, so it's your choice.'

'I'm afraid I'm not a fancy eater,' he said humbly.

Good God, thought Alex, it wasn't going to be the local fish and chip shop, was it? She was hardly going to get him paralytic there.

'There's a little restaurant out on the Bristol road that's quite nice, so I've heard,' he went on. 'I've never been there, so maybe that's not the right place. There's also a Berni Inn — '

'Let's find the little restaurant,' Alex said firmly. 'Just point me in the right direction and leave the rest to me. I'm Audrey, by the way. Audrey Barnes.'

She knew they were going to look like an unlikely couple. She was a head taller than he was, and she couldn't help thinking of Grace's hubby, who was also humble and weedy, and if she stopped to think about it, it didn't do her image any good to be seen in such company. Nick would say so, anyway. So it was just as well he couldn't see her now.

She was being bloody sexist and mean about the guy, who was probably as self-contained as she was in his own way

(Nick's words again, she noted) but he hardly said a word all the way to the restaurant apart from giving directions. When they arrived, Alex asked for a secluded alcove table, and didn't miss the waitress's raised eyebrows.

Which of them is the pimp? was the question Alex read in her mind, and she stared unblinkingly back at her until she gave a small shrug and showed them to their table. Keith stared at the menu as if he had never seen one before.

'Don't worry about prices,' Alex told him. 'Just choose whatever you want and I'll pick the wine — '

'Oh, I hardly ever drink — '

'Neither do I, especially when I'm driving,' she said, mentally crossing her fingers. 'Don't worry, I'll see that your honour is intact.'

The joke fell on concrete ears. He was twenty-six going on forty. Alex had the feeling this was going to be a pretty heavy evening if she didn't get him loosened up. And she had better remember her own words — she had to drive back to Bristol that night, so it had to be Keith's wine-glass that was being kept topped up, not hers.

By the time they had got through the first course of melon and raspberry coulis, and started on the peppered steak (good for the thirst) with all the trimmings and a few extras besides, she had ensured that he had drunk nearly three glasses to her one. He wasn't used to it, and the waitress clearly thought she was plying him with wine for her own dubious ends. Some chance! It was a shame to get him so pie-eyed and he'd have a hell of a head in the morning, but it was in the cause of research, and Alex was determined to get as much out of him as she could before he went into a stupor. By morning, it was doubtful if he'd remember anything he told her.

As yet, it wasn't very much. Yes, of course he remembered the camping trip that the six friends had arranged. Yes, of course he knew that Steven hadn't gone with them after all, but that wasn't surprising.

'Why do you say that, Keith?' Alex said.

He scowled, becoming more morose as the wine took effect, and more than ready to complain in his whining voice.

'We all thought he wouldn't come. His mother didn't want him to, and he was under her thumb, as well as his father's. I didn't know them — I told you that, didn't I? But Steven was always going on about them and saying he'd go off to India if Lennie would go with him. They were a daft pair, always making plans that we all laughed at.'

'Perhaps he did go to India, then,' Alex

said, knowing that he didn't.

'No he didn't. Nor did Lennie. They just liked to talk big, and some of that stuff they took didn't help, either.'

'What stuff? Drugs, was it?'

'Not the bad stuff. Just pot, mostly, and a bit of speed, but it made them boastful and stupid.'

'A lot of people think pot should be legalized, don't they? That it's no more harmful than tobacco — ' Alex said conversationally.

His face darkened. 'Oh yeah? Well, my dad smoked sixty a day for years and they said his lungs were as black as soot when he died of lung cancer, so don't talk to me about tobacco, or drugs.'

'You never took any, then. Pot, I mean. Not like the others.'

'No I never did. I wasn't so stupid. Of course, that wasn't how they saw it. They said I was a pansy and Cliff and Dave beat me up once when I threatened to tell what I knew — '

Resentment oozed out of him now, but Alex knew she had to go carefully. His thin voice throbbed with anger, and although they were in the alcove, other people were glancing their way. The last thing she could afford was to have a confession here and now, and for him to start shouting or blubbering, whichever way the mood took him.

'I think I should get you home, Keith. Black coffee sounds like a good idea to me, and if you'd be kind enough to offer me a cup before I drive back to Bristol, I'd be grateful. It's the least you can do after this lovely meal, isn't it?'

He could hardly say no, even though she guessed he didn't want her in his flat above the shop. Or anywhere else in his life. She was a threat to whatever he had managed to blot out of the events of ten years ago.

But she wasn't letting go of him now. She had hooked him on her line and she was ready to pull him in.

'All right,' he said grudgingly. 'But I don't usually have people in my flat, so I'd rather you didn't stay too long.'

'Of course not,' she said, giving him a sweet smile. 'We wouldn't want people to think the worst of us, would we?'

He looked at her blankly as she handed her credit card to the waitress, and couldn't resist giving her a sly wink at the same time. It would probably make her day, Alex thought, to wonder if the woman with the startling red hair and green eyes was really making a play for the drip in the glasses, and hoping that he was well-heeled — and man enough — to make it worth her while.

Alex mentally cringed at the thought. It was a pretty safe bet that Keith was definitely not a ladies' man, and it was possibly something else the others in the group had taunted him about — especially those thuggish Wilkins brothers. She wondered how he had got caught up with them in the first place. But she wouldn't ask. That wasn't the object of the exercise, and he was almost out on his feet by the time she got him into her car.

'You're not going to throw up, are you?' she said sharply. 'If so, I'd rather you did it outside the car and not in it.'

'I'm all right,' he growled. 'I just want to get home. I told you I didn't drink. I'll be better inside my own four walls.'

'Right then,' Alex said brightly. 'Home it is, and I'll be quite happy to make the coffee while we talk.'

'There's nothing to talk about,' he grunted.

'Don't you think it's sometimes easier to talk to a stranger about something that's been worrying you for a very long time, than to have to tell close friends?'

'There's nothing worrying me. Well, not really.'

She had to concentrate on the traffic going into the city then, but she knew the signs. He was ready to open up, seeing her as some kind of mother confessor now, and she didn't intend leaving him until she had got the truth out of him.

* * *

His flat was as she had imagined it, as cold and boringly neutral as its owner. No creature comforts here then. The furniture was worn, and she guessed it had belonged to his parents. Predictably, there was no sign of a young woman's hand anywhere. He pointed out the kitchen while he found some aspirin and turned on the gas fire, and she made the coffee quickly, feeling as if she were in a morgue.

'Now then,' she said finally, when the flat had thawed out a bit, though she still had her hands around her mug to warm them up. 'Why don't you unburden yourself to me about that day in the woods, Keith? You and the others were larking about, weren't you, and letting off fireworks? And then you were going to go on your camping trip. Isn't that right? And it's still worrying you not to be able to talk about it to anybody. Right?'

She kept his mind busy with questions, and although her tape recorder was switched on, she thought he was too fuddled to notice it.

But hopefully, not too fuddled to remember things.

'Why do you want to know? We've been through it all before. The questions always worried me. I don't like questions.'

He was becoming petulant, and Alex softened her voice.

'It's only for Mrs Leng's peace of mind, Keith — '

'You said she was dead!'

He wasn't that fuddled then.

'So she is, but I feel obliged to finish my report and then it will be filed away and that will be that. You keep proper books, don't you? Being a businessman yourself?' *Appeal to his pride . . .*

'Of course. But I wish all this Steven business would go away. I didn't want to get those letters — raking it all up again — '

'What letters were those?'

'Anonymous, warning me not to speak to anybody about it. I hadn't thought about it in years, and then suddenly it all got raked up again.'

'Did the letters have a postmark on them, Keith?'

Exeter, for instance?

He was close to tears now, his face pastier than ever, his eyes like marbles behind the rimless glasses, his voice jerky with panic. 'I never looked. I threw them away. It just made me sick, having to remember any of it. I mean, we weren't doing any harm. It was all a lark. Well, that's how it started, anyway.'

'And how did it end?' Alex said softly, feeling her heart thud at the thought that at last she could be on the brink of finding out exactly what had gone on in the woods that day.

'With the explosion,' he whispered, so quietly that she could barely hear him. The heat from the gas fire was soporific now, and without asking, she bent down and turned it down a fraction.

When she turned back to him she could see that he was away somewhere in a world of his own. A nightmare place that was somewhere in an old tumbledown hut in the woods where druggies and winos hung out, and a few members of a weird cult called the Followers may have tried to persuade some gullible kids that theirs was a good road to travel. Several of them had wild ideas about going to India and finding themselves, and a couple more would have scoffed and goaded the weakest link of them all to join in the fun.

'Did they persuade you to take any drugs that night, Keith?'

He gave a gigantic shudder. 'I never do. I always promised my parents I'd never do anything like that,' he said, his voice shrill now. 'But they made me. Forced me. Shoved it down my throat when I'd already had a few drinks — I told you I don't like strong drink, didn't I — and I'd lost my glasses in the grass, so I couldn't see properly.'

'Whose idea was it to take the fireworks to the woods and set fire to the old hut then?'

He swallowed. 'I don't remember. I think it was Cliff Wilkins. He hated the winos, even though they'd gone long before, but he said they'd left such a stink in the hut it was time to get rid of it. So the idea was just to set it alight and watch it burn. Then we were going to get out of there as fast as we could and go camping. Everybody thought we'd already gone on our trip, anyway.'

Alex resisted the urge to ask what kind of 'trip' he was referring to.

'So there was definitely nobody in the hut at the time?'

He shook his head violently, and then held it tightly as the headache kicked in. He'd have a hell of a hangover in the morning, Alex thought, with a touch of remorse, but you had to use whatever methods were available to you.

'So what happened to Steven? How did his hand come to be discovered a few weeks later by his father walking his dog?'

She punched the question at him, hoping to get a blundering response. It wasn't quite the one she had in mind. Keith suddenly retched, then clamped his hands to his mouth and rushed off to the bathroom to be violently sick. He tottered back ten minutes later, by which time Alex had switched off her tape recorder, and was preparing to switch it on again.

'You're not taping all this, are you?' he said, a mite sharper than before, his eyes full of new suspicion now. 'You're not the police, are you, because I'm not saying another thing if you are. This is harassment — '

'Keith, I'm not the police, I *promise* you. Look, I'll turn it off, OK?'

She made a great pretence of doing so, hoping the double click wouldn't alert him to the fact that she'd simply turned it off and back on again.

'That's all right then. God, my throat's sore,' he said next in an aggrieved tone, and she sensed that he couldn't concentrate on anything for too long.

'You were going to tell me about the discovery of Steven's hand. And what was this explosion you mentioned? Were the two things connected?'

He looked suddenly terrified as if memory was glazing his mind as well as his eyes. They had a distinctly glassy look now, Alex thought uneasily. As if . . .

'We didn't know, see? How the fuck were we supposed to know?'

The expletive shocked Alex as much as it shocked him. From the way his face was instantly flooded with colour she was quite sure he didn't normally use it.

'How were you supposed to know what, Keith? Take your time. Take some deep breaths — '

But he was too wound up to stop now. 'They had calor gas bottles inside, for cooking, see? For heating as well, I suppose. We didn't know that. How could we have known that? We were only there for a lark. We didn't know, we didn't *know*! We never looked around that much, and there were always old blankets and cardboard boxes and a lot of junk chucked about all over the place. It was a dump and it should have been condemned years ago. We were just helping it on its way.'

He was snivelling loudly now, his hands and arms making jerky movements, his eyes rolling in their sockets as if he was reliving every moment of that terrible day when the boys had probably all been high on drugs, however harmless they thought them, and everything was being viewed through a kaleidoscopic haze.

'So there was an explosion?' Alex persisted, when he swallowed convulsively several times, and she thought another trip to the bathroom might be in order. Another trip . . .

'Keith, did you take anything when you were in the bathroom?'

Oh, please tell me you didn't.

'It went up like an atomic bomb,' he slurred. 'And we all ran like hell. We met up ages later, crouching in the woods and listening to the fire engines. We couldn't find Steven, but we thought he'd gone home, knowing his dad would give him hell, him being a fireman and all. We eventually got to our camping ground, and we made a pact to say nothing — ever — and we swore on each others' lives that it had to stay our secret, no matter what. Lennie insisted on it. He threatened us if we didn't stick to it — ' he swallowed hard again as if his throat was closing up.

'*Lennie*? Not Cliff or David Wilkins? Not John Barnett?' She raked up the names from her memory. Gentle, peace-loving Lennie?

'He got involved with these people, and he said they had the power to do for us, whatever that meant. He was soft on the outside, with his music and all that stuff, but on the inside he was as hard as a rock. He scared me.'

He began shouting, belligerent with another swift change of mood. 'Why the fuck did you have to come here and stir it all up again? And I know who you are now! Somebody sent me a cutting from the Bristol paper with one of those stupid letters in it, and I've been puzzling over the name you signed in the restaurant. You're not Audrey somebody, are you? You're that private eye woman. Give me that tape recorder, you bitch.'

He lunged towards her, his eyes murderous, half-standing as he did so, but it was obvious that his legs were more like jelly than flesh and bone, and he keeled over on to the floor, panting like a fish out of water. Alex rolled him over quickly, and saw that his eyes were wide open, staring unseeingly. They were hugely dilated, and she knew the signs when she saw them. She rushed to the bathroom and saw the open medicine cabinet and the bottle of amphetamines spilled on the window-sill, even as she was dialling 999 on her mobile phone.

'Ambulance, as quick as you can,' she rapped out. 'It looks like an overdose. Amphetamines and drink. I don't know how many.'

She gave the address of the flat and

switched off without giving her name. She went back to Keith and tried to lift him on to the sofa again. He was surprisingly heavy for such a weed. Dead people usually were. Not that he was dead. Oh God, please don't let him be dead.

It wasn't her fault that he'd taken the pills, but it was down to her that he'd drunk so much wine when he wasn't used to it. Guilt made her rougher with him than she intended as she hauled him to his feet, put her arms around him and began walking him around the room. Dragging him was more like it, but she knew she had to try to wake him up and to get him as sensible as possible before the ambulance came. It was hard going. He much preferred to be out of it, and she only got a few incoherent words out of him now and then. But at least it was something.

She could imagine the headlines . . . 'Private Investigator accused in sordid drugs death'. The newspapers would have a field day. She might even be done for involuntary manslaughter.

She despised herself for thinking what all this was going to do to her reputation if it came out that way. But if it did, she knew she might as well pack up and take up knitting instead. The police would be ruthless with her, and so would Nick.

She continued dragging Keith around, shouting at him to wake up and mentally begging him not to die. That certainly hadn't been her intention when she came here to question him. How could she have known that he had a drug habit, when he'd been so adamant that he hated anything to do with drugs? But that's what druggies did.

She heard the sound of an ambulance siren and thanked God for it. Still hauling Keith around, she opened the door and let the paramedics in, a man and a woman in practical green overalls. Practically *Casualty* clones, she thought wildly, near to hysterics herself now.

'An overdose, is it, Miss? Boyfriend, is he? Name?' the man said efficiently.

'I think he took some of these,' she stuttered, handing him the bottle. 'We had dinner and he drank a lot of wine, and then he threw up in the bathroom. I suppose that's when he took the pills, and then he just collapsed. I didn't know he had them. His name's Keith Martin. He owns the hardware shop downstairs.'

'And you are?'

'Audrey Barnes. I'm just an acquaintance.'

God, if ever a suspect sounded guilty, she must do so now, she thought. She was desperate to get away from here. She wasn't heartless, but Keith was in safe hands now. They had put an oxygen mask over his face and his eyes had begun to roll a bit, instead of remaining glassily still. The woman medic was murmuring that he was stabilizing, and the sooner they got him into hospital and pumped out his stomach the better. He was lucky.

From the look the woman gave her, Alex guessed she was being considered a pick-up, a tart. With weedy Keith Martin? The thought was so ludicrous she could have laughed out loud, but if she did that she'd probably be blubbing too, because this night had turned out to be so nearly tragic.

17

She told the paramedics she would follow them to the hospital in her car, knowing she had no intention of doing so. There was nothing she could do for Keith, and she certainly didn't want him coming round to start raving at her in public. She managed to give the ambulance the slip at some traffic lights, and headed back the way she had come. All she wanted was to get home, crawl into bed, and wake up as if none of this had ever happened.

But she knew it was a futile hope. It was unprofessional. It wasn't the way Nick would handle things. Nor any of the police force. As she drove back to Bristol, going too fast around bends that she didn't know, and half-sobbing with nerves as she did so, she told herself to calm down and remember that she still had a job to do. She still owed it to Jane Leng to find out what had happened to Steven, even though she cursed the day she had ever met her and listened to her sob story. She should have listened to Nick instead.

Presumably neither Nick nor any of the

police investigtions had got wind of this pact to keep silent that the group of friends had made — the pact that Lennie Fry had orchestrated (good that, since he was a small-time musician, her fractured thoughts added). And the fact that they had all been so high on drugs when they scattered meant that none of them knew whether or not Steven Leng had actually gone home — or been inside the hut when it exploded. Or near enough for him to be blown to bits, with most of him perishing in the explosion — most of him, except for one disembodied hand that had been thrown clear a good distance away, to be found some weeks later, mouldering and maggot-ridden, by a dog ferreting about in the undergrowth. A dog belonging to Bob Leng, Steven's father.

She gasped as the vitriolic blast of a car horn reminded her that she was veering towards the white line in the middle of the road and hardly noticing where she was going. She slowed down and corrected the steering at once. A fat lot of good she would be to herself or anybody else if she was involved in an accident and pulled in for a breathalyser test. Worse still if she ended up in the morgue.

It was enough to sober her up, as far as driving more carefully went, but she was filled with an adrenalin rush of gigantic proportions now. She knew she was on to something. She *knew* it. Excitement shot through her every time the possibilities ran through her mind. She still didn't know *why* nothing of Steven's body-minus-one-hand had ever been discovered, even though the evidence said that the ferocity of the fire and the fire officers' frantic attempts to stop it spreading through the tinder-dry woods had reduced everything to ash and scattered it far and wide. Maybe it had also thrown Steven's hand . . . maybe it had been his ghoulish way of saying, hey, don't forget about me . . .

Alex tasted bile in her mouth then, and knew that the events of this night were having their effect on her, and she turned on her car radio to blot out the unwelcome images she was beginning to see in her mind, and also any suggestion of anything weird and unnatural.

Wait until you get home, Alex, she told herself grimly. There were some things that were best done in the privacy of your own bathroom, and throwing up was one of them. She just made it, weakly thinking what a bloody good waste it was of a couple of bottles of wine and an expensive meal at a good restaurant, when the two of them had ended up depositing all of it in various lavatory bowls.

Black coffee was next on her list of things to do, and then she was going to take a shower, simply because she couldn't settle to anything else until she had called the hospital and found out if Keith was all right. But it was too soon to do that. She had to give them time to pump out his stomach — ghastly thought, tube up the nose and down the throat — and then assess the outcome of his overdose. She wondered uneasily if he had meant to do it, or if it had been an accident as he fumbled for a couple of pills to calm him down — or pep him up as the case may be. In any case it had been a bad move, considering the amount of wine he'd drunk, and he must have known that.

She gave up surmising and made her coffee very strong, and her shower as hot as she could bear it. She found the local radio station to check if there was any information about a drug related incident in Bath that evening. But why should there be? These were depressingly all-too frequent. Except that this time, if Keith died, they would want to question the woman who had been with him and sent for the ambulance.

Her hand jerked over the radio and she knew she couldn't bear to wait any longer for news. She found the number of the Bath hospital in the phone directory, and dialled it with shaking hands.

'I'm enquiring about a young man brought in by ambulance this evening,' she said crisply, hoping her accent would impart efficiency, and thinking it was a good thing the woman at the other end couldn't guess at the way her stomach was churning.

'What name?' came the voice. 'Are you a relative?'

'His name's Keith Martin,' she said. 'I'm — his sister.'

'Hold on, Ms Martin. I'll check it out for you.'

There was an endless wait, and then a man's voice came on the line. Please don't be a police officer, she begged silently.

'Doctor Kane speaking. You were enquiring about Keith Martin, I believe.'

'Yes. I was told he was brought in earlier. Is he all right?'

'Mr Martin has had his stomach pumped and he should recover fully, barring a very sore throat. He's a very lucky young man and if it hadn't been for the quick action of the young woman with him, it might have been a different story. Do you know where we can get in touch with her?'

Alex slammed down the phone, relief

flooding through her so fast she thought she was going to faint. Keith wasn't going to die, and she had probably saved his life. It was the one tiny thing — the one *gigantic* thing — that she felt had justified the means she had employed. How was she to know he was addicted to amphetamines or anything else? He had so vehemently denied it.

Her coffee had gone cold by now, and anyway, she needed something stronger. She poured herself a large vodka and lime, and sipped it with something like relish before she played back the tape. She was so wound up with a mixture of terror and relief that there was no way she was going to sleep for hours. And now that she knew Keith wasn't going to end up in a wooden box she might as well try to make sense of all she had learned.

* * *

To her frustration and fury, the tape had run out before she reached the end of the conversation. It ended with the words 'larking about', which was something that had had more devastating consequences than any of them had bargained for, Alex thought. It also meant that she had no verbal evidence about the explosion and the calor gas bottles, and unless she could get Keith to talk again

. . . but she immediately discarded the idea of seeing him again.

In any case, she had probably frightened him off for good now, in the wake of some anonymous letters and a cutting he had been sent through the post containing one of Jane Leng's letters. The one naming *her*, presumably, which meant that whoever had sent it to Keith must have wanted to warn him to be on his guard in case she came snooping around. Which meant it could be any one of the six — no, five — boys involved, and anyone else who knew their names.

It left the field wide open. The case had been thoroughly investigated years ago, and the boys had been extensively interviewed in the press at the time. She knew that from reading Gran Patterson's press cuttings, and the newspaper archives. But that was years ago. Alex remembered how Nick had always told her to think laterally and never to take the obvious route as the only one available — rather like ignoring the motorway and taking an interesting side road to reach your destination. You never knew what bits of local colour you might pick up along the way.

So who else knew the boys' names, who hadn't been involved at the time? Other kids their age would probably have found it a nine days' wonder and then forgotten it. So who else had she been in contact with since coming here, apart from the newspaper guys, and Mavis Patterson and her Gran? She didn't think any of them qualified as a villain, even if the only villain she had in mind now was someone who sent threatening letters and stuff to Keith Martin. It was hardly big-time crime, but she knew from personal experience how threatening it could be.

Ray Smart hadn't been around at the time, Alex recalled suddenly. He would have been seven or eight years old then, but he'd seemed pretty interested in the case she was working on. She let her thoughts mull on him for a moment. Ray Smart, the nerdy computer whizz kid who had found details of the Followers for her, practically at the touch of a button and without too much input from herself. Ray Smart, who had been recommended by Philip Cordell, whom she didn't really know at all, but who had turned up out of nowhere when she first arrived in Bristol, and had seemed keen on following her progress, rather like an eager puppy — or a waiting Rottweiler.

Her heart was thumping now, and she told herself it was crazy to jump to conclusions. None of it fitted anyway. Phil was nice enough, even though he had never turned her on, and she had always had a slight sense of unease with him. It didn't mean he was involved with any of the camping group, nor that he had known any of them.

Think laterally, Alex. He was a head of sports tutor, and although he had initially led her to believe (despite his denial) that it was at the university, it was at a much smaller college, where he was friendly with lots of students and teachers. Presumably some of them would have known him before he got his present job.

She was clutching at straws, and was probably doing Phil an injustice in suspecting him. And what of, for God's sake? Keith had confirmed, along with all the newspaper reports at the time, that there were only the six students involved in the firework incident. There was no reason to think that a seventh person had had anything to do with it, or them. As far as she could remember, Alex had never asked him if he knew any of the boys. It was a shot in the dark, and it was fizzling out as fast as it had come.

She suddenly felt very tired as the events of the night crowded in on her, and she finally gave it all up and fell into bed, knowing she was doing no good by going over and over it and getting nowhere. Short of asking Phil if he had known them — and why on earth not, except for a gut feeling of not wanting to stir up suspicion in his mind — she had to go about this in a lateral way too. Like checking on his credentials and his background. So who could she ask? Not Ray Smart, for sure.

'I'll call you tomorrow, Nick,' she murmured into her pillow, seconds before she fell asleep.

* * *

'DCI Frobisher,' came his efficient voice at the other end of the line.

'Nick, can we talk?'

His tone altered at once. 'I thought I was coming down to see you soon. Don't tell me you've changed your mind — '

'No, of course not.'

Even if she'd completely forgotten it until this minute. 'I wondered if you could run a check on somebody for me? I don't think there's really anything wrong, but I'd feel easier if I knew for sure. I know I shouldn't ask — '

'What are friends for?' he put in. 'And if it means you're finally off the other dead loss affair, it'll be a plus, babe. What's the name?'

Alex was thankful he hadn't questioned whether or not this had anything to do with Steven Leng, and had just assumed it was a new case.

'Philip Cordell. He's in his mid-thirties, I'd say, and currently head of sports at St Joseph's teacher training college in Bristol. I'd like to know a bit more about him, in particular what his previous employment was — well, you get the idea.'

'It's a missing relative thing,' she added, when she didn't get any immediate response.

'I'll get back to you sometime, Alex, but I'm a bit tied up here now, so it may not be for a day or so. Sorry.'

'Oh yes, that's fine,' she said, even though it wasn't. 'It's just that I want to fill in a few blanks.'

He hung up, and she couldn't be sure if he believed that this was a new case or not. He had an uncanny way of sensing when she was uptight, or boiling with adrenalin at the thought that she might be on to something.

Right now, she had to admit she didn't really feel like that at all. It was just that she never ignored gut feelings, even when they sent her down a completely wrong trail. But sometimes they didn't.

She tried to assess Philip Cordell in her own mind. He was an upright citizen, as far as anyone could tell. But weren't they all? Even serial killers could look no different from the man — or woman — next door.

* * *

Chain reactions were the *pits*, she thought some time later. If it hadn't been for her instinctive call to the hospital to find out if Keith had survived, which in all common humanity, she had *had* to do, the night sister at the hospital wouldn't have reported to the local Bath police that there had been an enquiry from an unknown woman. And they wouldn't have registered the Bristol phone number and got on to their local branch to check her out. And she wouldn't have got the visit from DI Frank Gregory and one of his minions. Though since it was late the next evening, they certainly hadn't rushed, she thought, half-resentfully. Maybe they hoped to take her off guard at such an hour. Although of course, coppers never slept.

'Do they always send DIs out to investigate a perfectly innocent enquiry after a patient?' she countered the question, while she got her wits about her.

'It does when a patient is brought in after an overdose, and when the caller is known to us for meddling in a closed police investigation, and we'd like to know just what she was doing with a young man who was a known acquaintance of Steven Leng,' he snapped, his former pleasant manner gone in an instant.

The young constable with him was busily writing down everything that was said, Alex noted. She could have saved him the trouble by handing over her tape, but she was damned if she was going to be browbeaten by this arrogant attitude. Besides, it was still *her* investigation, and until she heard something more from Nick she was keeping everything under wraps.

'You know what I was doing,' she snapped back. 'You know very well I was looking into the Steven Leng case on his mother's behalf, and I'm still tying up loose ends.'

'There *are* no loose ends, Miss Best. The whole family is dead, so for Christ's sake let them rest in peace. And just for the record, I would remind you that if Keith Martin makes a complaint against you for harassment, you could find yourself in serious trouble.'

'Is that a threat, Mr Gregory?'

'It's a warning.'

And I wouldn't put it past you to get him to file a complaint against me either, you bastard.

'I'm only doing my job, the same as you're doing yours,' she said coldly.

He gave an elaborate sigh. 'You're becoming a nuisance, Miss Best. I advise you to leave things alone.'

'And they'll go away? Well, this case hasn't. Jane Leng saw to that — '

'And ended up dead,' he said brutally.

Alex stared at him. 'You said you'd got her killer. I identified the bogus window cleaner. I thought there was no doubt.'

'There isn't. But since he swore he thought the gun was loaded with blanks and that he'd just meant to scare the old girl, it may just be that someone else was pulling his strings. Or he may be a congenital liar. Take it or leave it.'

When they had gone, Alex was left thinking over those last remarks. Someone else pulling the killer's strings? Something similar had happened on her last case, and she knew damn well it happened with depressing frequency. Someone fired the gun and got done for the crime, but the real villain was the one who loaded it with bullets. Real bullets, not blanks. Who would have access to such things? It may be practically *de rigeur* in the States to have hand guns at home, but not here. Maybe a keen sportsman, a karate black belt, head of sports at a college, maybe someone who was a member of a bona fide gun club . . .

She was really letting her imagination go wild now, she thought angrily. Why would

Phil Cordell have the remotest interest in disposing of Jane Leng? He looked affluent enough, so presumably he didn't need her money. He hadn't seemed particularly interested in the Leng case, except for the usual probing she always got from people wanting to know what she did, and how she did it.

But he hadn't asked that, she thought suddenly. He'd just sent in Ray Smart, gullible, computer-mad Ray Smart, as her assistant — and just as quickly, Ray had backed out of the job because his parents hadn't liked the idea of him possibly getting into trouble. Or maybe Phil had decided he didn't need him there any more.

Her head was beginning to ache, because she still felt she was getting nowhere, and it was all pie in the sky, as so much investigation often was — leading her down wrong alleys and wasting time. Just like police probes, she thought, with a sliver of satisfaction. They hadn't found out what happened to Steven, either. But then the satisfaction faded, because maybe the trail really did end here. Keith had provided a lot more answers regarding the explosion from the calor gas bottles — but forensics had probably already got that on file. If so, it hadn't been reported in the press, which was nothing to write home about either. They weren't told everything.

She was sleeping fitfully when her mobile rang. Through squinting eyes she saw that it was just after half past five in the morning. It was far too early to start the day, she thought with a groan, so what now?

'Hello?' she croaked into her mobile.

'Did I wake you?' came Nick's voice.

She sat up too quickly and felt the room spin. 'Yes, but never mind about that. Have you found something?' It had to be important to call at such a time.

'Your Philip Cordell has quite a history, Alex. God knows how he managed to fool the authorities into giving him a college job, but the man's an accomplished liar so I daresay he created his own CV from previous fictitious employers.'

'I was right to be suspicious of him then,' she mumbled, still half awake. Not that it proved a thing, except that he was a clever con man. 'Is that all?'

'Not by a long shot. He's been in prison a couple of times for GBH and a bit of handling, and he's had a number of aliases — Patrick Walters and Grant Tobias to name but two. He's been clean for about six years now, but I wouldn't say he's the most savoury character you ever came in contact with.'

'I know.' She hesitated, and then it all came out in a rush. 'Nick, in case you get to hear it from that bastard Gregory, I went to see Keith Martin in Bath, and he ended up in hospital after a drugs overdose.'

'*Christ*, Alex, what's all this about now? I thought you wanted to know about this Cordell bloke — '

'I did. I do. But it came in the wake of my visit to Bath, and there's probably not the remotest connection — '

'I think you'd better tell me about this Martin geezer,' he snapped. 'No more hedging about now, Alex.'

She swallowed, feeling as if her mouth was as dry as the Sahara as she babbled it all out.

'All right. I wanted to hear his version of events, and I know I shouldn't have got him drunk, but he was such a nervy type I knew he was never going to tell me anything unless I did — but how the hell could I have guessed he'd take those pills? I thought he was just going to the bathroom to throw up — '

'And what did he tell you?' Nick said, cutting right through the waffle as usual.

'Nothing much. Well, quite a bit, actually.'

'I hope you taped it.'

'Yes,' she mumbled.

He was icily angry now. 'Well, now you've told me this much you'd better send me the tape by courier. *Do* it, Alex, first thing in the morning, and don't tell me I'm not involved.

If there's anything we don't know, you have a duty to pass on information. You know that, so don't give me any guff about client confidentiality. The client's dead.'

'I know,' she said miserably. 'And I failed her.'

'Rubbish. But it's time you realized you can't sort out the problems of the entire human race,' Nick told her a bit less censorially. 'We all do the best we can, Alex, and you should have left this one well alone. I told you that in the beginning, didn't I?'

'You did,' she said, humbly for her.

'Just send me that tape in the morning and I'll take it from there.'

'You mean you'll file it away and forget it.'

'Maybe. Maybe not. It depends what's on it.'

'Unfortunately the tape ran out before it got very far — and that's the truth, Nick,' she added, in case he thought it wasn't.

'Well, don't lose any sleep over it. I'll expect the tape tomorrow, OK?'

'OK,' she said.

But she was wide awake now, and reading through the lines she knew he was mightily keen to get his hands on that tape. It may be just to consign it to the recycle bin, she thought, with her new-found computer jargon, or it might not. In any case, she had no intention of sending him her only copy.

She got out of bed, shivering in the frosty early-morning air, and wrapped herself in her fleecy dressing-gown. This was no time for flimsy kimonos, and she pulled on some thick bootsocks as well before going down to her office with the tape, and setting up her machine to copy it on to two more separate tapes. Just for security.

Then she packed up the original, addressed it to DCI Frobisher, and looked up the name of a local courier firm to call as soon as it was daylight.

It was nearly that now, she realized, seeing signs of a pale dawn streaking the sky, and she wasn't going to get any more sleep. So she might as well turn on the computer and record all the information Nick had given her about Philip Cordell, which she found more and more disturbing.

There really was nothing to connect him with the group of boys who had set fire to an old hut in the woods for a lark. He would have been a lot older than they were, and she would hardly have called him a wino or a druggy . . . except for that one remark of Nick's. He had been in prison for GBH and handling, which could either mean stolen goods or drugs, and usually meant the latter.

Alex shivered, hating anything to do with

drugs. They were the worst thing ever to have come out of recent times, in her opinion, and ruined more lives than many diseases. It sent people out of control; made them do things they would never otherwise do; gave them a false sense of courage, bravado, or whatever; made them crazy; killed them.

She finished what she was doing and went back upstairs with the package containing the tape and the extra copies, putting them in separate places in her flat, just in case. She took a hot shower and made some black coffee to wake her up properly, and then as her stomach rumbled she decided to give in to a proper cooked breakfast as her Aunt Harriet would have said sternly, none of this going to work on a breath of fresh air.

She couldn't have said why Aunt Harriet came into her thoughts just then. Nor why she was still smiling when she went to answer her phone, and heard her cousin Jed's nasal Yorkshire voice.

'Is that our Audrey?'

18

The next hours passed in a total haze for Alex. She called the nearest motorbike courier and prowled around aimlessly until nine o'clock when he'd promised to collect the tape. By then she had called Nick, who said if she wanted to get off earlier, she could always take the tape round to DI Gregory.

'No,' she said, choked. 'It's you or nobody, Nick.'

'All right. Anyway, I'm sorry to hear your news, Alex, but you're not seriously thinking of driving to Yorkshire in this weather, are you? By all accounts it's pretty atrocious up there.'

'What would you have me do? Sit here twiddling my thumbs when I've just heard that my uncle's had a heart attack? I do have family feelings, Nick. Besides, they're all I've got left, and my cousin says his mother's in an awful state.'

She still couldn't picture it. Aunt Harriet was always strong and stoical, the competent daleswoman, capable of dealing with wind, weather and underlings. But according to Jed, she had completely gone to pieces when she found Uncle Bill frozen stiff as a board in the snow in one of his chicken houses.

'Dead as a dodo, he were, with feathers stuck all over him, and been there for hours, so the doctor said,' Jed had declared graphically. 'Me ma's crying all over the place and Amy and her Vic ain't much help, muttering and whispering and not knowing what to do for the best. Folk should be together at such times, so she thought you ought to know, you still being one of us, so to speak, and more sensible than most.'

'Of course I'm still one of you,' Alex had said, ignoring the bizarre turn of his conversation and trying not to visualize Uncle Bill, stiff as a board in the snow with chicken feathers stuck all over him as if he was taking part in some music-hall farce. 'Tell Aunt Harriet I'm going to throw a few things in a bag and I'll be with you just as soon as I can get there.'

She hadn't stopped to think. She just knew how it was when her dad died when they were all distraught, and had clung to one another for comfort and support. And if the rest of them weren't being much help, then Aunt Harriet would need her now. The sensible one, so to speak — though it was a long time since any of them had called her that, with her fancy boots and her soft southern lifestyle.

'Why don't you catch a train, Alex?' Nick's voice broke into her thoughts.

'What, and get stuck for hours while they go slow or break down or clear leaves from the line? No thanks. Besides, I'm not wasting time finding out about train times, so forget it. I'm leaving just as soon as your bloody courier arrives to collect the package. I wish I'd never told you anything about it now, then I'd have been on my way an hour ago.'

Everything else had to be put on hold: her vague intention of calling Keith Martin again to see if he was safely home, and to find out if he knew someone called Philip Cordell . . . or even taking him by surprise at his flat one evening and demanding to know more, since he'd already told her so much; her even vaguer plan of checking out the site where the incident had happened ten years ago and doing a little surveying of the area herself . . . none of it was so important as being with Aunt Harriet right now.

She smothered a sob, and knew how fond she still was of them all, deep down. The older ones, anyway, she amended. Amy and Jed were all right in small doses — they were family. She disliked Vic, but he was totally forgettable, and she found it easy enough to blot him out of her mind.

The sound of a motorbike startled her for a moment, with thoughts of Phil Cordell still lingering, but she saw that it was the courier arriving, and she handed over the package thankfully and got the necessary receipt for it. For a wistful moment, she wished it could have been her old mate Gary Hollis in his courier gear. It would be good to meet up again, and she remembered she'd missed the opportunity in refusing Charmaine's party invitation.

She realized that her thoughts were coming in disjointed bursts now, and she told herself severely that it was no way to be when she was about to drive on a long journey. Nick's idea of letting the train take the strain might suit some people, but being behind the wheel had its own way of calming her nerves, if only because she had to damn well concentrate and couldn't allow herself to think of much else.

* * *

Six hours later she was being ushered inside a warm and steamy farmhouse after a horrendous journey through driving sleet and snow, and had folded her Aunt Harriet in her arms. She had always thought her aunt a fairly tall and broad woman, but right now she seemed to have crumbled.

'I'll be all right in a bit,' she sniffed into Alex's ears. 'But I'm right glad to see you, lass, and so would he have been.'

He being Uncle Bill, Alex realized.

'Do you want to see him? He's not so bad looking now he's been cleaned and tidied and dressed in his Sunday best — '

'He's still here?' Alex said with a small start. What was wrong with funeral parlours and chapels of rest?

'Where else would he be but in his own home? They'll be taking him out of it soon enough.'

She gave a deep sigh. They had had a long marriage and shared a hard life, but love was there all the same, as strong as the soil they farmed. Alex knew they had never been folk for showing feelings, and it wouldn't be long before Aunt Harriet was back to normal, on the surface at least, hiding whatever she felt inside.

'I'd rather not see him if you don't mind,' Alex murmured. 'It will remind me too much of my Dad.' In any case viewing the corpse was nothing short of ghoulish in Alex's opinion.

Her aunt stared at her through red-rimmed eyes, seeing all the cowardice there was to see

— and the shame of it for not wanting to see a loved uncle dead in his coffin. And she finally nodded, understanding.

'Oh well, you'll not be forgetting him, I daresay, and if you'd rather remember him the way he was, we'll have some tea to warm us and then you can tell me how long you're staying. The funeral's next week, providing the ground's not too frozen for the men to dig his plot.'

Alex began to feel slightly hysterical. It had been a long and traumatic drive, she was tired and hungry and dying for a pee — and she was too afraid to go upstairs to the bathroom for fear of glancing into one of the bedrooms and seeing Uncle Bill laid out in his coffin. She should be ashamed.

'It's all right, lass,' Aunt Harriet said more gently. 'I daresay you see all sorts in your job, but 'tis different when 'tis one of your own, isn't it?'

'Yes,' Alex whispered. 'Oh, Aunt Harriet, I'm so sorry.'

'Aye, I know you are, but we all have to go sometime, Audrey, and your uncle's had a good innings. He always said it was the way he wanted to go, so how can we argue with that? He's in the front room, by the way, so you'll not find him upstairs if you want to put your things in the spare room.'

Alex fled, even more ashamed at her aunt's calm words, and feeling as vulnerable as when she was about six years old, when she'd come here to play with her cousins and her Uncle Bill had gently chaffed her for not wanting to help him feed the chickens. And now he'd been found dead in the snow, as stiff as a board with feathers stuck all over him, in one of his own chicken houses.

Bizarre wasn't the word for it, she thought, as the weak tears rolled down her cheeks. She was nothing like the tough nut someone in her profession was supposed to be. She had stood dry-eyed at Jane Leng's funeral, because it hadn't touched her personally, and she'd despised the way the obnoxious Grace and hubby had cried their crocodile tears. She'd been at the scene of other deaths, during her job, and at police investigations. She had attended funerals out of respect. But this was different. This was family. Her flesh and blood.

* * *

After a few days Alex realized just how stoical her aunt was, and admired her all the more because of it. She was continually irritated by her cousins whom she didn't admire at all, except that she knew very well they would rally round and look after Aunt Harriet as much as she allowed them to. But she knew she couldn't stand it here very much longer. She was stifled by the atmosphere of gloom and the deadpan faces, and by the people who came along to pay their respects to Uncle Bill, and looked her up and down and exclaimed at how bonny she was looking — whatever they secretly thought.

Translated, it meant that she looked far too slick and citified to be part of this close-knit farming community. She didn't belong any more, and she longed to get back to her own kind of normality, whatever that meant to a private eye. As soon as she could get away without feeling she was letting them down.

On the day of the funeral, thankfully not delayed because of frozen ground, her aunt spoke to her firmly when they had returned to the farm with neighbours and friends for the usual tea and sandwiches. She spoke with a sense of relief that a good man had been sent to his rest with all due dignity, and all the tears were done.

'You'll be needing to get back to Bristol now, Audrey,' Harriet said, 'and we won't delay you. I've been right glad to have you here, but your uncle wouldn't want you staying any longer on his account, nor mine.'

'I could stay another few days if you really wanted me to,' she said diffidently, praying that her aunt wouldn't take her up on it, but feeling obliged to make the gesture.

To her surprise, she got an unexpected kiss on the cheek.

'You're a good lass, Audrey, but I've got Jed here with me, and Amy and Vic will be looking in most days, so bless you for the thought. But mebbe the next time we see you, it'll be with happier news.'

Alex looked at her blankly and her aunt gave a small smile.

'Mebbe wedding bells? You're not getting any younger, and I daresay there's some young man who's got his eye on you. You come from good stock, Audrey, and you've got good child-bearing hips, so don't wait for ever.'

'I won't,' Alex said in a strangled voice, wondering whether it was appropriate to laugh or to feel totally insulted. In the end she did neither, but said that if her aunt was quite sure, she'd be leaving in the morning.

* * *

'She said what?' Nick said, when she reached home late the following afternoon and called him on his mobile just to hear a friendly voice.

'Child-bearing hips,' Alex repeated solemnly. 'And before you say any more, no, I'm not looking for a husband.'

'I wasn't offering,' he retorted. 'Anyway, are you really all right?'

'Well, apart from coming back to a freezing cold flat, yes. So what did you think of the tape?'

He hesitated before answering. 'Alex, I'm sorry — '

'You've sent it to Gregory, haven't you?' she said furiously. 'Nick, how could you? This is still my case — '

'Just listen a minute. There have been developments,' he said, in careful police-code for big news, 'and since you've had your mobile switched off for the past week I couldn't speak to you, and I didn't want to worry you at this time by sending a text message — '

'What's happened? For Pete's sake, just tell me.'

'Keith Martin was badly beaten up at his flat the night he got out of hospital, so he was taken straight back in again. It was touch and go at the time.'

'My God! Do they know who did it?'

Nick was grim. 'They're pretty sure *he*

knows, but he's not telling. Somebody scared the shit out of him, and he's being closer than a clam now.'

'Doesn't that prove something?' she said, adrenalin shooting through her again, reviving her.

'Yes. Leave it alone, Alex.'

She wouldn't commit herself to any such demands. Instead she changed tactics swiftly. 'When are you coming down here, Nick? I really miss you. After the homespun week I've just had, apart from my concern for my aunt, of course, I desperately need a bit of not-so-platonic company.'

She was damn sure Uncle Bill wouldn't have objected. Life went on, and in a farming community that was very much the way of things. She had heard his blunt philosophy often enough. You were born, you lived, and then you died. And if you didn't make the most of the time the man upstairs gave you, you didn't deserve to enter the pearly gates. Whether or not his views included making rampant love outside of wedlock, Alex didn't choose to question.

As she waited for Nick's reply, she knew he wouldn't have missed the fact that she didn't promise him to leave the case alone. But hopefully he would overlook it. She also knew she was being blatantly provocative with her invitation, and if he didn't respond, she'd start to think she was losing her touch.

She heard his low sexy chuckle, and felt her nerves settle. 'Thank God you're back on form, babe. With any luck I'll see you the weekend after next. There's no chance before then, but keep the bed warm for me. Better still, keep it good and hot.'

She was smiling as she hung up, but she sobered at once, remembering what he had told her. Keith Martin had been beaten up, and it was a sure bet it was somebody who was getting scared he'd start saying more than he should. But how did they know? Unless someone had been watching him — and her.

It was a less than comfortable thought, and one that she didn't want to dwell on. But she intended going to Bath tomorrow to find out just what else there was to know, and also to find out who had beaten him up. It was as well to know who they were both up against.

* * *

When she entered his hardware shop, she took one look at his bruised and battered face, the two black eyes and the broken nose, and gasped.

'What do you want?' he said stiffly through

the painful working of his jaw. 'I've got nothing more to say to you.'

'Keith, I'm so sorry this happened. You look terrible, and why haven't you closed the shop?'

'I have to earn a living, don't I?' he said sullenly. 'Now bugger off.'

His eyes watered, and he involuntarily held his ribs. Whoever had beaten him up had done a bloody good job, but she sensed that by now he was angry rather than scared.

'We never finished our conversation, did we? And I *did* save your life by getting an ambulance here for you, remember?' She was relentless now. 'You owe me for that, and you still need to rest, and I daresay you find it difficult to eat too. Look, close the shop and I'll make you a hot drink, or some soup — or whatever you want — as long as it's not pills. A couple of hours isn't going to make or break you, is it?'

She thought he was going to refuse, but then he shrugged and staggered across to the door, turned the Open sign to Closed on the window, and pulled down the blind.

'I've chucked out the pills, if you must know,' he said. 'I've done with all that for good. And no tape recorder, mind.'

Alex held her breath, wondering if this was an obscure way of telling her she was going to get at the truth at last. It took him a while to climb the stairs to his flat, holding his ribs all the way, but he finally eased himself into a chair and told her there were some tins of chicken soup in the cupboard. Once she had heated one up and served it to him, she had to wait while he painfully consumed it. It was like watching a child eat, Alex thought, in a fever of impatience.

'All right, Keith, so let's get down to it, shall we? I know you didn't tell the police who had done this to you, but my guess is that it was one of the Wilkins' brothers, right? I know they beat you up once before, and maybe you didn't tell the police that at the time, either.'

'Good guess,' he grunted.

'And the right one?'

When he didn't answer, she took it as a yes.

'So what is it they don't want anyone to know? Did they kill Steven Leng?' she asked brutally.

'Good God, no!' She had shocked him into a reaction now, his eyes as wide as they could go, considering the swelling that had reduced them to little more than slits. 'They weren't killers. None of us were. We were kids — '

'Kids can kill. It's not an exclusive adult activity.'

'We were just having a lark and it all went

wrong,' he said, in a panic now. 'Why must you rake it all up again? I want to forget it.'

'Mrs Leng didn't, though. It broke her heart, not knowing what had become of Steven. Can you imagine how that felt, Keith? The awfulness of not knowing? Not having the finality of burying her son, and always wondering, always imagining she could see him, in shops, on TV, always searching — '

'*Shut up!* Don't keep on about it!'

'Tell me what happened then. What really happened. You do know, don't you? Or do you want to live in fear for the rest of your life because of a stupid pact some schoolboys made years ago? That's not being very adult, is it? What happened to John Barnett, Keith?' she said, changing direction.

She saw him flinch. 'He was in a motorbike accident.'

'Do you believe it was an accident? Or was he too anxious about keeping quiet, the same as you've been all this time?'

'If he was, look what happened to him!' he lashed out. 'Do you think I want to risk that?'

'So you'd rather live in fear for the rest of your life, and risk the beatings from the likes of Cliff and Dave, would you?'

She was being a bitch of an interrogator and she knew it, and it wasn't fair when the poor guy was hurting and vulnerable. But if she didn't strike now, she knew it would be too late. One way or another.

'John had got unnerved about the whole thing and was threatening to go to the police, and Lennie tried to stop him. He was well in with this cult thing by then, and had got friendly with a guy called Patrick who was also involved in it. John called me one night and said this Patrick had put the wind up him, though he'd tried to brazen it out and said he'd tell if he wanted to. John said he was evil and warned me to watch out for him. He never got in touch with me though.'

He swallowed. 'Next thing I knew I got an anonymous phone call to say John had been pushed off the road on his motorbike and been killed. That was all, but I knew it was a threat to me, and I've kept my mouth shut ever since.'

Patrick . . . Alex knew there was something she should remember about the name, but for the moment it eluded her. And anyway, she was too near the brink of the truth to waste time on it for now. She spoke softly now.

'So what did happen to Steven, Keith? Your friend, remember?'

'I don't know, and that's the truth. But we'd discovered this well, see?'

It took a moment for her to register what he meant.

'Well? As in wishing-well, you mean?'

'No. Just an old well right behind the hut. There was no water in it and it was overgrown with weeds. But the druggies used to stash their stuff there, and we knew that. We sometimes helped ourselves, just for a lark.'

'Some lark,' Alex said. 'Didn't you ever stop to think how stupid that was?'

He had clearly given up pretending that he never took it, she noted. She had honoured his request not to have her tape recorder switched on, but she had a good memory and she was already halfway to the site in her mind. As he glowered at her, looking more like a gargoyle than ever with his battered face and piggy eyes now, she pressed on.

'So in your opinion, Keith, as a concerned friend, do you think it possible that Steven ended up down the well?' *Most of him*, she added silently.

'I don't know. It's possible, I suppose. The thing is, after the explosion the whole area was flattened and nobody ever mentioned a well in the reports. There was no way the druggies were going to complain about their stuff, and we weren't telling, either, or we'd be implicated in it, wouldn't we?'

'So you preferred to go off on your camping trip and forget all about your friend, did you?'

'It wasn't like that! I told you we thought he'd just gone home. It was only weeks later that we started putting two and two together, especially when his hand was found,' he said with a shudder, his breathing becoming rattled.

Alex saw him flex his jaw painfully, and he looked truly ghastly now. But she hadn't quite finished with him yet.

'You do know you've been withholding evidence, don't you, Keith? All of you. If you knew of the existence of this well, you should have told the police, and they would have found Steven's body right away — '

'I never said it was there, and you don't know it for certain.'

'But it's highly likely, isn't it?'

He didn't answer, and she knew it had to be right. But for one simple piece of information about a dry, overgrown well close to an old hut, this whole case would have been solved ten years ago. And Jane Leng wouldn't have gone to her grave never knowing what had happened to her son.

'I'm sorry, Keith,' she said, 'but I have to let the police know what you've told me. I imagine that an ordnance survey map of the area would show the existence of a well, but without your diclosure of it at the time, there would have been no reason for anyone to check on such a thing, would there?'

Appalled, she saw that he was crying now. With a temperament like his, he must have been going through hell all these years, and those so-called friends of his had attributed to it with their adolescent pact.

'Will you be all right?' she said, more gently. 'If you'd like me to stay for a while — '

'I want you to *go*, you bitch! I never want to see you again,' he raged, awash with humiliation at being seen like this.

'All right, and I'm sure someone will be contacting you soon. When they do, just tell them what you've told me, Keith, as calmly as possible — '

'*Get out!*' he screamed.

She obeyed hastily, aware that she was leaving him practically dissolving in his own misery and pain. She let herself out of the shop and walked quickly around the corner of the road to where she had cautiously left her car, rather than park it right outside. She was filled with pity for him, but she couldn't deny that it was pity marred by contempt.

She sank into the driving seat of her car, far more shaken than she had expected. It had all been so simple — if it was true. And she had no reason to think that it wasn't. She collated the facts in her mind. It was feasible enough, what with the fireworks and the huge explosion from the calor gas bottles. The boys had been hyperactive and hallucinated at the time, and probably none of them knew exactly where the others were.

Steven could easily have gone back inside the hut for something, or been near enough to the well to have been caught in the blast, blowing him to bits, and sending his hand hurtling through the air to some unknown destination until it was found weeks later, while the rest of him was disintegrating inside the collapsed well . . .

Then the vigorous attentions of the fire brigade had put paid to whatever other evidence there was, in a frantic need to quench the inferno before the whole wooded area became a forest fire in the tinder-dry air.

It was all feasible, however bizarre it seemed, and Alex found herself breathing erratically at the thought of just what those stupid kids had done in trying to cover up their involvement with dubious characters.

She started up her car, her eyes blurring with the horror of it all, and narrowly missed colliding with another car coming the other way. She hardly registered it. She knew she had to get back to Bristol and report her discussion with Keith Martin to DI Gregory. It was no longer her case. There was too much involved now, and if it was a criminal affair, then it was one that the police had to sort out.

She was nearly home before something triggered in her mind something she should have registered at once, if she hadn't been so intent on pushing Keith to the limit to answer her questions. She was remembering it clearly now. A guy called Patrick had been involved with the Followers and with Lennie, and John Barnett had called Keith and told him a guy called Patrick had warned him to keep his mouth shut. But John hadn't. And then John was killed.

And Patrick was one of the aliases of Philip Cordell.

19

Alex felt too agitated to go straight home. Once she reached Bristol she drove to the Downs and parked her car overlooking the suspension bridge and the dizzying drop to the river, from where Bob Leng had thrown himself. She sat there for more than an hour while she decided what to do next. In her heart she knew, but she was still reluctant to give up everything.

But in the end, she knew she had to do it. She drove slowly down the winding streets to the local nick and asked to see DI Gregory, and after he had kept her waiting a good half hour while she fumed, she related everything Keith Martin had told her in a torrent of words.

He sat with folded arms, looking at her as if she was an imbecile, and she had to admit she wasn't at her coolest.

'Do you really think we didn't scour the area for every bit of evidence at the time, young woman? Do you think we were unaware of the locale and even the old mine workings in that part of Somerset?'

'Old mine workings?' This was news to her.

'Forget it. They were abandoned or filled in years ago. All played out — '

'But what about an old well? If it had been somewhere in the vicinity of old mine workings, then maybe it would have collapsed even farther than was believed, taking Steven Leng with it. Did you know of this well's existence, Mr Gregory? I never saw any mention of it in the newspaper archives.'

She knew she was skating on thin ice. Coppers didn't like their research questioned, and in particular they didn't like young and headstrong female private investigators casting doubt on their results.

'I'm sorry,' she said quickly as she saw his eyes flash. 'But it seems to me that this was an easy thing to have overlooked, and if Keith Martin hadn't mentioned it none of us would ever have known.'

She let him off the hook, since it didn't matter to her either way who got the credit for this now. She just wanted the whole thing over and done with, and to get on with her life.

Finally he nodded. 'All right, Miss Best, we'll look into it. I require you to make a statement about what you've just told us, and I shall need confirmation from Keith Martin himself, of course. And after that I insist — *insist*, do you hear? — that you leave everything to us. Is that completely understood?'

'Of course. And don't forget Patrick's part in all this. Patrick Walters,' she emphasized.

She wanted him to register the name, but she didn't dare say in her statement that she suspected that Patrick Walters and Philip Cordell, respected Head of Sports at St Joseph's College, were one and the same. If she did, he would want to know how she knew that, and she couldn't drop Nick in it.

The police were jealous of guarding their sources, and she got too many privileges as it was, through Nick. But if Gregory was as astute as she thought, he'd start looking him up in police files and discover it for himself.

She left his office, feeling suddenly weak at the knees. It had been quite a time, what with the long drive back from Yorkshire after Uncle Bill's funeral, then hearing the news of Keith's beating and confronting him on his home territory. It was only when she was breathing heavily in the cold February air that she realized she was shaking and that it was hours since she'd had anything to eat. She had skipped lunch, and food must be her next priority.

'Miss Best! Just a minute, please.'

She heard her name being called as she was

unlocking her car. A police constable was running after her.

'What is it?'

'DI Gregory wants another word with you.'

Oh God, what now? Home and food had never seemed so attractive, but in the words of Rumpole of the Bailey, it was a case of *she who must be obeyed*, only in this case it was *he*. And she knew better than to ignore it.

Gregory was replacing the phone, when she returned to his office. His face was grimmer than before when he turned to her.

'That was the Bath police. A neighbour reported hearing a shot from Martin's hardware shop some time ago. They discovered that Keith Martin has been shot through the head at close range.'

She wasn't dumb enough to ask whether he was dead, just dumb enough to lose the faculty of speech for the moment. But her imagination wasn't so dumb. Being shot through the head wasn't the clean and tidy method of death as depicted in TV dramas, when the camera conveniently veered out of range for viewers' sensitivities. Being shot through the head at close range meant blood and brains being splattered over walls and floors and ceilings and anyone who happened to be standing near enough to catch the full disgusting blast . . .

'Miss Best, are you all right?'

She heard his voice as if through a haze, and then it rasped: 'Catch her, Constable. And then fetch a glass of water.'

She struggled to keep control of her senses, and sat down heavily on a chair, embarrassed and ashamed at such a show of weakness. She wouldn't pass out like some Victorian maiden in a novel about to swoon at the thought of a man . . . except that in this case it wasn't a lover, but a corpse, and one that she had seen alive and well, give or take some hideous bruises, several hours ago.

'Well? What have you got to say about this?' Gregory snapped at her, when she had recovered.

'You don't think I pulled the trigger, do you? I'd say you were a pretty good alibi, Mr Gregory.'

He wasn't, of course. The timing was wrong.

'No, I don't think you did it,' he was angry now. 'But in view of this happening and what you've already told us, I do think it's high time the rest of that infantile group was interviewed further and the investigation reopened. And by us. Do I make myself clear?'

'Perfectly,' Alex murmured, knowing this was his one concession that she could be right. 'I'm free to go then? You're not thinking of putting me in a cell for the night for safe keeping?'

'Flippancy will get you nowhere, and I'd advise you to remember that.'

As she reached the door she could hear him already going through the motions of getting a team together, barking out orders to his minions to look up files, to check addresses, and to put everything else on hold. Thank God. At last someone was taking Jane Leng's obsession seriously.

* * *

It was getting towards dusk when she got back to her car and she slid inside it thankfully. It was bitterly cold and she was ravenous by now, and she was distressed over what had happened to Keith Martin. He wasn't a likeable person, but nobody deserved to be shot in the head at close range, or any other range. But as she began to drive slowly in streets that were sparkling with frost, there was also a huge feeling of relief that it was in someone else's hands now. Whatever the outcome of it all the police would deal with it.

She felt the coldness in her neck at the same time as she heard the soft voice behind her. In a split second she had glanced in her mirror and seen the shadowy figure in the back seat of her car. In the same split second she remembered that she had gone back into the police station without locking it, and that the coldness in her neck was something very solid and very lethal — and probably the same gun that had recently blown Keith Martin's brains out.

'Drive, Miss Best,' the voice said in a husky whisper.

'I am driving,' she croaked. 'I'm going home — '

'Oh, I don't think so.'

'Where then?' she said, swallowing dryly.

'Don't you know?'

She was getting tired of this cat and mouse game, but not too tired to know that with one false move she could end up like Keith Martin. The thought of leaning on the horn, or veering her car and smashing it into the side of the road to alert passers-by didn't appeal, either. If this guy was as ruthless as she suspected, she'd be dead meat in a moment.

'I'm not a mind-reader!' she snapped, trying to ignore the ferociously rapid beat of her heart.

She glanced into her mirror again as they passed through some street lights, and saw the streaked highlights in his hair. Phil Cordell's hair. And she remembered instantly the big car that she had almost collided with in her haste to get away from Bath.

She had only noticed it peripherally, but the memory clicked in now. It had been a people mover with darkened windows. Phil Cordell's car, on its way to Martin's hardware shop to do the bloody murder of a simple guy. *Bastard*.

'Where are we going, then?' she stuttered. 'If you don't tell me, I shall just keep driving round in circles until the petrol runs out.'

And where were petrol blockades and shortages when you needed them?

'Wilkins' Haulage Company, bitch. I thought you might have worked that out already, since you're so clever.'

Alex swallowed. The image flashed into her mind of the last time she had been there with Ray Smart, when they had looked down from the road to the huge, water-filled quarry pit. But with the constant jab of steel pressing into her neck, she knew better than to refuse the command.

She supposed that to any outsiders, especially in the gloom of dusk now, they would just appear to be two people in a car, with the rear seat passenger leaning forward to give her directions. There was no way anyone would suspect that her passenger was Phil Cordell, respected teacher-cum-killer.

'Did you have to kill Keith Martin?' she said, before she could stop herself.

The gun stabbed into her neck, making her wince.

'Shut up and drive. You know the way.'

She saw the road sign to Backwell lit up by her headlights and she followed it in silence until she saw the turn-off she needed. Her petrol indicator *was* right down on empty, she noted with a sudden flare of hope. But even if the car stopped, what would she do and where would she go? Instead, she drove as slowly as she dared in the narrow lanes, praying she would hear the scream of police sirens behind her.

'Speed up,' Phil ordered.

'I can't, unless you want me to skid off the road. There's been heavy rain, in case you hadn't noticed, and we're in farming country now. They drive cattle through these lanes, and I don't fancy ending up in a pile of cowshit.'

Terror made her coarser than usual, and she bit her lip at being reduced to it by this lout. How could she ever have found him remotely attractive?

She heard him give a low chuckle.

'I always thought there was an earthy slut

beneath that classy exterior. If we had more time I'd put it to the test — '

'Screw you,' she said vehemently. 'If you think I'd fancy you in a million years — '

She cried out as he jabbed her harder with the gun and her neck throbbed.

'We could end this here and now, Alex,' he said, more harshly, 'but I don't want to deny my friends the pleasure of seeing you do it for yourself.'

'What do you mean?' she stuttered.

'You're not so good at guessing after all, are you? You're going to drive your car straight into the quarry pit. Do you know how deep it is? If not, let me inform you — '

'You're mad,' Alex said, panic-stricken now. 'You'll never get away with this. The police know where I am — '

'Oh, I don't think so. You left them playing their guessing games as usual, so don't give me that. You might as well get used to it, my dear Miss Best. You're going to die.'

His gloating words had the strange effect of calming Alex slightly. If she was going to die, then she was damn well going to hear the truth before it happened. It mustn't have been all a waste of time. And in her experience, pitiful though it seemed now, murderers relished explaining themselves. Otherwise, where was the glory? She shuddered, but forced herself to ask the question.

'So what did happen to Steven Leng?' she said in a choked voice. 'I'm quite sure you were involved, so don't pretend that you weren't.'

'Full marks! I think you'd nearly got there too. What a shame,' he said with mock regret. 'You're right, of course, and those bloody kids became far too interfering. Lennie and I had a good thing going. He was a good disciple — '

'Of the Followers, you mean?'

'Oh, that was just a convenient blind,' he sneered. 'I'm talking about my own operation.'

So much for peace and harmony then. Alex gripped the steering-wheel more tightly as the car slid on the muddy road surface in these sheltered lanes.

'Drugs, I suppose. You've been done before for handling, haven't you?'

The gun jabbed her again, though it could have been simply due to the uneven surface of the lanes they were driving through at a crawl now.

'You have been busy, haven't you! Yes, they'd been pinching my stuff, and I wasn't having any of that. Steven was Lennie's little hanger-on, and I think he wanted to prove himself by going back for more after they set the fireworks off. Only then the hut went up like an erupting volcano and he disappeared.'

'Down the well,' Alex supplied. Ding dong bell.

'Probably. Who knows? And who cares? It wasn't murder, anyway. It was an accident, and nobody can prove otherwise. And that's enough talking,' he said aggressively, his almost dreamy manner vanishing like magic as they approached the lane overlooking the Wilkins' Haulage Company.

Just as before, from the higher vantage point, Alex could see the impressive office building, the yard with its lorries totally still now at this time of day, and some distance beyond it, the quarry pit. It was quite dark now, but there was a thin sliver of moon in the sky, enough to light up the milky water of the fathoms-deep quarry pit.

As her car's headlights approached, three people emerged from the office building. She saw the two bullish Wilkins brothers, and a third man, whose blond hair was distinctive and recognizable at once. Lennie Fry.

'How did he get here?' Alex croaked.

'Oh, we had already decided it was time we co-ordinated ourselves and got rid of a few troublesome meddlers. A few phone calls did the rest.'

'And the troublesome meddlers included Keith Martin, did it? The poor sap wouldn't have done you any harm — '

'But he already had, you see. He'd talked to you.'

The soft, silky voice was more menacing than if he'd shouted at her. She longed for the safety of her own fireside, and doubted that she would ever see it again. She had never felt so vulnerable, and so sick with fear. If they were outside the car maybe she could have tackled him with karate, except that he was a black belt and she was well out of practice. They said it was like sex though. Once you'd done it, you never forgot how.

Her thoughts were disjointed and hysterical, and she was light-headed through the combination of a lack of food and sheer terror. They had reached the yard now, the three men were moving forward, and there was no escape . . .

'Stop the car. I'm getting out of it now,' Phil said in a hard voice, 'and you will continue driving to the edge of the quarry pit — '

'I bloody well will not!' Alex snapped, with a last attempt at bravado as she felt the hot, humiliating gush of urine inside her trousers. 'Do you think I'm completely off my head?'

'It makes no difference. There's enough

brawn here to do the job for you.'

Alex realized that the others had circled the car now. Cliff and David Wilkins flanked the driver and front passenger doors, and Lennie was at the rear, where presumably he and Phil would assist in pushing her car over the edge of the quarry pit into the deep, murky, freezing waters below.

Phil got out and slammed the car door, making her jump.

'Goodbye, Miss Best,' he shouted, and she saw the leering faces of the others as they began to manhandle her car forward. She slammed on the brake, but it made no difference. It simply went inexorably forward, and some mad instinct of saving her precious wheels from spinning and overheating made her take the brake off again. It was *completely* mad, in the circumstances, but she wasn't thinking sanely any more. Preservation was uppermost in what semblance of sanity she still had, for herself, and for this bloody car that was her pride and joy.

She was sure she was screaming inside as she saw the quarry pit approaching . . . except that it wasn't the pit approaching her, of course, it was the other way around, she thought incoherently. Or maybe she was screaming out loud. Or maybe it wasn't her at all, but the scream of something outside herself. Something that wasn't human at all.

In the next instant she realized the four men had let go of the car and were no longer forcing it towards the edge of the quarry pit. They had turned and run, and the whole area behind her and the slope leading down to the quarry was being filled with lights as police cars thundered towards the yard with all lights blazing.

It was the cavalry coming over the hill, she thought dizzily.

Then she realized that her car was fast gathering momentum on the slope towards the quarry pit, and there was no time to think about grabbing the brake again. Somehow her brain told her that if she did so, the car would probably go into a spin and end up submerged anyway. There was only one choice left.

She grabbed the door handle, opened it, and hurled herself out, seconds before the Suzuki upended itself like a splendidly miniature *Titanic* and disappeared from sight. She found herself scrabbling on the ground, clutching at mud to stop herself rolling over and following it, and sobbing into the filth as if she was making some glorious supplication.

Which she was, damn it. She *was*.

The next moment someone was pulling her

to her feet and yelling for a blanket to put around her. She could hardly see for the blindness of tears and mud clogging her eyes. All she could register was an overwhelming relief that she was alive by a hair's breadth, and that she was being held tightly in someone's arms. If she hadn't been, her knees would have buckled like the rest of her.

'Damn foolish young woman,' she heard Frank Gregory shout in her ear. 'But you're all right now, my dear, and we'll have these four bastards for attempted murder, if nothing else.'

Was that finally a touch of compassion for her in his voice? She hardly cared. What she desperately wanted was to crawl into bed and hide away like a wounded animal, since she had truly thought she was never going to have any of it again. But she couldn't quite let it go at that, even if she'd lost her bloody tape recorder and her bag, and everything else in her car. She heard herself give a high-pitched laugh, because it was such a paltry worry, when she'd just escaped with her life.

'You're feeling hysterical now, and understandably so,' Gregory said, as if he sensed the onset of typical female reaction.

'No, you don't understand at all,' she said through chattering lips. 'You have to question

Philip Cordell about drugs. And Lennie Fry — '

'Miss Best, you really can leave it all to us now,' he said, quite gently for him.

'And you'll excavate the old well to see if Steven did end up in there?' she persisted, even though her head seemed to be floating somewhere above her body now as he steered her towards a waiting police car.

Out of the corner of her eye she could see the four men being bundled none too carefully inside a larger police wagon. Thank God.

'Everything will be taken care of, Alex. Now let's get you home, and I'll arrange for a WPC to spend the night with you.'

'I don't want anybody — '

But she did. She knew she did. She wanted Nick, but she knew she couldn't have him, because he was miles away in London. And since she couldn't bear to be alone, she succumbed to having the WPC stay with her.

* * *

She told the woman she would never sleep anyway, knowing that her nerves were as taut as violin strings. She spent half an hour in the bath, weeping like a baby because she couldn't stop, and made no protest when the buxom WPC helped her out and dried her, pushed her unresisting arms into her nightdress and tucked her up in bed with a hot water bottle. She might have been back home on the farm with her mother's ministrations, or Aunt Harriet's, and that started the weeping again until she fell into an exhausted sleep.

Sometime towards dawn she awoke with a mild feeling of horror, because she was no longer alone in her bed.

Even though that person was on top of the bedclothes and she was inside them, someone was holding her tightly, and she prayed that she hadn't been mistaken in her assessment of the WPC . . .

'I thought you were never going to wake up,' she heard a familiar voice say close to her cheek.

'*Nick!* How did you get here? Oh *Nick* — ' she babbled, the weak tears starting again as yesterday's memory flooded in.

'Hush darling, you're quite safe now. Gregory called me as soon as they got you home. Apparently you'd been practically delirious in the police car, and were asking for me. I was flattered,' he said, making a joke of it, but the deepening of his voice betrayed how worried he'd been. 'I sent the WPC home, by the way. I got my leave brought forward and extended, and I'm here now.'

'Thank God. It was so awful, Nick,' she said with a violent shudder, the images still too vivid in her mind to dismiss.

'I know. I heard. And you'll be needing a new car now too.'

She managed a small grin at the incongruous remark. But she knew it was his way of dealing with things. Bringing her back to basics. To normality. Diffusing a bad situation. Caring for her.

'I do love you, Nick.'

'I know. And I love you too.'

And somehow she knew he recognized her words for what they were. The love of a dear friend. Maybe more. Maybe not. But not now.

Without warning she felt her stomach rumble, and they both heard it.

'Good God, what was that? It sounded like Concorde taking off,' he said.

'No, just me, reacting to the fact that I've eaten nothing since sometime yesterday morning.'

'Well, since I don't want you passing out on me, get up slowly while I cook us both a gigantic breakfast. What do you say to that?'

'I say this is no time for dieting,' Alex said solemnly, her mouth starting to water just at the thought of it.

* * *

A few days later they stood at the cordoned-off site of what had once been an old hut in the woods, now surrounded by all the paraphernalia of a police incident zone while the excavation of the dried-up well began. Alex hadn't objected when Nick said he had no intention of leaving her side for a while yet. Even though she knew she couldn't, and mustn't, be wet-nursed after every case. It wasn't the way she operated. But just this once.

The ground was appallingly heavy and sticky with continual rain and then hardening frost, but after what seemed like an endless wait the team reported that they had found some bones that could be human. They would have to go to forensics for final confirmation, but in Alex's mind it was confirmation enough that this was all that remained of a sixteen-year-old boy called Steven Leng.

Without warning she felt physically sick, and had to bolt for the trees before she disgraced herself in public.

'Here — use these to clean yourself up,' Nick said a few minutes later, handing her some tissues to wipe her mouth and streaming eyes.

'You should have stayed back there. I don't want you to see me like this,' she stuttered in embarrassment.

'Why not? I've seen you practically every other way.' His teasing voice changed, seeing her distress. 'It's time for us to go, sweetheart. There's nothing more we can do here.'

'But is Gregory convinced that the bones belonged to Steven?' she went on. 'It's important that I know, Nick.'

'He's as convinced as anybody can be at this stage, but until it's officially confirmed, he won't make any statements.'

'I know, but I just want a word with him,' she pleaded, knowing there was still something only she could do. She owed it to Jane.

She also knew these things couldn't be hurried, but Gregory promised to keep her informed until the comparison of bone from the exhumed hand and the bones from the well finally put the pieces of the puzzle together. It had begun as an adolescent lark that had all gone wrong, but the repercussions had happened because of the involvement with drugs and the evil Philip Cordell, and a pact of silence that had resulted in the deaths of two more of the group.

Once she was told that the facts were going to be released to the Press, Alex went to see

Grace and hubby. Nick went with her, still acting as unpaid chauffeur, as he called it.

The couple sat stiffly in their cottage while Alex told them of the police findings as gently as she could. Steven had been their nephew, and they would be upset to hear of his end. They heard her out and then Grace nodded decisively.

'That's that then,' she said. ' 'Tis a pity it all had to be raked up again, but I suppose we'll be expected to pay out for a proper burial now, will we?'

'It would be the proper thing to do,' Alex said in a strangled voice. 'I'm sure the police will inform you when the — when Steven's remains will be released.'

'They'll have to send 'em straight to the undertaker. He'll know what to do,' Grace went on. 'We've had enough of buryings lately.'

They were *inhuman*, Alex thought. Didn't they care at all?

Driving back to Bristol, Nick told her not to take it to heart.

'It takes all sorts, babe. You know that.'

'I do know,' she raged. 'But I was just thinking of my uncle's funeral, and how everybody remembered him and had good things to say about him. They were sad and supportive at the same time, full of concern for the rest of the family — and that poor kid is going to be stuck in the ground with his cold-hearted aunt and uncle just saying 'that's that then'.'

'And so it is. The case is over, Alex, and you've got to forget it and resist getting over-emotional about it. It's the way we work, isn't it?'

She knew he was right, of course. She knew too, that he couldn't stay with her much longer. He had to get back to London and get on with his job. He couldn't pander to a feeble private eye who fell to pieces when things got tough. And she had to admit that apart from this little excursion to see Grace and hubby, which she saw as the final thing she could do for Jane Leng, she had already begun to recover from the ordeal at the quarry pit.

She had her so-called Yorkshire grit to thank for that, and also the fact of knowing that the four men involved were safely in police custody now and awaiting trial. Everything was going to come out in the open, and a good thing too.

'Where are we going?' she asked suddenly, as she saw that he wasn't driving her back to the flat, but somewhere in the middle of the city. For someone who didn't know his way around Bristol, he had a copper's knack of finding places when he wanted to.

'Women like shopping, don't they?'

'Oh God, Nick, don't label me with all that sexist stuff,' she said in annoyance, knowing it was true, but not now, when she had never been in less of a shopping mood.

He laughed. 'I don't mean ordinary shopping, babe. You'll like this. At least, I think you will. And it's something you need, as well as want.' He glanced at her. 'A bit like me, really.'

She didn't bother to deny it, and a few minutes later they turned into the forecourt of a large car showroom, and then she knew. And he was right, as he usually was, she admitted. Her most sensible talking point in these last few horrendous days had been the necessity of getting a new car to cheer her up.

She couldn't allow Nick to go on being her personal chauffeur. He had already helped her so much. They had sorted out her bank statements and renewed her credit cards, and checked with her insurance company, and the other odds and ends in her car hadn't seemed important after all. Everything else could be replaced. But a car was essential in her life, and it would be the biggest thing to raise her spirits right now — apart from Nick.

'I wanted to make sure you'd got your car before I went back to London,' he told her as he applied the brake. 'I know how you like driving.'

His eyes challenged her, forcing her to admit that one drama in the job she had chosen wasn't going to make her give up one of the joys of her life. She leaned across and put her arms around him, kissing him full on the mouth, and ignoring the wolf whistles from a couple of yobs walking by.

'I do, and have I ever told you I think you're terrific?'

'Now and then, but I don't mind hearing it again.'

'You're terrific,' she repeated. 'So now let's go and buy a car.'

And she knew exactly where she was going once she had got the one she wanted. It hadn't been more than a glimmer of a thought until that moment. But now it was decided. She would go back to Yorkshire. Back to her roots — not for ever, but just for a brief spell of renewal with Aunt Harriet. Just to be Audrey Barnes again for a little while. She remembered that her dad used to call it recharging the batteries, which wasn't such a bad way of thinking.

'So what will you do next?' Nick said, when they saw the first available salesman heading their way with the usual gleam in his eyes at the thought of making a sale on a dismal

February afternoon.

'I'm going back to Yorkshire to spend a little more time with Aunt Harriet,' she said decisively.

'Pity. I'd hoped you might have second thoughts about coming back to London.' He paused. 'Or is this your subtle way of telling me you're giving up the job, Alex?'

She laughed, and she registered, almost with surprise, how good a sound it was. A very good, positive sound. Her voice became its classiest and sexiest, her eyes as bright as emeralds, as she answered.

'Not me, darling! So don't think you're going to lose me for ever. I promise you — I'll be back.'

THE END